PROOF

Colin Green

2QT Limited (Publishing)

First Edition published 2020 by
2QT Limited (Publishing)
Settle, North Yorkshire BD24 9BZ United Kingdom

This is a work of fiction and any resemblance to any person living or dead
is purely coincidental. The place names mentioned may exist but have no
connection with the events in this book

Cover Design by
Dale Rennard

Printed in Great Britain by IngramSpark UK

Cover photographs copyright

Chris Lishman Photography

A CIP catalogue record for the paperback format book is available
from the British Library
ISBN 978-1-913071-70-7

I would like to dedicate PROOF to Mam and Dad, both sadly no longer with us. Mam passed away in January 2015, whilst Dad died as PROOF was nearing completion. Wherever they maybe I sincerely hope they are both still playing golf, bowls, bridge etc. etc.!

P.S. And thanks to you both for just everything.

Acknowledgements

To Ruth for her love, loyalty and perseverance!
To Marje yet again, for her time, advice, support and encouragement.
To Anna for her help in the final read throughs during lockdown.
Without their assistance PROOF would never have been written.

Morpeth RFC and Morpeth Golf Club for permission to obtain cover photographs.

Chris Lishman Photography.

John Scurfield for the aerial views supplied of the 14th hole.

To everyone who purchases PROOF - Enjoy!

1

Susan Ibbotson

It was late morning in early April. Gary Thornton looked through the blanked-out window at Thames House, Millbank, home of the Security Service. You could see out, but you could not see in through the bomb-proof material that presented a barrier between him and the outside world.

He had just come from an audience with the director general. They had a problem. Thornton had thought it would be business as usual at the weekly resource allocation meeting for the increasingly stretched personnel dealing with international counter-terrorism. Understandably, Thornton's area of responsibility, Domestic Direct Action, had been pushed out of the spotlight because of the recent ISIS atrocities. He wondered if he was going to lose even more staff to the current threat.

Thornton had just chewed through the dregs of his shocking – but freely supplied – instant coffee and was about to gather his documents when the DG came to the final item on the agenda. 'Any other business?' he asked.

There were negative responses from around the table before the DG spoke, commanding their full attention. 'The PM wants to know what we are doing about right-wing groups. As you know, she's been very active in Europe recently and she's been talking with her counterparts. I gave her the normal rundown, Gary.' The DG looked across at Thornton. 'I think the politicians would refer to it as a holding statement. We have had some intel that British First are looking to hold a series of marches in city centres towards the end of the year. I'd like you to look at some proactive work around them. Can you update me personally by the end of April? I have a meeting diarised with the Home Secretary around that time.'

Thornton nodded, accepting his task, and collected his papers. As he walked purposefully back to his office, he reflected on the request. He was one of the service's most experienced officers; indeed, he could remember a time when Domestic Direct Action was the main focus of attention.

He grinned. 'What goes around comes around,' he thought with a glimmer of excitement. His area of work was back in the limelight. He was well aware of European unrest and the way in which the Far Right seemed to be gaining in popularity.

Back in the office he made a couple of calls and arranged a hasty meeting. As he looked out of the window at the murky waters of the Thames, adrenaline once again coursed through his veins. He'd planned to retire at the end of the year, but Gary Thornton was a dedicated officer.

His OBE, the norm for officers of his rank and with his years of service, was framed and placed strategically in his office. You couldn't miss it. In fact, if you took away his medal there was very little else by way of decoration in the room that would give any indication of what kind of person worked here.

Some twenty minutes later, Peter Havelock and Susan Ibbotson entered his office. Peter, his deputy, was in mid-career, dressed in an open-necked shirt and jeans in contrast to his boss, who always wore a collar and tie. Ibbotson, fresh from a recent deployment, was chewing gum; she wore a baseball cap, T-shirt and black padded gilet. Her bare arms displayed a couple of tattoos that would have to be removed or replaced, depending on her next job.

Susan was the department's best undercover operator; a poor degree from Teesside University was no bar to the fact that she had first-class honours when it came to their highly specialised area of undercover work. She carried a trendy bottle of Evian water in her left hand and took her place alongside Havelock whilst Thornton remained seated behind his desk.

Thornton spoke uninterrupted for nearly ten minutes. The strategy was clear: they needed to infiltrate British First. Susan would be deployed, and Havelock would provide the tactical support to enable this to happen. She would report to Havelock alone and Thornton would ensure that all necessary authorities under the Regulation of Investigatory Powers Act (RIPA) were in place. Contrary to what many people believe, the Security Service is under the same legal controls as any other law-enforcement organisation.

Susan's deployment would take place immediately to allow infiltration well before the planned British First demos later in the year. Thornton knew better than to rely purely upon a single strand of intelligence gathering and emphasised that they were hopeful of additional local reporting that would add to anything that Susan produced.

The usual 'Any questions?' from Thornton was greeted with the usual silence from Ibbotson and Havelock. As they left his office, Ibbotson deftly flicked her chewing gum into the small waste bin. Not a care in the world; it was an attitude that stood her in good stead.

She started her new role the following day not as Susan but as Shaz, totally unrecognisable from the individual who had attended Thornton's office. A menacing tattoo, depicting a swastika placed on the inside of her right wrist, together with a severe closely cropped haircut, she arrived at the Red Fox, a public house in London's East End for a British First gathering. Whilst her deployment was hasty, the event was already well known to the Security Service. There was a certain notoriety concerning the amount of alcohol consumed at these gatherings and therefore a late attendee suitably dressed would not attract undue attention. As an organisation, BF was far from surveillance conscious.

Shaz was wearing a pair of Doc Martens boots, denim jeans held up with braces that covered a Fred Perry polo shirt. She listened carefully to the increasingly drunken speakers and bided her time. No one noticed it had taken her over an hour to drink one pint of Crossbow cider. The speakers became shouters, with one particular individual who went by the name of Tel shouting the loudest and who seemed to have some influence over proceedings. As matters seemed to be drawing to a close, Tel walked past Shaz towards an exit door whilst tugging at a packet of cigarettes in his top pocket.

'Do you want a light, Tel?' Shaz asked, as Tel first peered and then leered at her through a drunken haze. Susan Ibbotson recognised the tell-tale signs; she knew there and then it wouldn't take her long to become a fully-fledged BF member.

2

Enid Benson

Enid Benson stood as upright as she could in the front room of her self-contained flat. She tucked the last visible snow-white curls of hair underneath her red and yellow floral-patterned headscarf. 'That's about as good as it gets,' sighed the eighty-two-year-old widow as she viewed herself in the mirror.

Despite her age, Enid was a very active and fit lady. But she was lonely, losing her true love, Alfred, some twelve years previously. It had been a devastating blow for Enid, and she missed her life partner every minute of every single day – her Alfie. It was a natural feeling following sixty-two years of marriage.

Her flat was practical for a single pensioner. As is the norm for a person of that age, it was constantly at a temperature that made the world seem incredibly cold when you stepped outside. The front room, which was a dining and living area, displayed a collection of family photographs: children, grandchildren and the most recent great-grandchildren, taking centre stage on her widescreen television, whose volume was set at a decibel level that made her many younger visitors shout to be heard. It was rarely switched off when Enid was at home; the television and her relatively new iPad were her best companions in the loneliness of old age. Bright floral wallpaper and similarly patterned carpets provided the background to the photographs. The flat was one of twenty similar units, each with a twenty-four hour alarm and response facility should the need arise. It was located approximately three miles from Parton city centre.

Enid was active in so many ways – art class on Monday and Friday mornings, her beloved upholstery on a Tuesday afternoon, and her bridge games on a Thursday. She was both talented and fit enough to teach upholstery, her favourite craft activity, although she was assisted by one of her younger nieces with some of the more physical aspects. Enid thanked her lucky stars that she could still get to these events, all of which took place at The Haven, a community centre near the pedestrian precinct in Parton. The community centre gave her life both meaning and reward, as it did for so many elderly people of the local area. She was currently a committee member, although she was not seeking re-election at the next AGM.

All in all, Enid Benson was an excellent advertisement for older people living a full and prolonged life. She was the original pillar of the community, loved by family and many friends.

Winter was just around the corner when she buttoned up her heavy brown woollen coat. It was 12.30pm on a Tuesday, late October, and she was anticipating an excellent afternoon's teaching. She had plenty of time to meet Muriel Eales, one of her closest friends and an upholstery class pupil, at the bus stop some fifty yards from her flat.

Just before heading out, Enid packed away her new Apple iPhone 5. It was a recent birthday present from her eldest daughter, Avril. It went with the iPad she had received the previous Christmas and, as Avril kept reminding her, helped her keep in touch with the younger members of the family as well as being useful for emergencies. Her phone secure in her handbag, brown-leather gloves covering her increasingly arthritic fingers, she walked outside, comforted in the knowledge that her niece would be assisting in this afternoon's class.

Enid closed the front door of her small flat totally unaware it would be for the very last time …

It was a sunny autumnal day, the week before the clocks make their annual trip one hour backwards. As far as Enid was concerned, the colours and crispness made this season the best before the dark and gloom descended in November and any daylight became so very rare and precious.

Some five minutes later, Muriel and Enid were at the bus stop waiting for the number 37 which would drop them off at the pedestrian precinct in Parton city centre. From there it was only a short walk through the precinct to The Haven.

'Well, what have you got in store for us today, our Enid?' enquired an enthusiastic Muriel.

'You'll just have to wait, Muriel. I think there is a total of six in today's class,' Enid replied teasingly. Six was a reasonable number; it allowed Enid the time and flexibility to give all the students a decent amount of tuition.

Muriel looked at the digital display in the bus shelter. The bright red flashing numbers and letters enabled both pensioners to read the message easily; the number 37 was due in a couple of minutes.

There was no one else waiting for the bus. The poorly maintained shelter saddened Enid and her friend. Litter accompanied the obscene graffiti. The state of the bus stop was often a topic of conversation between them and today was no exception; their discussion was only interrupted when the bright yellow single-decker bus arrived.

Bus passes at the ready, Muriel and Enid climbed on board. 'Good afternoon, my lovely ladies,' said Bert, their regular lunchtime driver. He never even glanced at the passes.

The conversation on the short journey into Parton covered the usual topics: their age, ailments and the weather. They were so engrossed with each other that they were oblivious to anything in the outside world.

'Come on, girls, you can't stay with me all day,' Bert flirted as they approached their destination.

After alighting, Muriel blew Bert a kiss as the bus headed off and the two of them began the five minute walk through the precinct. It was a relatively new development in Parton city centre and housed some notable high street traders. Whilst the area was pedestrianised, there was restricted access for licensed taxis and delivery vehicles. Still deep in conversation, Enid and Muriel walked towards The Haven.

Conor Tait and Zac Ewart were sitting on their mopeds at a junction that led into one of the many access roads to the precinct used by delivery vans. The two 18-year-olds, dressed in black hoodies and denim jeans without any insignias or distinctive marks, were waiting for their prey. Although they had only got out of bed an hour earlier, they were more than alert. This was their hunting ground, their sport.

From their observation point, Tait and Ewart saw the two pensioners enter the precinct, walking slowly and chatting merrily. Because of their vulnerability they were immediately identified as potentials. Yes, there were plenty of people in the precinct; it was a city centre shopping area at lunchtime, with people going purposefully about their business. Even though Christmas shopping had started, recent austerity measures meant visible policing was negligible. Neither Conor nor Zac had seen anything that would compromise their work.

Enid and Muriel had passed Dorothy Perkins and were near Primark before turning right at Marks and Spencer's when their destination, The Haven, would come into view. They failed to notice the two lads astride their machines. Why should they? Even if they had, would they have changed their routine?

As they approached Marks and Spencer's, the sound of

'Sweet Caroline' by Neil Diamond emanated from Enid's handbag. It was one of her favourite tunes, the ringtone supplied by her grandson who was called Alfie after his late grandpa.

Enid, recognising both the sound and its origin, stopped to unfasten her handbag. 'I'll just get this, Muriel.' Holding the bag with her right hand, she opened the gold coloured clasp with her left hand and removed the phone from her bag. At the same time, she dropped her small white handkerchief.

Conor Tait and Zac Ewart had seen everything, and it was just perfect. They didn't need to say anything as both black mopeds, again without any visible markings, left the junction and headed into the precinct. The machines sighed and whined, their instantly identifiable engine noise sounding like a very cheap hairdryer. Like hunters stalking their prey and making ready for the kill, the lads wove expertly through the pedestrian traffic.

Enid had removed the mobile and placed it to her ear with her left hand. It was her daughter, Avril. Tait had Enid's phone in his sights, ready to steal it, with Ewart acting as a distraction. They increased their speed as they neared their target that was now just twenty yards away.

'I'm just on my way to upholstery, Avril. Can I ring you back later, love?' Enid said to her daughter. 'I've just dropped my hanky, pet,' she continued, as she bent down to retrieve it.

Just at that moment Tait arrived on scene. His eyes were trained on the phone too late to anticipate Enid's movements. As she bent over, he grabbed at the mobile. Enid felt her hand holding her phone being violently pulled. Instead of releasing it, she instinctively gripped it even tighter. Tait pulled on her wrist and she hit the ground; suddenly, she was being dragged along.

Instead of plucking the mobile out of his victim's hand, Tait pulled her directly into his path. The rear wheel of his moped connected directly with the pensioner's head.

Muriel screamed hysterically then a total silence followed; it was one of those moments when everyone stops, stares, but doesn't move.

The silence was broken by Avril's voice down the open phone line, 'Mam, Mam! Speak to me, Mam! Are you alright?' The words were becoming louder and more frantic. The sound of Tait and Ewart's mopeds disappeared as quickly as it had arrived.

Geoff Sutton had just emerged from the adjacent Marks and Spencer's, having purchased flowers and tokens for girlfriend Debbie's forthcoming birthday. He was dressed in his usual green Barbour; he was rarely seen without it, whatever the season.

He surveyed the carnage in front of him: an elderly lady prone on the ground and another person, whom he rightly assumed to be her friend, screaming hysterically. He didn't require any medical knowledge to deduce that the woman who'd been knocked down had sustained a significant brain injury. He thought that she must have been wearing a coloured headscarf but even that wasn't clear, such was the extent of the damage.

Although it was his day off, Sutton clicked automatically into professional mode. Over thirty years highly regarded police service as a former detective chief inspector and now as a civilian support officer dictated his actions.

He was immediately on his phone, dialling 999, not giving the operator a chance. 'Geoff Sutton here. I'm a civilian officer with Parton Constabulary. My force number is 479. I need ambulance and police asap. There's been an accident in the city centre precinct outside Marks and Spencer's. There is an elderly lady with a significant head injury.'

Preservation of life was the priority; the information he gave helped the operator to appreciate the urgency, authenticate the caller and provide an accurate location. Sutton looked around; all eyes appeared to be trained on him.

Some people had their phones out, recording the events, and whilst some footage might be useful evidence, among them were a sad few focusing on the distressing sight of Enid.

His eyes scanned the crowd again and he did a double take when he saw his lifelong mate, Roger Strong. He quickly made an assessment; his priority was Enid. 'Strongy, round up anyone who saw what happened. Any potential witnesses,' he shouted.

Roger, initially stunned, accepted his task although he struggled to avert his gaze from the stricken elderly victim.

Geoff Sutton went over to Enid. Her eyes were closed, and blood seeped out of both ears, a clear indication of the seriousness of her head injury. She tried to speak but it was a mere gurgle of spit and blood. He had to physically push Muriel away as she sought to talk to Enid in between her screams. He shouted at a paralysed bystander for help. Fortunately, another younger member of The Haven arrived at the scene, realised the gravity of the situation, took Muriel by both shoulders and forced her away from Enid's prone body.

For Sutton, it seemed like ages before the ambulance arrived. It always did when you were in the thick of the action. The tell-tale noise of sirens getting closer and closer was punctuated by more emergency tones indicating that the *cavalry* was on their way.

It seemed that both police and ambulance arrived simultaneously. The paramedics took over from Sutton, who was able to impart scant details of how Enid had come by her injuries. He liaised with the two young uniform constables who were the first attenders from Parton Constabulary. Sutton didn't recognise them, which was unusual for someone with his amount of police service. No, he explained, he wasn't a material witness, but he'd asked his friend to identify any potentials. He pointed them towards Roger Strong. They immediately requested that their supervision attend the scene due to serious injuries sustained; then, whilst one of them secured the crime scene, the other accompanied Sutton to speak with Roger.

'I've got four names of potential witnesses. I managed to get their contact numbers. I'm sorry – things happened so quickly. Lots of people from the crowd seemed adamant that the first thing that attracted their attention was the screaming from the other woman. They didn't see the actual incident. But these four all say that two mopeds were involved and made off along Charters Street. One of the witnesses said that the woman who was uninjured might have seen the face of one of the riders because his hoody came off briefly.'

'Did you see anything, Rog?' enquired Sutton.

'Just the mopeds flying by, I didn't see the collision. Geoff, I feel so hopeless,' his friend replied, averting his gaze, chin nestling on his chest. Roger always felt better if he didn't look directly at anyone, and he was in a total daze at the scene he had just encountered.

Newly promoted Sergeant 8558 Steve Barker was engrossed in a messy complaint when the call came in. He dropped everything, grabbed the keys to the supervision vehicle and raced to the precinct.

It was some eighteen months since Operation Trust when Barker, at the end of his probationary period, had been the initial responder and witnessed the horrific sight of his murdered colleagues, an experience that continued to haunt him despite regular counselling sessions. His career though had started well; he'd been promoted before the fourth anniversary of joining Parton Constabulary and had been identified as more than promising.

'Sergeant 8558 at scene,' Barker said to the control room. He made a specific point of ensuring that the Critical Incident Manager (CIM) knew that he was the supervision 'on the scene'. He immediately recognised Geoff Sutton. 'Mr Sutton, good to see you again.' They quickly shook hands.

'Please call me Geoff – and many congratulations on your promotion.' Despite Barker's lack of experience, Sutton knew that he was going to be a great asset to the force and was genuinely happy for the young sergeant.

Barker, together with the CIM in the control room, followed the golden hour principles that allow the police to maximise all potential opportunities to gather evidence at the earliest stages of an investigation. The scene was secured, and the witnesses identified.

A quick review of the council's CCTV covering the precinct clearly showed that Enid and Muriel had been walking through the precinct when Enid was knocked over by one of the mopeds that failed to stop.

Further resources arrived and Barker supervised them impressively. 'Deano, shops on the north side, look for any CCTV or material witnesses. Jonesy, the same on the south side. Sandra, stay with the injured person and go with her in the ambulance. I need an update on her condition as soon as possible. We'll also need her clothing for forensics.'

Sutton chipped in, 'Steve, we need to secure the key witness who was accompanying the injured person at the time of the accident. She was taken off to the Haven by a friend. She didn't seem injured but she's quite hysterical. It may be a good idea to get her clothing as soon as possible. She may have had some form of contact with one of the offenders,' he advised.

For some unknown reason, Sutton felt the urge to turn back to see how the medics were doing and if Enid could be moved to hospital. He saw a paramedic glance across at his colleague. The look on his face told Sutton everything he needed to know: Enid Benson, a kind lady, a pensioner who had no enemies but a huge following of friends and family, had died. She had been senselessly killed. Head bowed Sutton cut a disconsolate figure as he slowly made his way to The Haven.

For the stricken Enid Benson, her next journey would be the one that reunited her with her beloved Alfie.

3

Ron Turner

At approximately the same time that Enid Benson left her home address, Assistant Chief Constable Ron Turner entered the main force conference room. It was the monthly tactical and co-ordination group meeting to combat the ever increasing problem of Organised Crime Groups (OCGs). Turner's portfolio included crime and he chaired the force's response.

The groups they were discussing all operated within the Parton Constabulary area. They would never be sophisticated enough to merit National Crime Agency intervention, but nevertheless these gangs created mayhem in the local community and played havoc with crime statistics and public confidence.

Dressed in a navy blue three-piece suit, with a crisp white shirt forming the background to a blue and white striped tie, Turner strode into the room. He had a presence; his audience stood up both in respect of his rank and with a certain sense of foreboding.

Turner didn't mince his words. Since his promotion to ACC, he'd become the leading light in ensuring that the force re-established its reputation after the recriminations following Operation Trust. 'Thank you, everyone. Got a coffee?' he enquired. That was the beginning and end of any pleasantries.

The format of the meeting was simple: each OCG had

been given an area lead officer and he or she was responsible for updating Turner about their progress in dismantling their criminal group. Each lead officer approached the meeting with some trepidation, desperately hoping that they could either report a drop in crime or – the icing on the cake – arrests and the dismantling of a group of criminals.

Turner wasn't known for his tact or diplomacy, but the officers had the utmost respect for him. After each update, the lead officer agreed a course of action for the next month although, in reality, Turner told them what they would be doing. Any other business was a discussion around emerging trends.

'Right, next one. Parton Smart Team – PST,' Turner barked. This was the name the force had given to a gang that was causing mayhem to the city centre crime statistics with a series of robberies. The offenders used mopeds to steal mobile phones and they targeted elderly victims. Naturally, the high-profile press coverage was increasing the force's problems. The name given to the group identified them with the Smart phones they were stealing.

Turner looked at Detective Chief Inspector Trish Delaney. She'd been dreading this moment, not only for the past forty-five minutes but since the last meeting. There had been six further offences and absolutely no progress from their enquiries as to who was responsible. She was aware that Turner would know that the offences were on the increase and would want answers. She shuffled her paperwork nervously before commencing. 'Sir, we've had six further offences…'

Turner butted in. 'I know that, Trish. More than one a week. What I want to know is what progress you've made in identifying those responsible?' There was an emphasis on the 'you' and a deafening silence around the room.

Delaney's throat was exceptionally dry; she wanted to take another sip of the bottled water she had brought in from her early morning gym session but thought Turner would note that as a sign of weakness. She cleared her throat. 'Sir…'

She was interrupted by a knock on the door. John Waterman, Turner's secretary, popped his head round. 'Apologies for the interruption, Mr Turner. I've been asked that you view an incident as a matter of urgency.'

Turner knew that Waterman would only interrupt if the incident warranted his attention. 'Stay here, everyone,' he commanded.

Trish Delaney let out a big sigh of relief. Little did she know…

***

Ron Turner was sitting behind his desk studying the log on his computer screen. The incident had occurred in the Parton city centre precinct. Being the operational animal that he was, Turner was itching to attend the scene, but his new role dictated that he take a far more strategic role; as well as crime, he also had force performance to account for. Nevertheless, he went through the log page by page, checking and rechecking to ensure that all that could be done was being actioned without delay.

A smile appeared on his face when he saw Geoff Sutton's name appear on Incident 235, 27th October. 'He just can't keep out of trouble,' thought Turner. That said, he also drew comfort from the fact that if Sutton was at the scene, albeit as a civilian, the initial actions would have been both thorough and correct.

Turner reached page 12 of the incident log, which confirmed Enid Benson's death. He sighed deeply as he rose from his desk. Head down, and without glancing around at the records of his many achievements adorning the walls of his office, he made his way back to the conference room. This was Turner in full operational mode.

He pushed open the door. 'Meeting over. DCI Delaney, follow me, please,' was all he said.

Delaney was in turmoil. She had made good use of

the interruption, sipping some of her Evian water and regathering her focus, but now she was being summoned to *his office*. She followed Turner like a well-trained pet but with increasing anxiety.

'Seen this?' Turner turned his computer around in its cup-like stand to afford her a view of the full screen whilst he returned to his swivel chair on the other side of his desk. He watched Delaney closely as she read the text.

Without realising what she was doing, Delaney put her hand up to her mouth. Despite her increasing apprehension, she took her time, reading the details supplied by the operational officers at the scene.

Turner allowed her to digest the contents, then took control. 'Trish, I need a full update by 5pm this afternoon. Included in that report, I want to know how you plan to detect this crime and dismantle this OCG. If I'm not satisfied with your response, I'll be appointing another Senior Investigating Officer.' His words sent a chilling message to DCI Trish Delaney: if you're not good enough, I will pull in somebody else.

Delaney left Turner's office, her head in a spin. She made her way out of the command suite, a fancy name for where the chief officer team and their respective staff were located in the headquarters' building. As she went to one of the supervision cars, she became aware of the late October weather. It had brought some cold northerly winds that knifed into her almost as much as Turner's words. She knew this was going to be a massive test.

A uniformed officer for all her career, she had applied and been successfully transferred to CID, with a view to making a significant step up the career ladder. The promotion from Chief Inspector to Superintendent was a significant one, both in terms of salary and pension. Her CID posting was a sideways step, which would hopefully develop her skills and make her a strong candidate for the next rank.

Delaney's move into the CID was supported by the new chief constable, Christine Mayling, a former assistant commissioner from the Met, who had been appointed to rebuild the force after the misery caused by Operation Trust. Mayling brought with her new ideas and a fresh outlook but she was no fool, and her first task was persuading Ron Turner to take an instant promotion and suspend his retirement for a few years. It was a masterstroke for the force – but perhaps not for Trish Delaney.

When Delaney was appointed to CID, Turner had raised concerns with the new chief that there was no substitute for detective experience. As far as Turner was concerned, this current operation was Delaney's real test.

'Lateral development, Ron. It will make her a better all-round officer,' Mayling had said when she'd refused to be dissuaded from Delaney's transfer.

Despite his reservations, Turner had heard good reports about Delaney from his numerous in-house informants but there was nothing like the true Turner test. This ongoing high-profile incident was Delaney's and she would sink or swim, irrespective of the chief's support.

Head down as she quickly gathered her thoughts, she heard her mobile ring. The ringtone was 'Wonderwall' by Oasis, the first dance at her wedding. Her pleasant memory ended abruptly.

'Ma'am, can I make you aware of Log 235 for today?'

Delaney interrupted the control room operator. 'I am aware. Put me down as attending the scene. I'll update you when I'm there. Thank you.' She ended the call and opened the door to the black Volvo, a pool car used for supervision, previously from the traffic department. Delaney knew that Turner would be watching the log all afternoon and she needed to make her presence felt.

Her mind raced as she made the five minute journey to the scene. She parked her car well away from the outer cordon to the crime scene and walked over to the civilian support officer who was logging everyone in and out of the area. Delaney produced her warrant card and waited, wanting to take in the sight of the investigation which was now under her control. The shiver down her back was caused not just by the cold but by her fear of making the wrong call. Momentarily she wished she was back having an infamous Turner grilling; it seemed preferable.

The precinct was now sectioned off with the customary blue and white barrier tape. All uniformed personnel were outside that zone; some with clipboards were attempting to identify any more potential witnesses. They had quickly established that they were looking for two offenders on mopeds. Delaney also noted that staff working in pairs had been despatched into the various commercial outlets to identify CCTV opportunities. Within the taped area, the white-paper-suited scenes of crime staff, all with hoods and looking like astronauts, went about their business meticulously.

Delaney seemed momentarily dazed by the sight. She had a vast amount of experience at being the first uniform supervision on the scene, but this investigation belonged to her. It was her first job as Senior Investigating Officer.

Trish Delaney didn't stay dazed for long and amongst the chaos quickly sought out Sergeant Steve Barker. She had been on his promotion board panel, recognised him immediately from that interview and remembered the positive impression he had made.

'Steve let's take a seat in the Volvo and you can update me,' she ordered. 'Inform the control room that I'm on scene.' She was making sure that Turner would be aware she had instantly assumed command.

Moments later, Delaney and Barker were back in the Volvo. Barker went through the events. 'Ma'am, briefly the current situation is this. Two elderly ladies were walking along the precinct heading to The Haven. One was knocked over as she was answering her mobile phone and she's been confirmed dead. The other is in a state of total shock and distress and she's been taken to The Haven by a friend. Scene is secure, not only where the incident took place but also the route we believe the offenders took. It's likely that they were observing their victims as they walked through the precinct. It has all the hallmarks of "The Parton Smart Team", ma'am.' Barker was referring to the OCG that had been causing significant problems in and around the city centre.

Trish Delaney knew it, but she hated Barker saying these words. Questions such as, 'Why was it inevitable?', 'What have you done about them?', or 'Why haven't you caught them before now?' would have to be answered. But this was the here and now.

Delaney climbed out of the vehicle and asked for a forensic update from Arthur Hails, the duty crime scene manager, as he emerged in his white suit from inside the cordon.

'It's early days, and at the moment I've just got one recovery of note. There's a skid mark where the moped hit the deceased. We've managed to take a lift from it – could possibly lead to a line of enquiry,' he reported. Hails was famous for his pessimism.

Once Enid had been certified dead, Hails and his staff had organised a tent to provide some privacy as they went about the gruesome business of treating the corpse as a scene in itself. The target for the offenders – Enid's mobile – had been photographed in situ, then bagged and tagged in an exhibit container. Hails pointed out the possibility of extracting a DNA profile from the item and Delaney asked for this to be fast-tracked.

Trish, somewhat despondent as she always was after a meeting with Hails, made her way to The Haven. She wanted to meet up with Geoff Sutton, whom she knew and had worked with previously, Barker had mentioned Sutton was one of the first people on the scene and had provided him with an initial brief.

It was Sutton's hope that Muriel Eales, the only real material witness, would now be able to provide some details. In his role as a part-time civilian, he could have easily walked away from the scene after initially providing assistance, but that course of action just wasn't in his DNA. He was straight back into operational mode, despite it being his day off.

DCI Delaney approached the white timber-framed building that was The Haven. Having been painted during the summer, the centre looked both clean and welcoming with its bold black lettering, 'Haven Helps', above the doorway. She was about to open the door when Sutton appeared.

'Trish, if you're looking to speak with Muriel Eales it's a complete waste of time,' he said without any prompting. 'She's so shocked that she hasn't even been told that her best mate has died. The paramedics are with her at the moment and someone from her GP's practice is turning out. It looks like the work of the Smart Team. Are you SIO?'

'I am – and I have to brief Ron Turner in a couple of hours. I'm open to any thoughts you might have, Geoff,' Delaney replied, a deepening frown appearing on her forehead.

Sutton glanced at his watch; he had to be away for 5pm at the latest for Debbie's birthday meal. 'Let's go somewhere quiet,' he suggested. 'Scenes are secure, and Arthur Hails and Steve Barker know how to get in touch with you. The detectives have a first account from the few witnesses we've identified, and Muriel is in no fit state to be spoken to.'

They left the area together, but not before Sutton had a brief word with his mate, Roger Strong. Roger's normally healthy complexion had drained from his face, the experience of the past hour or so taking its toll. 'Thanks for your help, Rog. See you on Saturday for golf and the rugby. Can't wait for it, Strongy. Take care.'

Roger Strong didn't respond; he just wondered how his mate slept at night. The sight of Enid lying prone on the ground with her head injuries had disturbed him far more than Geoff Sutton could ever have imagined.

4

Hilda 'Nan' Tait

At the same time that Sutton and Delaney were leaving the tragic scene at the city centre precinct, Conor Tait and Zac Ewart were safely housed in Hilda Tait's small, two-bedroom council bungalow on the north side of Parton, approximately four miles from the city centre. Conor used his nan's house as his home. He rarely saw his parents; he didn't want to, and never bothered with them. Nan had looked after him for as long as he could remember.

After depositing their mopeds in a carefully chosen, convenient and safe location, they arrived at Hilda Tait's to be welcomed by the usual questions, 'Would you like any lunch?' followed by, 'Any washing?' It was music to their ears.

Within fifteen minutes, the lads were sprawled over the sofa viewing a *Judge Rinder* rerun on Conor's iPad and tucking into Nan Tait's bangers and mash. Her new Blomberg washing machine contained their recently discarded clothing and was washing away any potential forensic evidence. A fast, full load was halfway through its cycle. Conor had given Nan the machine as a present to celebrate her seventy-fifth birthday. He'd deflected any questions about how he could afford such a present with lies and more lies. It had only cost him a dozen or so stolen Smart phones.

Hilda Tait loved the boys coming around. After being widowed in her early fifties, she had dedicated her life to bringing up Conor as best as she could. She had no contact with her only son, Conor's father. He and her daughter-in-law had moved away from the area for what was believed to be a drugs debt and in doing so they had abandoned their son. All this was too much for Hilda to understand; what she did know was that young Conor was hers for life.

When she was summoned to school in his early years to explain his truanting, Hilda defended Conor to the hilt. 'He's a good lad, you know. You need to support him.' If young Conor needed one thing, it was discipline with a capital D.

Hilda soon gave up any thought of forcing him to attend school and now eighteen-year-old Conor normally slept till lunchtime then went out with his mates. Sometimes they came around to her bungalow and, if she was not at the Haven, she had their company. 'Company' was a loose term as there was no real conversation, just a few grunts here and there as they took over the living room and continuously played on their phones; they always seemed to have a few of them at their disposal, whilst Hilda was relegated to the kitchen and kept busy with the continuous requests for food. They knew and addressed her as Nan Tait; Conor demanded that.

If Nan was honest with herself, she was frightened sometimes of Conor and his friends – but more so of spending time on her own. She usually attended The Haven in the morning when there were card games taking place in one of the side rooms. She indulged herself with a cup of milky coffee, always with two sugars, and a custard cream – none of this Americano or latte rubbish for Hilda and her companions. She had recently been introduced to mah-jong and never missed the Chinese board game on a Monday morning. Hilda always travelled to The Haven by bus. If it was a morning activity she returned in time to make her lunch and Conor's breakfast, if he was awake, although there had been a few occasions recently when Conor had actually been out and about in the mornings. 'A welcome change of routine,' thought Hilda to herself.

Hilda had many acquaintances who enjoyed her company

at The Haven. However, these acquaintances would never wish to be called friends. That had nothing to do with Hilda herself but because they knew of Conor's reputation.

Her bungalow was number ten, one of fifty that circled a well-kept grassed area known as Meadowland Crescent. They were all two-bedroom, council-owned properties, almost entirely occupied by elderly people, although council regulations allowed close, single dependants to live with them when there was a single occupant. This allowed their nearest and dearest to assist in a caring capacity for the elderly and relieved the pressure and costs on overcrowded care homes. Ironically, in Hilda and Conor's case the caring role lay with Nan Tait.

There had been one or two twitching curtains as Conor Tait and his friends started making an impact. On his way home a month or so earlier, Conor, in his usual outfit of dark hoody and baggy denim jeans and showing ample sight of his Calvin Klein boxers, was draining the contents of his Monster energy drink can, Smart phone jammed up against his ear. He'd tossed his can onto the grass curtilage of Charlie Drummond's property, one of Hilda's neighbours and another member of The Haven.

'Hey, lad, pick that up,' Charlie shouted, trying to communicate over Conor's phone conversation.

'Piss off,' was the immediate reply.

'I'll call the law,' Charlie threatened.

'I'll put your windows in,' came the immediate response from beneath the hoody. A shiver crept up Drummond's back as he recalled seeing Conor playing football on the green in front of his house on a hot summer's day. The swastika tattoo on the inside of his right wrist was an obvious sign of right-wing affiliation. It was a decoration that Drummond, a retired ex-military intelligence officer, would instantly recognise any day of the week.

Charlie took his time in deciding his next course of action, but Conor didn't. Charlie Drummond's kitchen window was smashed by a brick later that evening; 'don't mess with me or the Parton Smart Team,' was the message.

Drummond picked up the phone and contacted Parton Constabulary. He'd given his name and address and was about to tell the operator of Conor Tait's actions when he had second thoughts. He had been to Neighbourhood Watch meetings and they'd been a total waste of his time.

He put down the phone. 'Maybe if I was twenty years younger,' thought Charlie, 'But not now, not now,' he repeated to himself. Maybe he was a coward after all.

5

Roger Strong

Roger Strong left the city centre precinct and walked back to where his vehicle was parked in the NCP multi-storey car park. He noticed nothing and no one.

For Roger, retirement had come early in life, long before his other close rugby mates, Geoff Sutton, Stew Grant and Pete McIntyre. This was due to his insurance business being bought out by a larger company. It was an offer he couldn't refuse; he'd informed his mates on a winter Saturday some fifteen years previously, following a few beers in the Upper Parton RFC clubhouse.

Roger never let the grass grow under his feet; he made a complete career change, trained as a classroom assistant and got a job at Shoreton, a picturesque village some eight miles south-west of Parton. Roger loved this job; in many ways it was his saviour, as his wife had left him and started acrimonious divorce proceedings.

As the recriminations grew, their only child, now in his late teens, had been completely turned against him. As a consequence, Roger had totally lost contact with his son and, more understandably, his former wife. Initially he made numerous unsuccessful attempts to reinvigorate the relationship with his son but hadn't seen him now for some years. Such was the acrimonious nature of the split with his wife, it was rumoured she had unofficially changed their son's name. Roger hadn't a clue whether they remained in the

Parton area or had moved to another part of the country. For all he knew they could be living abroad.

He never spoke to his friends about his domestic circumstances and it would have taken a brave person to raise that particular topic. They remained blissfully unaware of the nightmare that haunted him. Roger Strong sincerely hoped that one day the situation would improve and the relationship with his only child would be rekindled, but he was a realist and knew full well that, as each day passed without contact, any hope of repairing what had been broken was becoming increasingly unlikely.

Nevertheless, Roger seemed resilient. When educational cutbacks forced him to take early retirement a second time, he did occasional gardening work, usually for pensioners, where the grass cutting was punctuated by long chats over mugs of tea when they put the world to rights.

His other great comfort were his close friends, with whom he played poor but regular golf, followed by a few pints and cruel but always entertaining *craic* down at his rugby club.

It was only recently that life had really picked up when, via internet dating, the lovely Cindy had arrived. Roger was in love. Everyone liked Cindy; she'd even passed her rugby club interview with Pete, Geoff and Stew! It was a whirlwind romance and within three months she'd moved into Roger's bungalow opposite the entrance to the rugby club.

As quickly as it had started, the relationship ended. Cindy had left Roger the previous day. She'd explained to him during a tearful conversation that everything was happening too fast for her; she wasn't ready, and he wanted more from the relationship than she did. She needed time to reflect and was going back to live with her parents. To say Roger was devastated was an understatement but he had told nobody. He intended letting the lads know after the match on Saturday.

His trip into town had been an unmitigated disaster.

With winter on the horizon, his gardening work was almost finished, and he'd needed to get out of the house. Now he couldn't clear his mind of the picture of a stricken Enid, lying prone, her head smashed in.

He made his way to Level 3 where the car was parked, struggling to remember where he'd left his Nissan X-Trail. He activated the key fob, climbed into the driver's seat and closed his eyes. Another flashback of Enid. He opened his eyes quickly, started the car and reversed out. It was back to an empty house for Roger Strong.

Conor and Zac Ewart lay on Nan Tait's long brown, fake-leather settee. Nan, without a Haven activity to attend, had been banished to the kitchen to listen to the afternoon play on Radio 4, as she finished Conor's ironing. She enjoyed the radio dramas and followed them keenly. She usually put the kettle on after they finished, but for some unknown reason this time she hadn't and now she was engrossed in a political discussion concerning direct action protest groups.

There had been a great deal of publicity, particularly about far-right groups that had embarked on a series of events in various cities across the country which were causing untold damage to property as well as involving organised violence. These groups were due to come as far north as Parton this weekend; the rumour was that Parton had been selected because of the recent influx of Eastern Europeans, among other nationalities. 'What an absolute disgrace,' Hilda Tait thought. 'Why can't people live together peacefully?'

Her two 'guests' were full after the bangers and mash, washed down with yet another can of Monster energy drink. An Inbetweeners rerun had just ended.

'What do you think happened to the granny?' Ewart asked.

'Granny,' was the word often used by the Parton Smart Team to describe the targets of their robberies. Sadly, as far as the PST was concerned a 'granny,' was purely another opportunity to steal and alleviate boredom. The manner in which they used the word was indicative of their lack of respect and care.

'Don't know, but it's a pisser not getting that Smart phone. Better lay low this aft, then we'll head out to Carsten later and meet up with the other two.' Conor was referring to another of their favourite hunting grounds, Carsten Plaza, where they would meet up with the other two members of the Parton Smart team, Freddie Ingles and Abbie Liston.

'Her mate could have seen something,' said Ewart quietly.

'What?' Conor asked, sitting forward on the sofa, taking a long swig from the can and looking directly at his mate.

'My hoody came off as you hit the granny,' Ewart explained. '

'Tosser,' came Tait's response.

'It was only for a second or two.' Ewart tried to downplay his error.

'CCTV and the other granny, that's the danger.' Conor correctly summed up the implications of Ewart's actions.

'I'm sure her name is Muriel,' said Ewart, attempting to minimise the damage. 'The one you hit called her friend Muriel just as she was going to answer her phone.'

'Muriel?' Conor mused. 'I've got an idea.'

He smiled as he walked through to his nan. 'How did the cards go at The Haven, Nan?' he asked, using his concerned voice.

'Not bad at all, thanks, Conor. Can I get you or Zac anything?'

'No, we're fine, thanks.' Conor looked at the pinboard on the back of the kitchen door. He was absolutely correct in his thoughts: Nan had an up-to-date list of the names and contact telephone numbers of some Haven members. It was essential that should bad weather force the centre to close, a ring-around by nominated people could be escalated to prevent needless journeys.

With his nan folding the last remaining clothes, Conor took out his phone and photographed the list. 'There wouldn't be many Muriels,' he thought to himself.

***

Roger Strong decided not to go directly home; there didn't seem any point as there was no one there. He drove down to the Parton West Marina. It was barren and cold, unlike the opulent East Marina with its vibrant quayside, large boats, fine restaurants and trendy apartments. He parked his maroon Nissan looking out over the sea. Bob Seger's 'We've Got Tonight' was booming out on his playlist.

His mind was a mix of emotions – losing Cindy, and then the precinct incident. He closed his eyes, but he could still see that poor old woman knocking on death's door, accompanied by her friend's screams.

The Beach Boys took over from Seger; 'Sail On Sailor' was the next track as the tears rolled down Roger's face. He felt awful. In a moment of inspiration, using the voice-activated hands-free system, he asked for Sutton from his address book.

Sutton's phone was turned off, so Roger tried the other two, Stew Grant and Peter McIntyre, but both calls went to voicemail. Irrationally, Roger felt let down by his closest friends.

'Where to next?' he wondered and banged his head violently on the steering wheel.

He decided to drive back to his empty home and slowly wiped away the tears that were streaming down his face. It was a ten minute drive back to his bungalow opposite the entrance of Upper Parton RFC. It was approaching 3pm and the sun was already starting to disappear as the shadow of darkness began its descent. The temperature was dropping too.

The cold outside matched the cold inside the house as Roger opened the front door. He called out Cindy's name in increasing desperation, clinging to the vain hope she might have changed her mind. It only took him a matter of moments to discover that Cindy hadn't returned; there wasn't even a note.

Roger sat down in the kitchen, pen and paper in hand, but not before he'd opened his best bottle of brandy. He filled his favourite Upper Parton RFC crystal glass. One large gulp followed another, then another. Before the next, he walked into the small utility room, through the door and down the two concrete steps to the ice-cold garage. It contained everything he didn't want in the house but might need 'one day.' Yet Roger knew exactly what he needed now and went straight to the old rope swing. His mind momentarily wandered back to the happy times he'd spent pushing the swing while his son screamed, 'Faster, Dad, faster!'

Still sober enough to cut off a decent length of rope, he climbed onto a wooden stool, reached up and secured it with a bowline knot around one of the three wooden beams that ran the width of the garage. He pulled the rope, making sure it was secure. He made a noose with another bowline, finally remembering something useful from his time as a Sea Scout.

Roger Strong retraced his steps to the kitchen. He sat down with the pen and paper but only after taking another large gulp of his brandy.

Geoff, Stew and Pete, he started …

6

Trish Delaney

Trish Delaney and Geoff Sutton had returned to her new office at Parton Central Police Station at the same time that Charlie Drummond, always tuned to the local radio station, stopped his housework when he heard the appeal for information following an incident in the city centre. Scant details were given of the accident, together with a hotline number. Instinctively he picked up his landline and phoned.

Seconds later, after supplying the name Conor, Drummond bottled it, not for the first time. Hand trembling, he replaced the handset, inwardly furious that he felt so vulnerable.

Parton Central Police Station adjoined the force's headquarters where Turner's office was sited. There had been no conversation between Geoff and Trish as the black Volvo snaked through the increasing afternoon traffic.

Delaney was trying to be as calm as possible, but the thought of what lay ahead was daunting. For the very first time she was in charge of what would be an undeniably high-profile case. That brought excitement, and adrenalin coursed through her veins – where it battled against apprehension and fear. If this went wrong, it would be career changing. Detective Chief Inspector Delaney would remain a detective chief inspector for the remaining years of her service.

As for Sutton, he was keeping his powder dry. He wanted to ask so many questions but knew this wasn't the time or place. He organised his priorities: he wanted a full intelligence picture regarding the Parton Smart Team. He'd heard about this ruthless gang who were able to reign through terror and had committed robberies on the elderly at random. It had threatened public confidence in the force which was the last thing it needed after Operation Trust.

This latest incident had taken the Parton Smart Team's activities to a different, but far more sinister, level. Sutton's vast experience had taught him that this type of crime spree always reached a climax. He hoped that this incident was the beginning of the end for the PST.

Black Volvo safely parked in the secure pound, they made their way to the top of the three floors that formed the command suite of Parton Central Police Station, the busiest area command in the force. Through the swing doors at the top of the stairs, Delaney's office was the first one on the right. 'Last one in, first one out,' passed through Delaney's mind as she entered through the unlocked door, ignoring the bold sign emblazoned on the door stating *Detective Chief Inspector*.

It was a good-sized office, which provided Delaney with a small gallery of her artistic achievements as well as her career accolades. Sutton knew Trish was a good amateur artist, good enough for the force to use her expertise to produce portraits from witnesses in previous years before technology took control.

'Coffee, Geoff? How do you take it?' Trish went to the customary coffee machine that Sutton hated with a vengeance.

He carefully placed his green Barbour over a chair, one of three around a small table in front of her desk. 'Milk, no sugar,' he said, knowing he would have to answer the next barrage of enquiries: cappuccino, espresso, latte or Americano? 'Just put the kettle on,' he thought to himself.

After what seemed to be an age, Sutton was supplied with a lukewarm cup of froth. He sat down and looked around the office; he always believed that the way an office was organised gave you a strong indication of the occupier. He liked what he saw: it was tidy and compact, with enough on display to confirm that Trish Delaney was both a competent police officer and had an active interest in art. A vase of freshly cut flowers stood on the right-hand corner of her desk. The flowers and coffee created a welcoming aroma, unlike most of the offices Sutton had visited during his service. He asked for a pen and paper to jot down some of the questions that had been forming in his mind during their journey back to the station.

Trish went through the investigation actions. Sutton didn't interrupt her, but he'd been at the scene and needed to satisfy himself that every possible angle had been covered. He knew that most of this information would already be on the incident log; he was more concerned about what Ron Turner would want from the imminent briefing. Turner would jettison Trish Delaney immediately if she didn't come up with the goods and provide him with a way forward that would dismantle the Parton Smart Team.

'Trish, what intelligence have we got on this OCG?' Sutton asked. 'We know they commit mobile phone robberies on the elderly. They boast about it anonymously through social media accounts.'

'Little or nothing,' replied Delaney, head down, not giving Sutton the eye contact that he sought. 'We have no informant coverage. Most of our assets don't fit their profile – for a start, they're a completely different age group. I think that the PST is a very small outfit, successful from their point of view, and happy to keep it that way. I've opened a hot-line asking for information but I'm not particularly hopeful. Any thoughts?'

Sutton was concluding that Delaney's role in this investigation was heading one way when his thoughts were interrupted by a quiet knock on the door. It was Detective Sergeant Joanne Firth.

'Yes, Jo, what is it?' asked Delaney, sounding unusually agitated.

'Ma'am, excuse me, but this could be important. We've had a few calls since the press release and the precinct incident hotline was set up. Most of them are naming the usual suspects but this one has caught my eye because it's a name that means nothing to me: Conor Tait. I carried out a subscriber check from the number and it originates from a guy called Drummond, Charles Drummond. Now, the very same number rang our switchboard a couple of weeks ago, provided his details and mumbled the name Conor Tait before putting down the phone. We tried to ring back but couldn't get a reply. It would seem he was reluctant to speak at that time.'

'Do we know where Drummond lives?' asked Sutton.

'Yep, I've done a voters' check. It's 11, Meadowland Crescent, Parton. His neighbour is listed as Hilda Tait, who lives at number ten. The enquiry team down at The Haven have confirmed they are both regular attenders.'

'Jo, you and another detective go to The Haven first thing in the morning when people start arriving. We need to speak to Charlie Drummond away from his address and find out exactly what caused him to make those calls. Make sure you speak to a few different people so as not to raise any suspicions, particularly as Hilda Tait will probably be around. A story that you're making background enquiries into Enid Benson's background and her recent movements should suffice.' Delaney immediately sounded more confident. 'Thanks, Jo. That's good stuff.'

Sutton took control. 'Ron Turner needs that, Trish. He needs to know positive actions are being taken and this is your best line of investigation to date. I'd also pursue the forensic recovery with the skid mark and the potential of a DNA hit from Enid's Smart phone. That would be a major breakthrough. I suggest that an enquiry with various garages may give a better indication of the mopeds they used, possibly where you'd purchase tyres and any places specialising in their servicing. Although that's supposition – they may well do their own vehicle maintenance.'

'Thanks, Geoff. You've been really helpful, particularly as you aren't on duty. Do you mind if I give you a ring tomorrow? Are you at work?'

'I am. Unfortunately, Wednesday is one of my workdays!' he said with some relish, having recently reduced his working hours. 'Ring any time – and I mean any time.' He didn't give a second thought about the implications of that comment.

They left her office. For him, it was to go to a happier event and celebrate Debbie's birthday. He checked his mobile and noticed a missed call from Roger Strong; he wondered if Roger had somehow remembered another witness. 'Trish, just hold on a moment, this may be something important,' he said, as he rang his good mate.

The phone rang then went to voicemail. Sutton ended the call. 'Must be nothing. Sorry.'

Delaney faced a return to the lion's den that constituted a meeting with Ron Turner. She made her way from the city centre police station to Parton Constabulary HQ located next door. It was 4.50pm. Her slow walk through the adjoining corridors gave her further time for reflection. This is what she'd wanted, to be the officer in charge of a major investigation. By the time she reached Turner's office she was feeling a steely determination – if she was going down, it would not be without a fight.

She waited in the secretariat of the force's senior officers, mirrored by two large TV screens giving an update of Parton Constabulary crime figures, community work and appeals, the most recent being the precinct incident. It was the usual police message that assured anyone who gave information that it would be dealt with in the strictest confidence.

'Trish, come in.' Turner beckoned, immaculately dressed

as ever, as he approached the waiting area. It was exactly 5pm when Delaney followed him and walked confidently into Turner's spotless office; there was nothing on his large desk other than a laptop. He took his seat behind the desk whilst Delaney sat down opposite. There was no cosy coffee table in front of Ron Turner's desk.

'First question: what are you going to do to sort out these bloody bikers? It is the biggest problem we have at the moment and the impact on the Parton Community is reaching a critical stage, as is their confidence in ourselves.' Turner emphasised *you,* placing even more pressure on his DCI.

Delaney, her voice faltering initially, went briefly through the actions at the scene, then, as Sutton had directed, she moved to the proactive work around Charlie Drummond and the tyre mark. She also mentioned the potential of DNA from Enid's phone.

Turner didn't interrupt, just looked directly at her, taking in her every word. When she finished her briefing, he sat back. 'What about informants? Have we got any reporting on them?'

'Not at this stage, sir,' said Delaney openly.

'What re-sources do you need?'

Trish had already prepared for this and she listed incident room staff and an outside enquiry team. She also placed great emphasis on an intelligence cell because of the way the PST were operating and the current lack of informant coverage. She ended by making a specific request. 'Sir, is there any chance I could have Geoff Sutton on this enquiry?'

A broad smile appeared on Turner's face. 'He's going to love you. I'll ring and ask – but I can't force him, Trish. I'll sort out your resources. Brief me on a daily basis. Now I need to update the chief. It will obviously be a high-profile enquiry, given the circumstances.'

Delaney left Turner's office. 'Now the hard work begins,'

she thought.

***

During the time Delaney was in Turner's office, Stew Grant and Pete McIntyre had noticed missed calls from Roger Strong. As was natural with the group, both had tried to call back at the earliest opportunity but, after a couple of rings, Strong's phone had gone to voicemail. Couldn't be urgent, was the obvious conclusion.

7

Freddie Ingles and Abbie Liston

Clothed in a different set of grey hoodies and baggy denims, Tait and Ewart had decided it was now safe enough in the cover of late October darkness to make the journey over to Carsten Plaza. The only difference in their clothing was the trainers: Tait with Nike's and Ewart with his new Skechers.

'Bye, Nan,' said Conor, as he and Zac left the warmth of the house, they automatically put their hoods up.

If she was honest, Nan was more than pleased to see the back of them, having been banished to the kitchen all afternoon. It was now 6pm and, although she had missed Pointless, she could catch up with Eggheads, another quiz game, and although she found the questions far too hard, there was always the attraction of that charming Jeremy Vine.

There was never any purpose in asking what time Conor would be back, where he was going or would Zac be staying, as she never got an answer and it always seemed to irritate Conor, even though Zac was always polite and respectful.

Carsten Plaza was a good indoor venue for the PST to meet, particularly when the dark and cold nights arrived. It was a warm shopping centre, open late in the evenings, where there were numerous eating and drinking outlets. They never considered this a place to use their vehicles and commit crime as the modern design made their use almost impossible. In addition, as opposed to the city centre precinct, the Plaza didn't have the natural viewing areas where they could spot their potential prey. The in-house CCTV system was state of the art; the multi-agency forum of designing out crime was currently a success.

However, the main reason for the PST using Carsten Plaza was SAMS, a mobile phone repair shop that, as well as supplying new batteries, screen replacements and SIM cards, provided accessories such as car chargers, headphones and the like. It was located in a part of the plaza where other shops were closing, unable to keep up with the online shopping bonanza and the escalating rents.

SAMS was the PST staging post for their crimes; they got a monetary reward from supplying Nevil Samuels with phones and it was a safe location for them to meet, despite having internal security cameras. Nevil asked no questions, he had little or no self-confidence. Dominated at home, to the point of being bullied by his totally unsympathetic wife, Joyce, life at the shop was no better, as he allowed the control of his business to a group of terrorising teenagers known in the community as the PST. Unusually, his shop doubled as a small café for youngsters moving towards their late teens. At their request he constantly played music from Goth rock artists, such as The Cure or Sisters of Mercy, which was popular with the customers despite not being the music of his choice. He ignored the odd spliff and youngsters often took their first puff of weed in Nev's premises. He looked upon these sacrifices as necessary to maintain his business.

Due to its location and the fact that many other shops were closed, SAMS was ideal for the PST. Nev made just about enough money to make ends meet and, importantly for Conor and his team, they intimidated him enough, so they had access to a discreet lock-up, which Nev owned, and where the team stored their mopeds. He charged no rent for the garage as long as the stolen phones kept coming. It was all part of their unofficial deal.

The relatively recent income from the phones had become crucial for Nev in ensuring SAMS made a profit. Online shopping had also hit small businesses. He took the stolen items, removed and destroyed the SIM cards then sold them on, making a healthy profit. In an attempt to avoid detection, those that he knew or suspected had been stolen locally by the PST were shipped on to his twin brother, Eric, who had a similar enterprise more than 300 miles away on the south coast.

As for the four members of the Parton Smart Team, it was a love-hate one-sided relationship, kept alive because they enjoyed the thrill of committing crimes. Any remuneration was a bonus. Charging around on their mopeds, attacking the vulnerable and making a few bob in the process was appealing. What else had they got in their lives? And if an old lady happened to get in their way because she was picking up her handkerchief that was her fault.

Conor and Zac approached SAMS. Its window was plastered with small, brightly coloured cards in the shape of stars covered in prices scrawled on them with a felt-tip pen. Instead of turning immediately left to face the sales counter where Nevil stood, they ignored the owner and walked straight ahead to the four tables and chairs which constituted SAMS café. They were deliberately placed near an old-fashioned gaming machine, which was employed almost constantly when the PST were in town. Behind the table and chairs on the back wall was a serving hatch with sliding wooden shutters, where Nev's eldest son occasionally served.

Freddie Ingles and Abbie Liston were already present, Abbie glued to the gaming machine, her eyes staring, hypnotised by the lights, numbers and figures. Dressed in a maroon hoody, she was oblivious to anything or anyone.

Freddie sat at one of the tables, both hands wrapped around his green and black energy can. He was the youngest of the PST. Totally disaffected with his divorced parents, the seventeen-year-old spent most of his time at Abbie's; they had become an item over the past year.

Abbie's mam, Paula, who worked long hours at the local pub, never had the time or energy to pay much needed attention to her daughter, whose eldest brother had married and moved out last year. Paula had raised the two children as a single mother; they had different fathers who didn't provide for them and were not interested in their respective offspring.

These arrangements suited Abbie and Freddie; they could live together at Abbie's mam's house, coming and going as they wished. They even had their own shared bedroom. It was a simple life; by the time they were out of bed, Paula had left the house for her afternoon shift. Their entertainment was with the team and meeting up at SAMS.

Nevil finished his phone call and beckoned Conor over. He had obviously heard the news about the old lady in the precinct and he knew who was responsible.

Conor reluctantly approached the counter. Before Nev could say anything, the cocky Tait took the initiative. 'Piss off, Nev. I'm going on the machine.'

'It's a bloody step too far, Conor,' Nevil pleaded and tried to have a reasoned conversation. 'I'm going to tell the law.'

'Fuck off, Nev. You're as guilty as anyone. Make sure the shutters are down tonight,' said Tait threateningly, as he looked around the shop.

'Yeah, fuck off, Nev,' Abbie joined in after overhearing the conversation, and then deliberately poured her drink over the floor.

Nev, mouth open but unable to speak, could only cower from behind the counter. It was open defiance and there was absolutely nothing he could do; furthermore, all this had been witnessed by his frightened son who was peering through the serving hatch. Utter humiliation. The four members of the PST weren't aware, nor would they have cared, that the humiliation Nev suffered at his shop was mirrored on the domestic front.

They all returned to their table as if nothing happened. Conor spoke – and when Conor spoke, they all listened. 'Got a problem. The other granny in the precinct might have seen Zac's face.' No further explanation was required.

The other three listened intently; they had already received an account from Zac. 'We're going to make sure this doesn't go any further,' Conor said. 'I've found her address from Nan's list of Haven members. Off we go.'

8

Muriel Eales

'It's really very cold tonight,' thought Terry Murton, as he switched on yet another bar of the electric fire. 'Bloody short days and long nights.' It was approaching the time of year when he felt the loneliness of old age and saw fewer people.

It was 8pm and *EastEnders* was just finishing. He hummed the closing bars of the theme tune as he picked up his remote, one of his very best friends during the cold dark months. With the help of his grandchildren, he could now use catch-up television. He was about to try it out with a rerun of one of the autumn rugby internationals, England vs Australia, which had taken place the previous Saturday. He hadn't seen the game live as he supported his club, Upper Parton RFC; due to his long and dedicated service in various roles, he had been rightly awarded the status of honorary life member. Terry never missed a Saturday down at the club; it was the highlight of his week during the season.

After the euphoria of watching the rugby, he was settling down to watch more TV when he was disturbed by a loud knock on the door. He wasn't expecting visitors, particularly at this time of night; as a wise, fully competent eighty-two-year-old, he was apprehensive at opening the door for unannounced guests at any time. He'd had enough of youngsters during the summer nights knocking on his door and running off; good fun for them but not for his ageing limbs.

Terry had been completely unaware of the activity taking place next door at Muriel Eales' home. He had drawn the curtains before he cooked his tea and had missed Muriel returning home, assisted by a doctor from the health centre and two detectives. The doctor had examined Muriel thoroughly. As he left the premises, the experienced practitioner turned to the two police officers, looked them straight in the eye and said, 'I appreciate you have a job to do, but you will not speak to Muriel tonight about today's incidents. Is that understood, officers?' It wasn't just an instruction it was more of a threat and was acknowledged by them both.

When Terry answered the door, he was confronted by DS Joanne Firth and DC Pete Hallett, both of whom produced identification sufficient for Terry to release the security chain and allow them into his front room.

'Mr Murton, I hope you can help us. Your neighbour Muriel has been involved in a nasty incident this afternoon—' Joanne Firth explained.

Terry interrupted her. 'Is she alright? I saw her go out to get the bus – it would be about 12.30pm this afternoon. She goes to her class at The Haven every Tuesday without fail.'

'The doctor has just left. She's in shock, which isn't surprising, as her friend Enid Benson died in an incident this afternoon.'

Firth was already aware that Murton wasn't a friend of Enid's, but the old man probably knew of her through Muriel. So far, they had tried but failed to find any members of Muriel's family.

'She's got no family that I know of,' said Terry, in shock himself but still trying to be helpful. 'I'll go and see her.' He wanted to do something to help his neighbour of more than ten years.

'Terry, can I sit down?' Firth purposefully used his Christian name in an effort to put him at ease. 'Poor Muriel has witnessed a tragic incident. I don't know if you've seen the news?' The officers rightly assumed that Terry wasn't a follower of social media.

'No, I was just going to catch up now.' Terry pointed the remote towards the TV with one hand and passed the other across his wrinkled brow. He took off his glasses.

'Terry, Muriel and Enid were walking through the precinct when Enid was hit by a moped and died as a result. The enquiry is at a very early stage, but we think that the two lads were trying to steal Enid's phone. Muriel is our prime witness. Obviously, we can't speak to her at the moment – she's too upset.'

'Awful. Awful.' Terry replaced his glasses but had no wish to make eye contact with his guests; he was struggling with the shock of the news. 'Is there anything I can do?' The widowed, long retired bus driver was recovering his emotions. He'd always had a soft spot for Muriel; with no family of her own, she made a big fuss of his grandchildren and was always making small butterfly cakes for them with 20p pieces wrapped in rice paper hidden inside. She loved having them call round for their treats, even though they were always accompanied by worried parents. Terry's children were rightly concerned that one of their offspring might digest a small coin.

'Muriel is in bed. She's okay, but obviously upset. We aim to visit with her doctor at about 9am tomorrow – hopefully, she'll be in a better state by then. She has your landline number if there is a problem.'

'That's absolutely fine by me,' said Terry, happy to help. 'Muriel gave me a key a few years ago in case of emergencies.'

Pete Hallett, who had let his sergeant do the talking, handed Murton his card containing his contact details.

'Would you like a cup of tea?' Terry immediately regretted his offer; it seemed so out of place considering what they'd just discussed but for him it was the right thing to do – and he had to do something.

The officers left. Terry sat back in his special chair, carefully placed with the best view of his widescreen television. The remote control had been replaced with a large Upper Parton RFC crystal glass of his favourite tipple, Courvoisier VS Cognac Brandy. He usually drank it during the course of a celebration but sadly that wasn't the case now.

His mind wandered between poor old Muriel and 'What has life come to?', then to anger that anyone should be so cruel. 'Those bastards,' thought Terry. His mind was working overtime; for once he wasn't focused on the television, which remained switched off after the officers left.

Terry took a large swig of brandy and looked at the clock above the fire, 9pm. How long till bedtime? He normally turned in shortly after 10.30pm – it was almost time to plug in the electric blanket.

For a moment he thought that he heard a car close by, but it couldn't be; his bungalow was on a green, and the nearest parking bays were about twenty yards away. That was where he kept his white Ford Fiesta.

He picked up the TV remote. At the same time, he heard a thundering crash from what he presumed was his bedroom window. Dropping the remote, he walked as quickly as he could via the kitchen to the bedroom at the back of the bungalow. Switching on the light, he was relieved to see everything intact. Then he heard it: almost animal-like screaming coming from the other side of his bedroom wall.

He knew the layout of Muriel's flat – it was coming from her bedroom. Terry Murton would never forget that scream; it would live with him for ever. He again heard what he thought was a vehicle – or maybe two – in the distance as he went to get the key for Muriel's bungalow.

Moments later he was next door, searching for the light switch. The screams were getting louder and louder. As he went into the living room and then the kitchen, Murton shouted out, trying to be heard, trying to calm her, and desperately trying to stop that noise. 'I'm here, Muriel, I'm here,' he repeated.

Murton turned on the main bedroom light and stopped suddenly, unable to move. A cold northerly wind was blowing through the net curtains, causing them to billow into the room. There was shattered glass everywhere, glistening against the bedside light like stars on a clear frosty winter night.

Muriel was sitting up, screaming and screaming, with rivulets of blood running slowly down her face into her constantly blinking eyes. Amazingly, she was still clinging onto the book she was reading, a Mills and Boon romance – she was addicted to them.

Despite his fragility, Terry Murton was a man of action – but even he was transfixed by the sight and the noise. 'Bastards!' he shouted. 'Bastards!' No one heard; Muriel lived in the end bungalow.

As his neighbour continued to scream, something clicked into gear for Terry. He approached her and, ignoring the glass fragments and the seeping blood, sat on the bed and took her into his arms, cradling her like a newborn baby. 'It's okay, Muriel. It's Terry. You're safe with me.'

He rocked her backwards and forwards and gradually the screaming subsided. He tried to pull away, but she dug her nails deep into his upper arms; she wouldn't let him go. Some minutes passed by as Terry continued his soothing words and gentle rocking. It seemed like an age, but it gave him an opportunity to gather his thoughts.

He needed to call an ambulance and get Muriel the attention she needed. He looked at the bedside cabinet and saw she had a phone by the bed. With one hand he reached over, grabbed the handset and placed it next to him. He dialled 999, his other arm still firmly wrapped around his friend's shoulder.

He asked for the ambulance and gave his name and

address as well as Muriel's. He briefly told the operator her condition and pleaded for them to be quick.

'It's okay, Muriel, it's okay,' he continued to repeat.

Terry's thoughts turned to the offenders and the police. Again, with one hand, he reached into his pocket, only to remember he'd placed the police contact card on his mantelpiece next door.

It was then that Terry had a brainwave. He knew Geoff Sutton very well; some years back Terry had coached the first team when Geoff was at the end of his playing career. More importantly, Terry could instantly recall Geoff's mobile number. He repeated his actions with the phone but this time he called Sutton.

***

'I really like it here, Geoff,' said Debbie.

The couple had been given a table in the quietest corner of Antonio's, a local Italian restaurant. Geoff had made a special request – it was the same table they'd occupied on their first date nearly eighteen months previously, shortly after the end of Operation Trust.

As far as their relationship was concerned, it seemed longer than 18 months. Initially it had seemed ideal. Debbie was in recovery after an abusive relationship, and Sutton had lost his wife, Maria, some fifteen years earlier following a long battle with cancer. The first month was full of laughter and conversation but, after the honeymoon phase, they both came to realise that they were accustomed to their own company and routines.

Although her violent ex-partner was out of the way, Debbie was often withdrawn and even frightened when the doorbell rang. Fortunately, she had just agreed to try some counselling after much persuasion from both Sutton and her brother, Billy. She was happy working at The Parlour Café that she owned, next door to her brother's newsagents. Billy Dillon Smith liked to keep a close eye on his sister, and he was thrilled she was now going out with Sutton. He'd dropped more than a couple of hints to Sutton to ask her out.

There was little intimacy in the relationship, although Sutton yearned for it. This was still a major hurdle for Debbie, who was still coming to terms with the fact that Paul had repeatedly raped her during their desperate time together. Holding hands and the occasional goodnight kiss was as far as she and Geoff had advanced, with the scars from her previous abusive relationship far from healed.

Sutton had knowledge of domestic abuse victims and he knew he had to be patient if the relationship had any chance of success. The fact that Debbie had agreed to counselling was a major step forward.

Despite the problems, there was both friendship and companionship. They really enjoyed each other's company and, for the most part, they laughed together. There was a genuine understanding between them that, if they were patient and took matters slowly, there would be a positive outcome. It was this belief that kept their relationship alive.

'It's the scene of our first date,' said Sutton, looking deeply into Debbie's gorgeous brown eyes.

His phone rang, the ringtone of 'Local Hero' immediately providing a distraction. He initially ignored it until Debbie asked, 'Aren't you going to answer it?'

After he'd rummaged around in his Barbour pocket to find his phone, Sutton didn't recognise the number on the screen. 'It could wait,' he thought. They could leave a message if it was necessary. Seconds later, the phone rang again before Sutton had a chance to re-engage with Debbie. She rolled her eyes as he retrieved it and this time answered without delay.

'Geoff, Geoff, I need the police.' Sutton immediately recognised Terry's voice.

'Terry, what is it?'

'Geoff, I need the police *now*! I'm at my neighbour's. I've already called an ambulance.'

'I'm on my way and I'll call it in.'

***

'Did you hear the granny squeal?' Zac Ewart shouted across to Conor Tait above the noise of their mopeds as they made their way back to the lock-up. Ewart always wanted to make an impression on 'the leader', wanting to be Conor's favourite gang member in a childish sort of a way. They had been joined by Freddie and Abbie; Conor had decided they would do the job as a team. It didn't take much planning; Muriel's address was easily identified from Nan Tait's call-out rota.

They'd waited for a couple of hours before making the journey from the lock-up. It was no more than five miles and almost devoid of CCTV as they travelled via pavements, bridle paths and minor roads. Not that they would be easily identified in their dark hooded clothing, astride their mopeds.

'What a bloody noise!' Freddie joined in, laughing along with Abbie.

***

Sutton immediately scrolled down his list of contacts and rang Steve Barker, who he knew would still be on duty. Barker took the details; blue lights illuminated, he was soon on his way, single-crewed, shouting what details he knew to the control room so the incident could be created, and also asking for further resources.

He had no idea what lay in front of him as the adrenaline began to kick in. He had few officers at his disposal, partly due to so many of them still being deployed at the city centre precinct for scene preservation and partly due to the continuing reduction in police numbers.

'Sergeant 8558 at scene,' he reported as he pulled up at the nearest parking area to Muriel Eales' address, next to

Terry Murton's Ford Fiesta.

He ran across to the house without any thought of danger to himself and saw the open door and lights. 'POLICE! POLICE!' he shouted loudly. This was met with a blood-curdling scream from Muriel as Terry hugged her more tightly and called out, 'In here.'

Barker followed the noise and entered the bedroom, his movements mirroring those of Murton a few minutes earlier. He stopped for a moment to take in the scene: the broken window; the shattered glass and billowing net curtains; the two pensioners glued together. Muriel was sitting up in bed with her hair matted with blood, holding on to her neighbour for dear life. Barker immediately recognised Muriel from the precinct incident.

He didn't even hear the ambulance and paramedics arriving as he regained his composure. 'You okay? It's Terry, isn't it?'

'Yes, officer, I'm okay. I'm Muriel's neighbour. I heard this horrible crash and found this.' His eyes scanned the damaged room.

The paramedics arrived moments after Barker had extricated Terry from Muriel's grasp. Barker wasn't concerned about the crime scene; preservation of Muriel's life was the obvious priority, and he needed an update about her condition. Whilst the medical staff did their job, he did his and took Terry Murton back next door to get an account of what had happened. It was the briefest of accounts; in fairness, Murton hadn't seen a great deal but merely reacted to the crashing noise and Muriel's screams. He did tell Barker that he thought he heard more than one vehicle in the immediate vicinity, which was unusual.

Barker was joined by Sutton, fresh from a brief and fairly fraught explanation to Debbie about why he had to leave her birthday meal. 'I'll ring later,' was his final response as he abandoned her and ran from the restaurant. She appeared about to burst into tears but, unfortunately for her, Sutton was in operational mode.

'You okay, Terry?' Sutton asked.

'I'm alright, Geoff, thanks. Muriel isn't. What a noise she made when her window went in. Never heard anything like it. I was just explaining that we do get kids being a nuisance during the light summer nights, but it's harmless stuff like knocking on doors and running off. This was meant, Geoff – she was a target. Muriel wouldn't hurt a fly.'

'Thanks, Terry,' was all Sutton could manage in response.

A paramedic appeared at the door. 'Can I have a quick word, guys?'

Both Sutton and Barker went into Murton's kitchen to speak to her. Sally Robson, dressed in her green uniform, spoke calmly. 'Muriel is in a really bad way. We've stabilised her and we'll be blue lighting to Parton General. The injuries to her head are basically superficial but it's the shock – she is one severely traumatised elderly lady. She really is struggling.' With that, she left them.

'Shit!' thought Sutton. He needed to contact Trish Delaney; as the SIO, she needed to be updated. This attack on her prime witness was the last thing she would want to hear.

Barker called for Scenes of Crime and also requested a glazier to secure the property. Sutton, Barker or Terry Murton could not have anticipated that Muriel Eales would never return to the neat little bungalow and community that she loved. Indeed, kind Muriel ended her days in a psychiatric unit for disturbed elderly residents, unable to recover and come to terms with the events of that Tuesday in late October.

For the Parton Smart Team, it was another success; they didn't care. For the police, it was a witness they would never be able to use. For Muriel Eales – she would have been better off dead.

9

Jim Glasson

Sergeant Jim Glasson was early for his daily bacon roll at the almost empty canteen that still just about existed in Parton Constabulary HQ. It was 8am on the Wednesday morning. With a class of fifteen probationer constables awaiting him at 9am, some more eager to learn than others, he wanted some sustenance, particularly after the six pints of Theakston's hand-pulled bitter he'd drunk the previous evening at a colleague's retirement do.

He took a bite of the large roll, causing the brown sauce to ooze out and almost land on his pristine uniform if it hadn't been caught by the strategically placed napkin. There were a few officers and civilian staff around, but many tables were unoccupied. The general consensus was that the facility wouldn't be in existence this time next year; the force canteen would be yet another casualty of austerity.

His thoughts were interrupted when Geoff Sutton arrived at his table. 'How you doing, young Geoffrey? The rumour was you tended to eat somewhere else in the morning,' Glasson winked at his long-time colleague, referring to Geoff's romance with Debbie. 'Such was the gossip that flew around the force, it was often better than Facebook,' thought Sutton. At that particular moment it was the last thing that Geoff wanted to hear; he had purposefully given Debbie's Parlour café a wide berth after last night's abrupt exit from Antonio's. He'd also tried again to ring Roger Strong on his way to work but there'd been no reply.

'I've got to see Ron Turner after his morning briefing. It might be the end of the road. I've heard lots of rumours about further civilian redundancies. Anyway, I can't complain, although it'll leave a bit of a hole. Not long for you now, Jim?' Sutton enquired.

'Two months,' came the immediate response. 'I'll be sad – I've had a great time – but it's time to go. I'm not having a do, but we can have a quiet beer together, Geoff. It's your round again.' A wide grin appeared across Glasson's ruddy features.

'Bugger off, Jim.' Sutton matched his smile. 'Well, what are you teaching today?'

'Theft act, followed by a practical on shoplifting,' came Glasson's response.

'Any star pupils in this lot?' asked Sutton.

'No stars, but I've never met a more confident and arrogant little shit in all my service,' said Glasson with feeling, referring to one of the constables in his current syndicate. 'Dominic Charlton is his name. He looks about an eighteen-year-old, like a choirboy. Thin as a rake, thinks he knows everything. How on earth he got through the assessment centre I just don't know. He thinks and acts as if he's James Bond. Apparently, one of the other pupils had to be pulled away from him in self-defence class because he was going to sort him out. If he gets through his probation – and it's a big if – I pity the poor sergeant who has to deal with him. Cocky isn't the word.'

Sutton was surprised with Glasson's vehemence; Glasson had always seemed to be a laid-back individual. 'What's his background?' he asked.

'Kingston Uni, some crap degree in Politics I think, who just fancied Parton. He has an aunt who lives somewhere in the county. First-class prat is my view,' said Glasson. 'You know, Geoff, we all need to be part of a team. I've never met anyone who is so unsuitable as a team player. And he can talk his way out of a paper bag, he's so bloody confident.' The sergeant finally finished his tirade and paused, hands gripping tightly around his empty tea mug. Glasson was a dedicated officer who, even at the end of his service, cared deeply for the force. He, like many members of Parton Constabulary, was deeply hurt by the widespread criticism following Operation Trust.

Sutton smiled to himself. He had seen all kinds of cops, the good, the bad and the ugly. He was intrigued by Glasson's account of Charlton; Jim wasn't one to exaggerate but this kid had certainly got under his skin. If this meeting with Turner wasn't the end of his own service, he might contact Jim and ask if he could be an actor in one of Charlton's training scenarios. It sounded as though it would be more than entertaining.

Sutton gave Glasson a summary of the past 24 hours, the incident at the precinct, followed by the damage at the home of the elderly witness. Glasson listened intently; he'd obviously heard of the precinct job and wondered if there had been any arrests. 'Who's the officer in charge?' he asked.

'Trish Delaney,' Sutton replied.

'She's a good operator. She was my boss when I had a spell as custody sergeant a couple of years ago. Not a great deal of CID experience. This will be a good test,' Glasson commented, raising his eyebrows.

'It will be a bloody good test, Jim. Turner has her in his sights. Could be interesting!' Sutton responded.

'You recovered from Op Trust, Geoff?' Glasson asked, still concerned about the force's reputation.

'Getting there. Ron Turner is pivotal if the force is to move forward. I just don't know how long he'll stay. He's past retirement age. But the new chief seems impressive and the word is that Ron and she make a good team. He has total confidence in her and that's fully reciprocated. Total turnaround from the previous regime,' Sutton summarised.

Sutton and Glasson smiled at each other before Glasson's attention was drawn to the swing doors to the canteen. A short, very slim male walked into the canteen wearing a dark brown hoody, baggy denims and trainers. Sutton followed Glasson's gaze. It wasn't much of a walk; it was more of a swagger.

'That's him, that's bloody PC Charlton,' Glasson almost spat the words out. 'You know, Geoff, I've always had a mantra when I've been training officers. If a member of my family had an issue and needed the police, anyone who I've trained should be both capable and sensitive enough to walk up their garden path and deal with them both appropriately and professionally. I rest my case.' His eyes narrowed towards his pupil.

Sutton could see immediately that young Charlton and his tutor were not going to be a match made in heaven. It was approaching 8.30am. Charlton was due in class at 9am; he still had enough time to get changed and sorted, but he was leaving it late. Sutton observed him and was intrigued. The lad hadn't a care, seemed completely oblivious that he was in the force canteen where senior officers and visitors could easily drop in. He hadn't even removed his hood!

Glasson seethed. 'Prick,' he muttered but not loud enough for others to hear. A couple of minutes later, Charlton was tucking into his full breakfast, oblivious to everyone.

'I've seen enough. Ron Turner beckons,' Sutton said, ending the conversation. They exchanged a firm, but warm handshake. As Sutton left him, Glasson wondered about changing the curriculum. Riot training rather than the Theft Act would give him a better opportunity to bring some reality into Dominic Charlton's life.

Sutton went directly to Ron Turner's office. It was best not to be late, though he doubted that young PC Charlton had the same outlook. The door was open; Sutton could see Trish Delaney was already updating Turner on last night's incident and the poor health of Muriel Eales, who was still hospitalised.

Turner turned his stare towards Sutton and beckoned him in. 'Close the door, Geoff,' he commanded. Turner might have been promoted and his office might have moved but the surroundings remained the same, a mixture of awards and commendations interspersed with landscape paintings of the Lake District.

Sutton took his seat alongside Delaney and opposite Turner, who remained behind hisdesk.

'Geoff, I want you in on this enquiry.' It wasn't a request. 'Put it down as being in the wrong place at the wrong time. You have the knowledge and expertise that will be of a great assistance to Trish. Indeed, Trish has specifically asked for you.'

Sutton knew this was as much as he was likely to get as a compliment from Turner.

'I've been updated on last night's incident. It's tragic but we can't dwell on it. I want ideas.' Typical Turner in full operational mode – shit happens, now let's move on and get this sorted.

Both Turner and Delaney looked at Sutton. He'd given the matter considerable thought, particularly after the incident at Muriel Eales' bungalow. He'd had a poor night's sleep, his mind in overdrive partly about Debbie and partly about the precinct enquiry. Yet he did have an idea.

10

Charlie Drummond

After outlining his ideas with Turner and Delaney, Sutton was excused. He exited Turner's office, leaving Delaney to go through the actions before she headed for a team briefing. Geoff Sutton couldn't have been further from the mark in thinking that he might lose his ad hoc civilian job; he was wanted again on another major enquiry.

He was off to The Haven. Leaving the building, he was happy to be in the fresh air, his green Barbour keeping out that cold easterly wind, which was a feature of the Parton weather, particularly during the late Autumn. He reflected on the last twenty-four hours. In no particular order, he needed to contact Roger Strong and ring Debbie to apologise not only for last night but also that he was going to be out of action for a while. Sutton pondered his instant decision in accepting a role as an integral part of another enquiry, just as he had in Operation Trust. Yet again, when asked, he had never given it a second thought. 'I bet Dominic Charlton would have told Turner to go and do a running jump,' he smiled to himself.

He walked over to his new bright red Skoda Karoq. He'd decided to ditch the Insignia, giving in to what was, for him, some extravagance. He'd had the car for about six months; it easily housed his golf clubs in the boot, and the new vehicle would be helpful if ever his daughter Maggie moved from her rented place in Watford. It also had a few appealing bells and whistles.

Sitting comfortably in the car, Sutton made a quick call to Maggie; he had a few calls to make, but family came first, and he hadn't heard from his only offspring for a few days. There was a chance he would catch her on her way to work – they seemed to start and finish later down south.

Using the hands-free facility, he tried her number unsuccessfully and left a message. 'It's not urgent, Maggie, just a catch-up.' Sutton then tried Debbie's number but again there was no response. He thought about leaving a message but didn't know how he could begin to explain. He would try later.

Now Roger. Again, the same response: no answer. For the first time Sutton thought it strange that, after receiving a call from his good friend, there hasn't been any further message or contact. It was unusual. Finally, he rang another lifelong friend, Stew Grant. This time he got an answer. 'Now, Stew. How's things, mate?'

'I'm good, thanks. Just about to go shopping with Tina. It'll be hell but at least I'll earn my day out at the weekend. You okay with the tee-off time for Saturday?'

'That's partly the reason I'm ringing. I could be struggling for golf – work, I'm afraid. The other thing is, have you heard from Roger? He rang yesterday but I can't get in touch with him.'

'Strange, I've had a similar experience,' replied Grant. 'I haven't had a reply. Look, you're obviously busy. I'll pop round to see him later after shopping. It'll give me a good excuse when I get bored and rescue the credit card from Tina!' he laughed.

It was after 9.20am and it took Sutton 15 minutes to get through the remainder of the rush hour traffic. After his phone calls, he listened to Radio 2 with Chris Evans doing his stuff before handing over to Ken Bruce. It had been announced that Evans was leaving the breakfast slot. 'Just in time,' thought Sutton, as Evans really had started to get on his nerves to a point that he often preferred the dulcet tones of Nicky Campbell on Radio 5 Live. He switched stations; Campbell was presenting his daily phone-in.

Geoff locked the car at one of the many parking bays available at The Haven and immediately recognised a blue Astra CID car occupying a neighbouring bay. 'That's enough for now, Nicky,' he said to himself, as he pressed the pad that stopped and started the vehicle.

He zipped up his coat and walked across the car park, noticing the Union Jack at half-mast above the front door of the popular community centre. It was a timely reminder of the purpose of his visit.

The Haven was a typical old-style village hall, with wooden flooring and beams and a large stage hidden behind long dark red curtains. There was a dozen or so fold-away tables with similarly designed chairs scattered around the main hall area. Electric fires were giving out necessary warmth on this cold October morning. No doubt the hall was set up for the bridge club, which took place every Wednesday morning at 10am. There were windows along one side of the room and three reasonably sized meeting rooms along the other.

He noticed that DS Joanne Firth, together with her colleague DC Pete Hallett, had already commandeered one of the meeting rooms and a cup of coffee. Firth was chatting with a man dressed in a boiler suit who Sutton rightly guessed was the caretaker. The members of The Haven Bridge Club were arriving in the hall and making their way to a serving hatch, behind which a couple of club members were rostered to make coffee in the small kitchen.

Sutton thought that The Haven had a really welcoming atmosphere, although it would be very sombre this morning following yesterday's tragedy. He knew there would be only one topic of conversation, the tragic death of Enid Benson; hopefully, last night's news about Muriel Eales hadn't yet filtered through. Whilst death was inevitable, the manner in which Enid died had caused even more trauma for her many close friends.

Sutton had already spoken to Firth, after first obtaining approval during his meeting with Turner and Delaney. The plan was to interview approximately ten Haven members, primarily to gain some background information about Enid. It was conceivable that they could uncover an important witness, although the appeals and requests had resulted in a poor response so far. Among the ten would be Charlie Drummond and Hilda Tait; there were specific questions to be put to those two.

It was Hilda Tait's turn on the coffee rota and Drummond would have to be persuaded to talk during a break in his bridge match. Pete Hallett and Joanne Firth started the interviews whilst Sutton walked to the hatch.

'Yes, sir, can I help?' asked a pleasant voice.

'Hilda is it tea or coffee?' demanded another voice from further inside the kitchen.

'Coffee, Hilda. Milk and no sugar please.' Sutton made his request. He'd identified Hilda without trying.

'There you go, Officer. It's tragic, isn't it?' she said.

For a moment Sutton paused, looking down at the very milky drink and remembering times past when his grandparents made coffee with Carnation Milk. His stomach was still recovering.

'It certainly is. Please call me Geoff.' Sutton checked that Hilda's assistant was far enough away not to hear their conversation. 'How well did you know Enid?' he enquired.

'I've known her for over ten years. We met through coming here.' Hilda's eyes welled up. 'Sorry,' she said, and reached inside her apron for a handkerchief to dam any tears before the floodgates opened. 'Enid was the loveliest lady you'd wish to meet. She was a committee member and still so active and sharp.'

Sutton changed the direction of the conversation. 'You seem to be doing very well yourself, Hilda. Live locally?' he continued softly.

'Yes, not far from here but in the opposite direction to Enid. She normally travels in with Muriel, another absolute diamond. I'm surprised she's not here this morning.' Hilda continued, 'I love the company here, although I have Conor at home.'

'Conor?' enquired Sutton, feigning surprise.

'He's my grandson who lives with me. Lovely lad, but his parents didn't want anything to do with him and I've brought him up,' she said proudly.

Sutton saw the tears appearing again in Hilda's eyes. He had the information he wanted for the moment. He'd only known her for a few minutes, but Sutton recognised Hilda Tait was yet another diamond. It was patently obvious that this crime had made a significant impact on The Haven community. 'Hilda, if you hear anything that may assist us in our investigation, please give me a ring.' He gave her a Parton Constabulary card with his details and contact numbers. He took his coffee cup away from the hatch, hoping he'd find somewhere to pour away the contents.

A few more bridge players had made an appearance while he was talking with Hilda. He studied the group. There were about 20 or so members, predominantly female. Some were in deep conversation, whilst others were visibly upset having just been given the news about Enid. Muriel's circumstances had still not been disclosed. Sutton intended to discuss how they were going to relay that information with Joanne Firth before they left The Haven; far better for them to hear the news from the police than someone else.

As Sutton tried to identify Charlie Drummond, Firth addressed the group. She asked if they would be so kind as to speak to the police about yesterday's tragic events. It would be an informal chat; they wanted to create a picture of Enid's lifestyle. Also, someone might unknowingly have pertinent information. The interviews would take place in Meeting Room Two.

Sutton was impressed by Firth. He'd never worked directly with her before, but everyone spoke highly of her ability. She was calm, firm and spoke confidently. She'd been promoted early in her career and had plenty of experience as an acting inspector, but she was almost unique in being an officer perfectly content with her rank.

Jo Firth was in her mid-forties. She'd married her schoolboy sweetheart, only to find out quickly that it had been an awful mistake. After a quick divorce, Jo had concentrated on her career; a hardworking ethic, assisted by some excellent arrests, saw her successful career thrive, with a move to CID and promotion to sergeant.

Pete Hallett, on the other hand, had only recently been appointed to the CID. Young and enthusiastic, Sutton thought he wouldn't get a better tutor than forty-five-year-old Joanne Firth.

Immediately after she'd addressed the group, Firth and Hallett went into the meeting room closely followed by a tall man dressed in dark brown corduroy trousers, shiny brown brogues, checked shirt and a thick woollen jumper. He was immaculate, walking very upright, almost marching – a man on a mission. That would be Charlie Drummond. 'Must be ex-services,' thought Sutton, as he followed him into the office.

Firth allowed Hallett to go through the normal introductory questions. How well did Drummond know Enid? Who were her close friends? Unlike Hilda Tait moments earlier, Drummond showed no emotion. He was experienced with death.

Then Firth took control. 'Charlie, have you got anything that may assist us in the investigation into Hilda's death?'

It was a completely open question and Drummond

hesitated momentarily. 'No, nothing. She was a lovely person and it's a tragedy,' he replied confidently.

'Charlie, why did you call the hotline? And please don't say it wasn't you.' Firth leant forward on the desk, her eyes never leaving Drummond's.

Charlie took more than a moment, his eyes fixed on Firth's. 'He's been here before,' thought Sutton, sitting at the back of the room.

'Well, officer, it's a stab in the dark. Hilda Tait is my good neighbour, a lovely and devoted lady. She lives with her grandson, Conor. She doesn't say much about his circumstances, but if you want my opinion, she's intimidated by Conor. He was abandoned by his parents and Hilda was left with him. He's a shit,' Drummond said with conviction. Using such language in front of a female didn't sit well with him, although Firth had frequently heard a lot worse.

Drummond continued, 'A month or so ago, I asked him to pick up some litter he'd thrown on my grass. He became abusive. I threatened to call the police then thought better of it, and he put a brick through my kitchen window. I thought about reporting it but bottled out, it would be his word against mine. Hilda doesn't need the grief and I suppose, at my age, I don't either. A few years ago, I would have sorted him.' After a short pause and without any prompting, Drummond asked, 'Why? Do you think he's maybe involved in the Parton Smart Team? (the notoriety of the PST was ever increasing particularly amongst the elderly people of Parton) Well, he sometimes has company at Hilda's. I'm nearly sure that on one occasion, from a distance I saw him pushing a moped that must have broken down. It was a few months back. I couldn't positively identify him – normal thing, hoody up. But I tell you, this Conor Tait is capable of something like this and he wouldn't give a toss.' Drummond spat out the last few words.

'Poor Hilda looks after him like a prince, and she won't

have a bad word said about her lovely Conor, but I tell you he's a shit.' Drummond repeated himself as if to emphasise how he felt about his young neighbour. He neither remembered nor thought it relevant to mention Tait's tattoo that he'd recognised.

There was silence in the room as everyone digested his honest, heartfelt words. The peace was broken by Sutton who pulled up a chair and sat next to Drummond. 'Mr Drummond,' he said, deliberately using Charlie's surname out of formality as well as respect. 'I'm Geoff Sutton and I'm also working on this enquiry. Could you please help us?'

Drummond pulled his eyes away from Joanne Firth and looked directly at Sutton. 'Mr Sutton, why should I help you? We have the usual disorder around here, youngsters gathering consuming drink and probably drugs, a bit of graffiti here and there. We always report it as we've been instructed to by the police. Everyone who lives in Meadowland Crescent is elderly and we're all, to a person, law abiding. Form a Neighbourhood Watch, we were told, so we did. What did we get from it? Bugger all, Mr Sutton, bugger all. And please don't take this personally. You haven't got the resources to tackle the issues that affect our daily lives. I don't know how I can help you and I certainly don't want anything I do to cause Hilda Tait any more problems. She's got enough on her plate already with that lad.'

Sutton took his time; Drummond's comments were valid criticisms. Eventually he said, 'Charlie, Enid Benson is dead. The person or people responsible haven't been apprehended. Conor Tait may or may not be involved, but at the moment he's the only lead we've got. Am I right in saying that you live in a semi-detached bungalow, with your living room adjoining Hilda Tait's?'

'That's correct,' Drummond replied immediately.

'With your permission, we'd like to install some technical equipment – a listening device – in your premises that would allow us to record the conversations that take place next door. We would arrive disguised as plumbers, so you'd need to have some cover story – maybe say you're having boiler trouble that you want sorting before winter sets in.'

Drummond sat bolt upright in his chair, looking down at his gleaming brown brogues, chin hard against his chest.

Sutton didn't let up the pressure. 'Enid was run down, Charlie. And, just to let you know, Muriel Eales, who was with Enid at the time, had her windows smashed last night. She's currently in hospital. We need your help, Charlie, and we need it now.' He had played his final card.

There was a prolonged silence. Drummond seemed to be in a trance until his military experience of obeying orders kicked in. But it was more than just obeying orders; it was the old adrenalin beginning to flow through his ageing veins. Charlie Drummond was actually excited. 'Yes,' he finally replied. 'When will you come?'

'This afternoon when you get home. I'll need the official authorisation and also to organise the equipment. If you give me your mobile or landline number, I'll tell you exactly who will be coming around and at what time. Thanks, Charlie,' Sutton said sincerely, placing his hand lightly on the pensioner's shoulder.

Drummond pushed back his chair, shook hands with everyone in the room, turned tail and marched out of the meeting room back into the hall to his impending bridge match.

'Great stuff, Geoff,' said an admiring Joanne Firth.

'Well, it may or may not be successful, but Conor Tait requires some scrutiny. He's made a lasting impression on Charlie Drummond,' said Sutton hopefully.

'I'll phone Ron Turner and get the authorisation. Jo, can you liaise with Technical Support and sort out times for deployment? I'll also have a word with Trish and bring her up to speed.'

'That's all good, Geoff. Pete and I will continue interviewing for an hour or so, you never know what we might uncover,' Firth smiled at Sutton.

He finally walked out into the hall and waved at Hilda Tait, who was still serving milky coffee through the serving hatch. His stomach retched slightly as he left the community hall.

His phone rang, it was Debbie and any thoughts of sickness evaporated.

11

Stew Grant

On that same Wednesday morning, the Grants made their way to the Carsten Plaza in separate vehicles because they anticipated going their separate ways after shopping. The Plaza had easy parking and most of the shops that Tina liked; although there were a few empty premises caused by the massive increase in online shopping, it remained a pleasant environment.

'If that's what Tina wants, anything for an easy life,' thought Stew as they both parked up at 10am. It had been Classic FM for Stew during the journey, one of Beethoven's less well-known symphonies.

An hour or so later. 'Come on, Tina, isn't that enough?' Stew pleaded hopefully, as the pair of them moved from House of Fraser to River Island. He knew his credit card felt the same way as he did. Despite the trauma of William's death, their last ever foster child, and the fact that their fostering days had finally come to an end, some things never changed. Tina, shopping for England was one of them. Purchasing Christmas presents for all the foster kids with whom they still had contact was another.

'I've promised to go and see Roger,' Stew sighed.

'You also promised to come Christmas shopping with me.' Tina grasped his hand even more strongly and dragged him along, like a mother controlling a naughty child. 'One more, Stew,' she said, as they entered River Island. Tina led the way, with Stew almost tripping through the door such was her insistence. She knew that once Stew had disappeared, she'd have a bit of me-time and could get her nails done.

It was after 12 noon when Stew finally gave his wife a peck on the cheek. His job now was to haul the bounty back to his car, load up and head out to Roger's. He felt like a Sherpa helping a climber on his trek to base camp.

He walked past SAMS as he made his way to the underground car park where his white Lexus SUV was parked. They didn't need a car of that size, but it really looked the part; Stew could get his golf clubs in the boot and Tina loved the black-leather heated seats. Her chiropractor had recommended them, although Stew thought that was hardly a reason to buy such an expensive car. But, crucially, Stew had noted that Tina had taken a distinct liking to the young car dealer which just about sealed the deal.

He loaded up the presents and exited the car park. Using the hands-free system, he again tried to call Roger, but it rang out, similar to the previous calls.

Roger Strong's three-bedroom detached bungalow was immediately opposite the entrance to Upper Parton RFC and Stew knew the route like the back of his hand. It took twenty-five minutes of Elgar, followed by Tchaikovsky's 1812 Overture, to accompany him from the underground car park to Roger's home. He was relieved to see his friend's car parked on the driveway; 'not a wasted visit,' he thought.

Stew parked on the roadside and walked down the short driveway to the front door. As a frequent visitor he knew the layout of the house. There had been many Saturday evenings after his wife and son had left him when Roger had invited Stew, Pete and Geoff back to the bungalow after they'd called time at the club for more booze and excellent craic.

Stew rang the doorbell three times but there was no answer. He was puzzled as he walked backwards from the door and looked at the front of the premises. In the porch there was a pair of muddy golf shoes. That would never be the case in the Grants' house; Stew was immaculate everywhere, never more so than on the golf course, whatever the conditions. Immediately to the right of the front door and porch was the attached garage. To the left of the door was the main living room; the curtains were closed, and he couldn't see if there were lights on inside.

He decided to walk along the path that circled the house. As Stew walked past the living room, he paused and put his face up against the window, hoping to find a clue as to Roger's whereabouts. He saw nothing but the long draped curtains blocking his view – strange at this time of day. He reached the gate that separated the front and rear gardens and undid the bolt on the other side.

His heart started beating faster. He thought back to moments earlier, when he'd strode confidently down the driveway towards Roger's front door. That confidence had evaporated as he continued his slow and now cautious walk, still on the path. He reached the corner of the house; the path turned sharp right and followed along the rear of the property. Two of the three bedrooms looked out over the small back garden. Roger enjoyed the garden and he liked to keep his plot tidy.

Stew paused, looked at the back garden and the last autumn leaves scattered around like brown confetti. Heart pounding, he continued. He passed the first bedroom. The curtains were drawn so there was absolutely no view of the inside. At the second bedroom, he was again faced with the closed curtains. He knew this was Roger's bedroom and he banged repeatedly on the window, calling out above the sound of the thumping in his chest, 'Rog, Rog, it's Stew.'

Rather than complete the walk around the bungalow and the attached garage, Stew retraced his steps to the front. He opened the letterbox and called out for his lifelong friend. Nothing. Nothing. Curtains closed at midday at Roger

Strong's house – it just didn't make any sense, not to those who knew him well.

Stew raised clammy palms to his cheeks. His mind was racing, trying desperately to keep up with his heart rate. He decided to retrace his steps and go back around the house, banging on each window and calling out for Roger as he did so. He reached the living room, shouted, banged his fist; pressed his face against the glass at different angles, trying desperately to glimpse anything behind the curtains. At the rear of the premises he repeated the process. Still nothing. Absolutely nothing.

Stew stood, hands on hips then reached into his trouser pocket for his mobile. Shit, no signal. Half a smirk crossed his face as he remembered that one of the benefits of their extended drinking sessions was the fact that it was always difficult to be contacted when they were at Roger's.

He continued to follow the footpath that would take him around the garage and return to the front of the property. He might as well see if there was any sign of life through the garage windows, which he knew had net curtains. He'd been in Roger's garage a couple of times; that's where his friend kept a ready supply of beer, as well as some of his better wines.

He stopped and faced the garage window. From where he was standing, Stew could see the legs of his good friend dangling down, one shoe on, one off.

He ran around to the larger window, passing a small wooden door on the side of the house that faced out onto Roger's neighbours. He thought his heart would explode as he pressed his face against the glass. He could see clearly now: Roger's eyes bulging, his face discoloured, tongue protruding, neck distorted and partially covered by rope deeply embedded into his skin.

Stew's eyes slowly followed the rope upwards, tracing the loop over the beam that formed part of the garage roof. His eyes went further down to the overturned chair, near where Roger's feet would have been. A brandy bottle lay on its side, some of its contents spilt onto the garage floor. He saw a pen and paper lying next to the bottle.

His heavy breathing was making the window mist and he frantically swiped his hand across the glass to assist his view. He would always wish that he had never wiped that window clear. The sight before him, caused his knees to buckle and he dropped to the ground, hands covering his face, crying uncontrollably.

He stayed in that position for some time, unable to move. His knees became numb. 'Get a grip!' he shouted to himself, 'get a bloody grip, Grant!' Slowly he managed to get back to his feet and felt the blood returning to his legs.

He went back to the wooden door, his thoughts slowly clearing. He tried the handle; it was no surprise that it was locked. He shoved with his shoulder and it gave slightly. Stew looked at the frame. He kicked at the door and it groaned; he kicked again and now there was the sound of wood splintering. He stood back and put his shoulder to the wooden structure and there was another groan from the door surround. He stood back and aimed a kick at the lock, kicked twice more and the door gave way.

He was confronted by the hanging body dangling forlornly from the garage roof. The scene was too much for Stew Grant; his recovery ended abruptly. Stew's legs gave way, and he dropped on his knees again, adopting a prayer-like position in homage to one of his closest friends. He had loved Roger Strong.

'Why, Rog? Why?' Stew repeated out loud. He looked to his left; the internal garage door was open to the kitchen and the welcoming sight of a telephone attached to the wall. He tried again to win the battle over his emotions. He needed help, and he needed it quickly.

Struggling to his feet, he went into the kitchen; his legs

didn't seem to be part of his body. He lifted the receiver and punched in 999, deliberately turning his back on the ugly scene behind him.

Stew didn't allow the operator to speak. 'Please help. Please help,' he repeated. 'My mate is hanging from his garage roof. He's dead! He's dead!' Stew began sobbing again.

'Where are you, sir?' came the polite, calm voice at the other end of the line. 'Roger's house,' Stew said without thinking, a stupid but obvious reply.

'No, sir, what address are you ringing from?' asked the patient voice.

'32, Round Park Lane, Parton.'

'And your name, please?' was the final enquiry. 'Stew Grant.'

'Stew stay where you are. Help is on its way.' The operator ended the call.

Stew placed the receiver back in its wall mounting and slumped against the kitchen wall. His legs gave way and he slid slowly to the floor. Staring through the open kitchen door into the garage, he looked at Roger Strong. His uncontrollable sobbing started again.

12

Nevil Samuels

Nevil had opened up SAMS at about 11am on Wednesday morning, the usual time for him. His clientele never, ever arrived earlier. Many of his regulars never got out of bed before lunchtime.

His passing trade came from people either parking in, or collecting their cars from, the multi-storey underground car park nearby. It was always worth opening for passing trade, particularly in the run-up to Christmas. His phone accessories were popular because he was cheaper than the major distributors such as Apple and Carphone Warehouse, both of which had outlets near the centre of the Plaza.

His early start gave him time to replenish stock and complete any repairs such as screen replacements, which were always popular and a good source of regular income. As were the stolen items that Conor Tait and his cronies supplied. Nevil, however, was becoming increasingly concerned about the Parton Smart Team. Conor Tait was more than a nasty piece of work.

Samuels was basically a law-abiding citizen but the pressure of falling trade and his wife's ability to spend money had caused him to reconsider his business. The relationship with Conor had started platonically and Nev was grateful to fence their stolen property, even if he was consumed with guilt. It made him money, which he could keep outside his till, satisfy his wife Joyce's expensive tastes and hide from

HMRC. He didn't make great amounts from the stolen property he handled, but any money was gratefully received. Nev was careful not to bring those small profits into a scenario where his wife started to question him.

The events of the last twenty-four hours had convinced him that he needed the PST away from the shop and, most importantly, away from him. He'd struggled to sleep last night having heard the tragic news about Enid Benson. He knew full well who was responsible and Nev's conscience told him that he himself was implicated in her death. Yes, he took in a few nicked phones, but he didn't kill old ladies.

It might seem perverse, given his criminal activity in handling stolen goods, but Nevil Samuels was fundamentally a good man. If Joyce ever found out he was dealing in stolen goods, his life wouldn't be worth living, not that his domestic life was a bundle of roses. Her behaviour towards him had altered in recent times and she treated him with total disdain. Initially he'd thought it was her idea of humour, but he had come to realise that her humiliating comments were meant with a passion.

He was now caught in a difficult situation. Conor Tait and his crew treated him like Joyce did, and had even begun humiliating him in front of his own son. It hurt Nevil and he needed out but where was courage when it mattered?

It was shortly after 2pm when Conor, Zac, Freddie and Abbie gathered. The café section of SAMS didn't open till then. There wasn't a great deal of conversation. Conor looked at Nevil, almost as an order for him to plug in the gaming machine and start playing the music of their choice. Some ten minutes later, with a track from Synthesis by the American band Evanescence blaring out and energy drinks in hand, the PST were momentarily happy. They would soon start on the gaming machine and Nevil, unable to concentrate, would give up trying to check his stock and repair customers' phones.

As Nevil watched them waste their time, he started to think of a way to end his business relationship with the Parton Smart Team. His major concern was not if they would agree to his proposal, it was whether he had the bottle to deliver the news.

The basic outline of Nevil's plan was that SAMS always closed down for ten days in early January, just after the sales. This was the time when he and his entire family, including grandparents and children, left the winter chill and flew to the Canary Islands, a holiday they couldn't really afford. The kids missed a few days' schooling, but Joyce demanded the trip went ahead, leaving Nevil the aggravation of dealing with the Education Authority. The threatening letters from them were also another annual event.

He'd tossed and turned last night but had finally decided he would tell the PST that he was selling the business after his annual holiday and SAMS would not reopen. He'd say he'd been offered a job at the Carphone Warehouse in the Plaza carrying out phone repairs – good money, no rent to pay and a lot less hassle. He would tell Conor to sling his hook – but not in so many words.

Of course, the truth was that it would be business as usual but without the extra income from their stolen phones. He'd given some thought to potential reprisals from the gang when they found that SAMS was still open. He would tell Conor his wife had changed her mind over his career change – simple as that – and that Nevil would no longer be taking in his stolen mobiles. Easy to plan, now he needed the courage to deliver.

Nevil shouted over to Conor – he had to shout because of the volume of the music.

Conor was busy on the gaming machine. 'I'll be over when I'm finished,' he grunted from beneath his hood. 'Stupid shit.' He didn't care if Nevil heard him.

'It was always on Conor's terms,' thought Nev, similar

to the way that Joyce controlled their marriage. A couple of minutes later, Conor and Nevil were facing each other in the back room of the store. It was a disorganised mess, full of ongoing phone repairs and sales magazines, with another small laptop just visible. Normally Conor would produce a couple of phones in return for the agreed amount of cash, although recently he'd been more demanding and his behaviour increasingly extreme.

'What is it, Nev? I'm busy,' Tait started, annoyed at being interrupted.

Despite him being more than twice this lad's age, he was being intimidated – no, positively frightened – by Conor's presence. Nevil was a slight man, both in build and height, and he felt himself shrink further as he spoke. 'Just to let you know – and you're the first I've told – after our usual winter break in January I'm moving out of SAMS. Packing up. Been offered a new job at Carphone Warehouse. Better money and no bloody rent,' he said with increasing confidence.

There was a pause while Tait stared at him, steely eyes piercing right through him. Then, 'You're not,' came the short but emphatic reply.

Nevil tried to muster the courage to make his point. 'I am, Conor,' he said, deliberating using his Christian name in an effort to befriend him. 'This is the best decision for my wife and family, and they come first.' He couldn't make eye contact with Tait, a fact that wasn't missed.

'You're not,' Tait repeated. His steely eyes hunted out Nevil, forcing him to look directly at him.

'I'm sorry, Conor, but I have to make the right decision for my family,' Nev repeated and pleaded. But if he wanted to appeal to Conor Tait's good nature, he had totally misread the situation.

'You're not, for two reasons. One, you're guilty of handling stolen property. And two, I think you're lying.'

Nevil put his hand out to steady himself. He hated Conor

Tait, but he believed everything he said. 'Conor, SAMS will not exist in the New Year. It's a simple as that.'

Tait fumbled in one of the many pockets in his baggy denims. With a swift movement, he produced his knife. An expert flick of his thumb on a silver button produced a sickening click coupled with the appearance of a four-inch blade that glistened in the gloomy room. It didn't end there. Tait closed the gap between them as the blade was released.

Nevil backed off; he'd never seen Tait with a weapon before. He stared at the blade and noticed the swastika tattoo on the inside of Conor's right wrist.

It was not a planned move, just one of self-preservation as he stumbled backwards over the table where the laptop was located.

Tait followed him, eyes never leaving Nevil, leading with his flick knife. 'Business as normal, Nev. Business as normal. You're a feeble shit. Next thing you'll be telling me we can't park our bikes at the lock-up. Bugger off, Nev, it's not happening.' Tait pushed the blade towards Nevil's face and the menacing tattoo was fully revealed. Then he turned away, laughing to himself and carefully folding the knife as he left the storeroom. He walked back to the gaming machine, ignoring the others, eyes focused on the flashing lights and sounds of the mesmeric machine.

As for Nevil Samuels, he just wanted to lock the door and stay in his storeroom.

Later that night, Nevil spoke to Joyce as they lay in bed. He knew exactly what her reaction would be. Their relationship had deteriorated gradually over the years. She regarded him as a pathetic excuse for a husband, working long hours but barely making a living; it certainly wasn't the life she had anticipated on their wedding day.

'Joyce, I had some trouble at the shop today. I was threatened with a knife, by some youngsters,' he said.

'Report it. I've told you before,' came her impatient

response. She didn't look up from her Maeve Binchy novel. 'Stop being so useless, Samuels,' she added venomously.

'This lad has a swastika tattoo on the inside of his right wrist,' said a troubled Nevil.

Joyce closed her book and switched off the reading lamp at her side of the bed. She knew her pathetic husband wouldn't report the matter; he always ignored her advice and any further discussion would be fruitless. She had an early start and was attending her weekly Pilates class in the morning. She fell asleep immediately, dreaming of a new life, while Nevil tossed and turned before leaving for yet another night in the spare bedroom.

The following morning was the same as any other: Joyce ignored her husband and made sure the children were ready for school. Armed with her exercise mat, she set off without even saying goodbye to Nevil. The saddest part of her deep frustration was that Joyce loved Nevil Samuels. She always would.

***

Geoff Sutton was in a briefing with Trish Delaney. Joanne Firth had organised the technical equipment at Charlie Drummond's, the only slight hiccup being when his neighbour Hilda Tait had knocked on the door with cake and milky coffee for the 'workmen' just as they were about to have a test run. With some excuse about having another urgent job to attend, the 'workmen' were able to avoid any problems. The monitoring for the equipment was in place and the recordings would be studied each morning and actioned accordingly. Other than that, progress in the investigation had been slow and Trish wasn't anticipating any plaudits at her forthcoming appointment with Ron Turner.

The council had proposed some measures to make life more difficult for moped thieves by placing bollards at strategic points in the main crime areas but installing them would take time. The news from the hospital about Muriel

Eales' condition was tragic: mentally shot, the chances of her ever being a competent witness were fast disappearing. Their hope of some forensic evidence from the tyre mark at the scene had so far drawn a blank, and the DNA profile from the recovered phone had been fast-tracked through the system but no matches had been found on the national database. The walls were closing in on Trish Delaney's investigation.

'Geoff, we need some ideas,' Trish said. 'We can't just rely on the technical from Conor Tait. We haven't any proof on his involvement, other than that he's a nasty piece of work.'

Sutton looked around Delaney's welcoming office. His phone had been going crackers over the past ten minutes, but he'd put it to silent, as was his custom when he was in a briefing. He wanted to ensure he was giving the investigation his total concentration. It was difficult because he had several ongoing distractions; a phone call to Debbie as well as discovering whether or not Stew or Pete had contacted Rog.

Despite these external matters, Sutton put them to one side as he summed up the investigation. 'Trish, we need proof,' he said emphatically. 'We have no intelligence other than Charlie Drummond's opinion, which is a tenuous link at this stage. We have nothing of forensic value either from Enid's death or last night's incident at Muriel's bungalow. We know that the tyre marks found at the precinct were identical to those found in the mud close to Muriel's, but there's no DNA match from the phone recovered at the scene. What about trying to put someone in – a human source?'

Delaney paused for a second, considering Sutton's comments. 'The problem with Tait is that we don't have anyone who would match his profile,' she said. 'We have him at his nan's but nowhere else. It would be far too obvious if we deployed a couple of hoody types to roam the streets and bump into him. We need someone far younger than any of our available undercover operatives. What about a decoy job?

We could easily dress someone up to act as bait, an officer made up as a pensioner using a mobile phone, equipped with CS gas. We'd need other responders close by – perhaps a stinger to shred the tyres of the mopeds in the event of a pursuit. It would be resource intensive, but it might work. Do you think Turner would authorise it?' Sutton could detect a certain amount of desperation in her voice.

'If you're looking for a senior officer with bottle who's willing to put his neck on the line with authority, Ron Turner is your man. But be prepared, Trish, because he'll rightly interrogate you about such an operation before he allows it to happen. However much prep you do, he'll always ask you a question you haven't considered. But if we could catch them in the act, crime in action,' Sutton nodded his approval.

Both of them knew that Turner would expect arrests and they were nowhere near that. Sutton continued slowly, 'I may have another option, if we can sell it to Turner? It's fraught with risk and all I'm going on is a recent conversation I had with a training sergeant who has a nightmare student. Apparently, he has the necessary attitude. I've seen him in the flesh from a short distance and he also seems to fit the physical profile.'

Their discussion was halted by an impatient knock on the door. One of the Area Command secretaries poked his head around the door.

'We're really busy.' Trish made it clear that he was an unwanted guest.

'I know, but this is urgent,' came the clear and concise reply. 'A male by the name of Stew Grant rang in an incident about ten minutes ago and now he desperately needs to contact Mr Sutton. He's ringing from a landline number. The address is 32, Round Park Lane, Parton.'

'Shit! Rog,' Sutton said. 'Sorry, Trish. I've got to go.' He picked up his green Barbour and ran out, giving no explanation or affording Delaney the chance to ask why.

Once he'd left, she looked up the incident on her laptop: unexplained death, the address, 32, Round Park Lane, typed neatly underneath.

It took Sutton twenty minutes to arrive at the scene. An ambulance and two marked police vehicles were parked outside, together with Stew's Lexus SUV and Tina's Audi TT. Without a thought of anything or anyone other than his friend Roger, Sutton ran into the house. He didn't even notice the officer just inside the porch, who looked up from his clipboard and tried to grab him.

'Stew! Stew!' Sutton called out repeatedly. He entered the kitchen and saw Tina cradling her husband. The paramedics were completing the formalities confirming Roger's death. Stew was in shock and needed their help.

Tina didn't say anything but, with a flick of her head, indicated the open door which led to the garage. Sutton looked at Roger Strong, still hanging from his self-constructed gallows.

Forensic officers were on their way, together with the duty detective inspector. Force protocol dictated what happened next. He or she would make the decision whether or not the matter would be dealt with as 'suspicious,' even though all the initial indications suggested this was a tragic suicide.

Sutton couldn't move. Why hadn't Rog said something? He suddenly felt anger towards his friend and bitterness swept over him time and time again, like small waves. His thoughts were only interrupted when DI Henry Foster entered the kitchen.

Foster looked at Stew and Tina before turning to Sutton. 'Geoff, can I have a quick word please?' He was a mid-career inspector who, after working with Sutton, had recently made a sideways move from Professional Standards, the complaints department, to take up a CID post as an operational detective supervisor.

As Sutton walked towards him, Foster responded instinctively, taking Sutton in his arms and hugging him close. Henry Foster hadn't a clue what connection Sutton had with the deceased, but he immediately recognised his need for comfort.

Some twenty minutes later, Geoff Sutton and Stew Grant were sitting in Roger's living room briefing Henry Foster who, together with the crime scene manager, had already inspected the garage and read Roger's note. Foster had asked that the knot on the rope be preserved as an exhibit, as well as the note and brandy bottle. The scene had been fully photographed and they were waiting for the undertakers.

Foster judged that Roger's death was suicide and could be handed back to uniform personnel but, before doing so, he wanted to gain as much background information about the deceased as possible.

Fortunately, Stew had recovered a little, thanks more to Tina's words of advice as opposed to anything the paramedics had been able to offer, but he was still confused. 'I never knew Cindy had left him. He never mentioned it. Why, Roger? Why this?'

Foster was patient and let Sutton speak in his own time. 'He was a divorcee – his wife left him about seven years back. She took his son, who will be about seventeen or eighteen now. Roger really struggled because he could never get to see the boy. I think the ex-wife had something to do with that. Understandably it was a major issue in Rog's life – he always hoped that one day his relationship with his lad would be rekindled. So far that hasn't happened. I heard she's gone back to her maiden name and presumably that's now also the son's name. Haven't a clue what that might be or where they are living.'

Sutton continued, 'Then there was Cindy, who was good fun. They met on the internet and things seemed to be going smoothly, but lately it seemed that Roger wanted more from the relationship than she was prepared to give. I never knew she was thinking of leaving him. Roger was one of the first people on the scene at the precinct yesterday when Enid Benson was killed. He was very distressed, but I never thought it would come to this. He rang me, Stew and Pete McIntyre. We all tried ringing back but there was no answer. Then Stew came around and here we are.' Sutton looked down, his voice faltering.

Each line of Roger's brief suicide note ended with the word SORRY.

The doorbell rang; a uniformed officer went to the door to be confronted by Pete McIntyre. 'No! No!'

Both Sutton and Grant recognised Pete's voice long before he ran into the living room. They stood up and all three joined in a prolonged embrace. It was an emotional sign of love and loss. Foster left the room for a moment so that their grief could be shared in privacy.

'Why, Rog? Why didn't you tell us? We should have acted on that phone call,' Stew said to everyone and no one. Each of them felt that same guilt.

Foster gave them a few moments before returning to the living room. 'Do you know who would be his next of kin?' he enquired.

'That's a really good question,' said Pete, who'd rushed here from childminding his grandson Ben, his Upper Parton RFC scarf wrapped untidily around his neck. 'I think it would be his brother Alan – he lives in Cumbria. Definitely not his former wife or his son. Nope – Alan, I guess.' He looked at Stew and Geoff for confirmation.

'Yep, Alan,' said Stew. 'They saw each other regularly. Alan came over to watch some of the games at the club. Nice bloke.'

'I noticed a few phone numbers pinned on the kitchen wall,' Sutton chipped in.

'Thanks for your help,' Foster said. 'It'll be a matter for

the coroner now. We'll search the premises but sadly there's nothing to suggest anything other than Roger took his own life. Even though there's so much more happening around mental illness awareness, it seems that no one was actually aware of how acute his problems were. Please don't blame yourselves – although that's easy for me to say. I'll give you a ring if anything comes to light from the search, Geoff, but I'll be handing the incident over to uniform personnel. I'm sure you'd rather be somewhere else than here. The undertakers are expected within thirty minutes,' Foster said, and handed each of them a leaflet advertising various counselling services.

The three men walked out of Roger's bungalow. Tina was sitting in her Audi, trying desperately to repair her smudged mascara. She'd already left the house to allow the police to start their search; she certainly didn't want to be around when the undertakers arrived.

'Let's go to the rugby club,' said Pete. It was late afternoon and darkness had already descended.

'Will it be open?' asked Sutton.

'It bloody will be. The Under-15s have training after school on a Wednesday,' Pete stated with some authority.

'Leave the cars. We'll sort them tomorrow. Come on.' Stew shrugged at Tina who rolled her eyes. 'See you when I see you. Give me a kiss.' She pursed her lips.

Pete, Stew and Geoff walked across the road and up the driveway to Upper Parton RFC's warm and welcoming clubhouse. Without the need for any words, they draped their arms over each other's shoulders as they passed the first team pitch. They failed to look around and see Tina, whose temporary mascara repairs had failed again. The tears were rolling down her cheeks as she watched her husband walk away from her with his two best friends. She knew there should have been four of them.

***

The Parton Smart Team had whiled away the afternoon at SAMS, taking it in turn to play the gaming machine, listening to the music and having yet more cans of energy drink. Conor Tait was determined to stay as long he possibly could in order to piss off Nevil even more. They'd agreed that, after the previous twenty-four hours, the best plan was for them to keep their heads down. It was unanimously agreed, although they always agreed with what Conor suggested. But for how long would they be inactive, their criminal activity was a drug for the PST, a drug which had become increasingly addictive.

It was 6pm when they left SAMS. Everyone ignored Nevil. Conor walked out with Zac; he was going back home to Nan's. Freddie and Abbie went back to her mam's. They knew she would be out working, and they'd have the house to themselves to do as they wished.

'Hello, boys,' said Hilda, as the two of them, hoods up, entered her bungalow. 'Time for tea. What about fish and chips?'

'Cheers, Nan,' Conor replied. 'Can I have salad cream on my chips and some bread and butter?' he added.

'Same for me, Nan,' said Zac.

After placing their orders, they took control of the living room and TV remote. Hilda hunted out the chip pan, knowing she'd be confined to the kitchen for the evening. Whilst not unheard of, it was unusual to have the boys at home during the evening. She immediately banished any potential wrongdoing from her mind. It was her Conor, bless him. She would cook the tea then tune in to Radio 4, where she hoped that she'd pick up a rerun of one of her favourite quiz shows, Just a Minute.

Conor sat with the remote, flicking through the screens mindlessly. After a few seconds, he threw it away. 'Nothing on,' he announced, as he set up the PlayStation 4 and threw some controls in Zac's direction. Conor had chosen *Red Dead*

Redemption 2; 'Suitably violent,' he thought.

'Had a word with Nevil this afternoon,' he said.

'Anything in particular, Con?' asked Zac as he grappled with the control wiring then lounged back on the sofa alongside his hero.

'The shit told me a pack of lies about selling SAMS after his winter holidays. Load of bollocks.'

'What did you say to him?' Zac asked with interest.

'I didn't say much really,' said Tait. 'Just put a knife to his guts.' He smiled to himself.

Previously Zac had seen Conor with his flick knife, but he'd never seen him use it. He didn't really know how – or if – he wanted to continue the conversation. 'Let's see who wins, Conor,' he said, tackling the buttons on his controls. But they already knew who would win; Conor Tait won at everything.

Meanwhile Nan was frying away, apron on, trays at the ready. She'd already taken through the salad cream with slices of well-buttered bread. Conor and Zac said very little, let alone thanked her.

***

Back at Upper Parton Rugby Club, Pete, Stew and Geoff had been in the clubhouse for an hour and a half. They'd pulled up the high chairs with their nameplates screwed onto the rear and placed them around 'their' table. They made sure that Roger's empty chair was with them and Pete had wrapped his Upper Parton RFC scarf around it. It was more than appropriate.

When they'd arrived, the Under-15s had finished training and were in the club having a fizzy drink whilst waiting for their stressed parents. Within half an hour the place was empty, and the men were alone with their thoughts. They informed Rozanne, the club steward, that Roger had passed away and, despite being asked the obvious question, they tactfully didn't disclose any further details.

Whilst Rozanne made herself busy preparing for an evening party that was being held this coming Friday, the three continued to drink and reminisce about Roger. They told funny stories about their lost friend, yet between each yarn was the question: why? Why hadn't they spotted that their friend was in so much trouble? Why hadn't he mentioned something to them? Didn't they know him best? Weren't they the closest of friends?

Then there were the personal recriminations as to why they hadn't answered his first phone call. If they had done, would Roger still be with them? It was the fact that none of them had detected Roger's inner turmoil and mental health issues that hurt so deeply. They would have to live with the consequences of Roger's death and they'd never come to terms with their failure to notice the problems that had driven him to hang himself.

It was after 9pm when they called it a day. Tina came to take Stew home; she would drop Pete on the way. Geoff preferred to walk back up the hill.

They said their farewells to Rozanne and stumbled from the toilets near the front door and out into the cold October air. They embraced one more time before Sutton set off across the first team pitch. He tucked his chin deep into his coat and approached the picnic area near to the bridge where, some eighteen months previously, he'd spotted the vehicle that contained the bodies of his two murdered colleagues which had sparked off Operation Trust.

He stopped at the bench that commemorated those officers and, despite the cold, chose to sit for a minute or two. He sat, elbows on his knees, hands supporting his heavy head. He looked briefly at the plaque in memory of his colleagues. Strangely, he felt safe here but also emotionally weary as the last few hours of alcohol began to take their toll.

He checked his phone. There were now four missed calls from Debbie; they still hadn't spoken since he'd walked out of the restaurant during her birthday meal. He looked upwards, appealing for help. Then, with a huge effort, he got to his feet and began his lonely ascent up the hill to the sanctuary of home. Thoughts of Conor Tait and the death of Enid Benson had been completely banished.

'Why, Roger? WHY?' he repeated to himself.

A few hours later, at 3am the following morning, Stew awoke screaming, his nightmare of discovering Roger swinging from the garage rafters, eyes bulging would reoccur until he sought necessary counselling. He clung to Tina for the remainder of a very long night.

***

Trish Delaney had just returned to her office after another face-to-face briefing with Turner, who had wanted a report on the progress of Operation Proof, the name now allocated to the investigation of the Parton Smart Team.

She'd hoped that Turner's mind would be fully occupied with planning for the British First march, taking place in the city centre this coming Saturday. She'd tried her best to be positive. Turner had seemed to like the idea of infiltration and installing the listening device, although she'd never supervised such a specialised op. Turner's final question about when he could expect an arrest was something he knew Delaney couldn't answer.

Where was Sutton when she really needed him? Delaney knew she'd have to wait for Geoff to contact her. But, knowing Sutton, she'd be very surprised if she didn't get a call first thing the following morning.

13

Debbie

Sutton awoke at 6.15am the following morning. He had collapsed into bed the night before some time shortly after 9pm. He smiled as he slowly remembered last night's conversations with Stew and Pete, but his smile disappeared, as he thought back to the scene at Roger's bungalow. 'Why, Roger? WHY?' he asked himself yet again, those thoughts completely blocking his blinding headache. The recriminations would never leave him.

He forced himself out from underneath the duvet and walked into the kitchen where he gulped down orange juice, quenching his raging thirst and washing down a couple of Anadin Extra, before returning to bed with a large mug of tea.

Despite his epic hangover, his mind was extremely active. They'd agreed that Pete would keep in contact with Roger's brother, Alan, and assist with anything the family needed. As far as Sutton was concerned, he needed to get back to work and find out from Trish Delaney if there had been any developments. The thought of taking a day off after Roger's death never entered his mind. Geoff Sutton was back, working on another major enquiry.

He lay in bed as the rehydration and headache tablets started to take effect. He thought about Debbie and decided he would start the day at her café, The Parlour. Not only would that give him chance to explain the last twenty-four hours, a fry up was particularly appealing in his current condition.

He turned on his old Binatone clock radio and listened to Radio 5. After finishing his mug of tea, he fell in and out of sleep until 7.30, when he crawled out of bed and stumbled into the shower. The power of the water bouncing off his shoulders helped bring him back to life as he stood, head down, feeling the water envelop him and gather around his feet. 'God, that feels better,' he thought, as he tried to relax, and droplets eased into his pores. He reached blindly for the shower gel which nosedived into the shower tray. With a massive effort, he stretched down, grabbing blindly to retrieve the object, his hangover headache momentarily returning.

A few minutes later, invigorated, Sutton picked up his Barbour and went out of the door. He ignored the Skoda; a walk to the café would offer some exercise, fresh air and an opportunity to clear his head before meeting Debbie.

The weather was definitely becoming colder. He checked the car windows and noticed just the faintest marks of frost. It was only a five minute walk from his house to the line of shops where The Parlour Café was located in the Springfield Green housing estate. He walked through the car park at the rear of the Falcon pub and decided not to buy his usual paper, *The Times*, from Dillon's newsagents next door to the café. He was anticipating a busy day, with little opportunity to read and try the small crossword. Also, the newsagent was owned by Debbie's brother, Billy Dillon Smith, and the last thing Sutton needed at this particular time were Smithy's wisecracks about him and Debbie.

Sutton walked into The Parlour. Thursday was a quiet day for the café, and it was too early for the school run customers; it was empty but for a couple of contractors sporting luminous yellow tabards, waiting to pick up sandwiches to fuel the day ahead.

Debbie appeared with two bulging white paper bags and Sutton realised what attracted him to her: a slim curvaceous figure and gorgeous, deep-brown eyes. Those eyes seemed to light up when she saw him. She was wearing her work outfit, the purple pinafore with *The Parlour Café* printed over her left breast.

'Two sausage and mushrooms, lads.' She handed over the bags. The two men left the café and Debbie's eyes followed them; then her eyes met Sutton's.

'Hi, Debbie. Can I have a full breakfast, please?' Without warning, Sutton suddenly felt emotion rock his body like a deep tremor. The sight of her triggered a natural reaction to the events since they had abruptly parted company, and he desperately tried to keep his composure.

Debbie had started to walk towards Sutton but, sensing all was not right, she paused and stood still. Sutton was fighting, fighting so hard, trying to keep his emotions in check because that's what was expected.

Debbie stood still for what seemed like an age. A large part of her wanted to take him into her arms but she recognised that he needed to win his personal battle. She turned, head down, and went back to the kitchen to give him the time and distance he needed.

A few minutes later, she was sitting at his table and Sutton was attacking his breakfast. His emotions temporarily under control, he was tucking into his fried offering as if nothing had happened. Such was human nature. Between mouthfuls, he gave Debbie a full account of the events after he'd left her at the restaurant. He purposefully didn't mention Roger until he'd finished his meal.

He looked around, checking that no one was just about to enter the café, then took hold of her hands and looked into her eyes. 'I've got some really sad news. Roger Strong died yesterday.'

She took her hands away from his and covered her mouth.

'But how? An accident?' she asked, eyes wide.

'He hanged himself. Committed suicide,' Sutton said abruptly.

'What? No!' She shook her head.

'Debbie, Roger left a note. Apparently Cindy had left him, and he still couldn't contact his son. He must have been in a right state. We never knew. It's bloody awful, Debs. He rang us all before he died. Although we rang back, we never got an answer, so Stew went around yesterday afternoon and found him. We all feel so very guilty Debbie,' he said with conviction.

'I'm so sorry, Geoff. So sorry.' Debbie had only known Roger for a short while, but it hadn't taken any time at all to appreciate the strong bond between the four friends. She really didn't know how to respond. Debbie struggled being close to anyone, particular a man, something that she'd only realised since her relationship with Sutton had begun. It was the knock-on effect of the violence that she'd suffered. Her therapy sessions were due to start that afternoon. It had taken nearly eighteen months for her to accept that she needed help to move on from the past, and this was a crucial day in her recovery.

Sutton looked at her closely. He was strongly attracted to her but, in a moment where both would have benefitted from physical contact there was an immovable barrier between them. It had been apparent the first time they'd kissed. Sutton had forgotten the number of times Debbie had pulled away from him, apologising as she did so.

'I'm at work today. I'm on an enquiry. That was why I got that call and had to leave the restaurant. Haven't a clue when Rog's funeral will be. His brother Alan is liaising with Pete.' Sutton spoke quickly, wanting to give her as much information as possible.

'I'm so sorry, Geoff,' said Debbie. 'Look, give me a ring later when you can. I have my first therapy session today.'

She tidied the empty plates and mug from Sutton's table, placing a tender kiss on his cheek as she did so.

'Good luck with that,' he said with genuine feeling, his recently kissed cheek burning. He rose from his seat as his phone began to ring in his inside jacket pocket. When he saw the caller's name, Joanne Firth, appear on the screen. 'I'm sorry Debbie. I have to make tracks, work I'm afraid,' Sutton said quickly, allowing his phone to ring off.

Debbie shrugged and went back to the kitchen as he scurried out of the café, now wishing he had driven to The Parlour. He walked quickly back to his house. Reversing the Skoda out of the driveway he rang Joanne Firth, who answered almost immediately.

'You okay, Geoff?' were her first words. She was fully aware of Roger's Strong suicide having been informed by Trish Delaney.

'Yes, I'm alright. Thanks, Jo. How's the investigation?' Sutton enquired.

'That's why I was ringing. We've had a development from the listening device at Drummond's place. How far away are you? I'm meeting DCI Delaney in thirty minutes.'

'I'll be there,' said Sutton enthusiastically. The news changed his mood completely.

As he drove, Sutton felt the adrenaline course through his veins, wondering what had been found on the listening device. It took him twenty-five minutes to make the journey to the police station. He used the time to phone both Pete and Stew, more of a welfare check than anything else.

Pete was meeting Alan, who'd travelled from Cumbria the previous night. Tina had ordered Stew to go out for brunch then take a walk together along the marina. They both seemed fine but, then again, so did Roger.

Sutton frowned as he manoeuvred through the security gates and parked in an unallocated bay.

He walked across the car park, meeting training sergeant

Jim Glasson along the way. 'Hi, Jim. How is PC Charlton?' he asked.

'Don't talk about that shit,' spat the smart uniformed sergeant. 'He has a tutorial with me and the chief super this morning. They're looking to pedal him,' Glasson smiled before adding, 'Not before time. He's got his police federation representative all lined up but, after walking out of an assessment yesterday without giving any reason other than stating he thought it was a complete waste of time, he'll be extremely fortunate if he gets another opportunity.'

'Maybe it just isn't the job for him,' said Sutton helpfully.

'I know, Geoff, and I've had a few like that, which is absolutely fine. But it's the way he's gone about it. It's as though he joined with twenty-five years' service behind him. His arrogance is beyond belief, it really is,' said Glasson emphatically.

They parted ways, Glasson to the training department in the main headquarters block whilst Sutton made his way to Delaney's office, coat over his arm, Parton Constabulary fake-leather document holder in his hand. Despite the cold, it was hardly worth the effort of wearing his coat for the thirty yard walk.

He walked quickly, excited at the possibility of a break-through in the enquiry.

Sutton let his concentration wander, thinking back to his recent meeting with Debbie. He thought back to when their relationship began; he was on cloud nine, captivated by her. On his days off he helped out at The Parlour Café; if he wasn't playing golf, he was cleaning tables and doing the washing up. But he couldn't get close to her; there was no intimacy and he craved that after being on his own for so long. Yes, he understood about her horrendously abusive relationship; yes, he was patient – but he felt that everything was on hold. Hopefully, these therapy sessions would be the answer. It had taken some time to persuade her to seek professional help. Debbie's brother, Billy, had been forced to step in when he realised that Sutton was struggling.

Sutton had always been quite shy with women, although alcohol fuelled his bravery from time to time. Since his wife's death some years previously, he'd been celibate. He'd also seen so many police officers' marriages evaporate because of other relationships, usually within the organisation. That was not for Sutton; he was both loyal and professional at all times.

He climbed the stairs to the offices of the area command hierarchy, where only yesterday he'd been given the news of Roger's death. He shuddered as he remembered. He knocked on the door and entered Trish Delaney's friendly office. Sitting in front of her desk was Joanne Firth, who immediately stood, as Sutton entered the room, not as a sign of respect but to take her mug of coffee recently delivered from the modern machine. It was a silent, awkward moment when no one knew what to say.

She finally gave him a sympathetic smile. 'Hi, Geoff. You okay?' She repeated the question she'd posed during their recent phone call.

'Yes, thanks, Jo. We hadn't a clue he was so ill.' Sutton hoped that a short explanation would put an end to talk of Roger's death and they could focus on the enquiry.

Without asking, Delaney supplied Sutton with another mug of frothy liquid and handed it to him before sitting behind her desk. 'Right, Jo, shoot,' she said.

'We've had our first translation from the listening device at Charlie Drummond's house,' Joanne said. 'Conor Tait and another youth went back there in the early evening and played some computer game, but they did have a short conversation about an incident that had occurred earlier. It appears they have a connection to a place called SAMS. Conor had an altercation there, something about the owner wanting to finish trading. That didn't go down too well with our Conor, who used a knife to threaten him.' She took a large mouthful of coffee. 'We've done some research on SAMS. It's a phone accessory business in Carsten Plaza owned by a bloke called Nevil Samuels.'

'Is he recorded or known?' Sutton interrupted.

'No, nothing at all,' Firth replied confidently.

'It's looking more promising all the time,' said Delaney. 'We just need a little more.'

'At least it's a starting point,' said Sutton. 'Let's see if we can get someone into SAMS. It will need absolute secrecy, and it will have to go through Turner. We haven't got the time or profile to go national, but I have an idea.'

'Geoff, I've never run an undercover operation like that,' Trish Delaney objected. 'I'd be really concerned about the risks.'

'I think we've got to level with Turner. We'll need his authority and I personally think he'll need to consult the chief, because what I have in mind would fall outside the normal process and she may disagree.'

'Why don't we just lock Tait up? We have reasonable suspicion and we are investigating robberies where phones are stolen. Now we have a name of someone who frequents a shop that may be dealing with those phones,' Firth summed up.

'We've got no other evidence,' said Sutton. 'We need more.'

'A search following his arrest could recover more evidence against him,' Firth retorted. 'We could approach Nevil Samuels on the quiet and interview him. He's not recorded, but he could be the key to getting at the main people. We may recover some stolen phones and be able to put him under pressure.' It was a reasoned argument.

'Yep – and we could lose our best lead if Samuels says nothing and then informs Tait of our interest. But it's an option for Turner to consider,' Sutton said.

Trish Delaney leant back in her chair and puffed out

her cheeks. She had listened intently to both sides of the discussion. Partly because of her lack of experience, she would have opted for Firth's plan because it was less risky, but she was wise enough to consult Turner and allow him to make what would be a crucial decision. That was his job.

She picked up the phone and dialled an internal extension. 'Sir, it's Trish Delaney. Can I have a short meeting with you? It's urgent.'

After a moment, Turner replied, 'See you in five minutes. I then have the British First March to prepare for.'

'I'll have Geoff Sutton and DS Firth with me,' Delaney said. Turner didn't hear; he had already put the phone down.

It was exactly five minutes later when the deputation arrived outside his door. All three were in different mental states. Delaney was nervous, rightly so; this investigation, which would make or break her career, was ramping up. For Joanne Firth, this was her first visit into the lion's den, namely Ron Turner's office, something highly unusual for someone of her rank. As for Sutton, he was smiling to himself. He'd been here before and he knew the score: put your cards on the table and then let Ron decide. Sutton knew one thing was certain: there would be a decision, maybe not immediately – but there would be a decision.

Delaney knocked. 'Come in,' came Turner's sharp response. Trish looked anxiously over her shoulder at the other two as she entered the office.

'Mob handed, Trish,' said Turner. There wasn't a sign of any unfinished business or outstanding matters on his desk, nothing. He took a mouthful of coffee but didn't offer a cup to his guests . He wanted them to know that this unplanned meeting was an unwanted interruption in his busy schedule.

Delaney skilfully summarised their recent briefing, bringing Turner up to date on what was on offer. Turner looked at Sutton. 'Geoff, how on earth are we going to infiltrate this lot? The profile we're after is younger than any undercover cop we could get.'

'Sir, I bumped into Sergeant Jim Glasson the other day. They have a nightmare probationer who thinks he's James Bond. He's arrogant as anything, not known in the area, looks half his age and, from what I've seen, wears clothes similar to those of the PST. He's so cocky and rebellious that they're looking to get rid of him,' it was half a question and half a statement of facts from Sutton, just to gauge the reaction.

'Geoff, you have got to be bloody joking?' Turner said in a slightly higher pitched tone. 'A young lad, no bloody experience, who's struggling to be a cop – and you want to place him into a highly dangerous situation. And, to cap it all, we think this gang may be using weapons. Don't waste my time,' Turner said with feeling.

'So, we go with the other option of arresting Samuels, get nothing, and Tait knows we're onto him. We'll have nothing and the chances are that the gang will continue their activities,' Sutton said, not with any bravery but because he knew Turner rated his operational experience.

Delaney and Firth watched the proceedings with some trepidation. There was a silence in the room as Turner and Sutton looked at each other.

Finally, Turner put his hands on the front of his desk and pushed back his chair. He looked down at his brown, highly-polished brogues. 'Right, Geoff, have a chat with your man. He sounds a bloody nightmare, but I've worked with you long enough to respect your opinion. The lad must agree and not be pushed or enticed in any way. I don't want him to think that success in this particular job guarantees him passing his probation. I'll then decide on our course of action and give you a decision this afternoon. I'm also hoping to persuade the chief that we'll train up some personnel so that if there is a moped chase, they have the training and the authority to pursue and make tactical contact. It will be supervised by the critical incident manager in the control room.'

The three left the room. 'Sutton has some balls,' Turner thought, 'Wanting me to authorise a nightmare probationer for some undercover work. Typical Sutton.'

But these were desperate times.

14

Dominic Charlton

Charlton sauntered across to the training block. He'd been summoned by bloody Glasson, the old fart. His mood wasn't helped because, whilst others in his syndicate had been given time off to study for a forthcoming exam, he had a meeting with Glasson and a chief superintendent. 'Bollocks,' he thought. He'd planned to use the study time for a far more important task: he was about to go online and book tickets at the O2 for Sisters of Mercy. The dates had been published that morning, but bloody Glasson had knackered that.

Shoulders slumped, hands in his pockets, his police issue high-viz jacket and black cargo pants seemed to emphasise his slight figure. His epaulettes, showing his force number, followed the line of his sloping shoulders so that his rank and numbers were unreadable unless you were standing next to him. If there had still been a minimum height requirement for recruits, Charlton's police career would never have even reached this stage. His regulation black boots were dull; he couldn't be bothered to polish them, unlike his fellow classmates who took pride in their appearance and felt privileged to wear the uniform. In fact, had he been wearing his hat, Dominic Charlton would have looked more like a cartoon character than a keen and eager rookie cop.

Life hadn't turned out the way he'd planned for twenty-one-year-old Dominic Charlton. He'd graduated from Kingston University where, as an only child, he had continued living with his elderly parents. His 2:2 in Politics and Economics showed that Dominic, yet again, had failed to achieve his academic potential; that had been a consistent theme throughout his education after he attended a private local school as a day pupil. He spent much of his leisure time locked away, either playing media games or listening to his music. Not for him the social activities normally associated with people of his age. He didn't attract many friends, although there were a few who admired his sharp words and quick responses. He might have spent a fair amount of time on his own, but Dominic Charlton wasn't short of a word or two. He was quick-witted, never overawed or fazed.

Then Charlton had shocked his parents by telling them he was applying for a post in Parton Constabulary, a provincial force in the north-east of the country. If he was successful, he'd live with Aunty Rita. As a family, the Charltons used her house as a base for their annual summer holiday. The unspoilt coastline of Parton was popular with the 'townies' from suburban London.

Dominic's parents didn't pay much attention to the formal vanilla-coloured envelopes that appeared addressed to him. Nor did they ask too many questions when Dominic made three separate visits to Aunty Rita's, while undergoing assessment centres and formal interviews as he progressed through the application process. They believed that this was something that young Dominic had to get out of his system. The chances of him being successful and becoming a fully-fledged police constable were remote, to say the least.

For Dominic, the challenge of going through the assessment centres, interviews and psychometric testing was one of the main reasons why he wanted to join. He thought the whole rigmarole was a bit of a laugh – although his pleasure was marred by the rigours of the fitness test, which he only just passed by feigning injury.

After the final envelope arrived and he was formally

offered a place with Parton Constabulary, Dominic decided he'd have to embark on some reasoned conversation with his parents, something more than a few grunts when he acknowledged a meal or two.

But things had not turned out as he hoped. The euphoria of passing the recruitment process had changed dramatically when he started his training. He didn't take kindly to a disciplined approach and, when he questioned anything, he and his training sergeant Jim Glasson were poles apart. No one seemed to appreciate his outlook on life.

The only aspects of his new career that appealed to Charlton were the practical scenarios. In many instances, whether it was a public order arrest or a shoplifting offence, he was able to sabotage Sergeant Glasson's well-planned lesson by changing the script or providing some unplanned comment or action that ruined the intended outcome. No wonder Glasson was calling time on his protégé.

Dominic decided to knock on the door as opposed to just entering. He had previously arranged for a police federation representative to be present and look after his interests but, typical Charlton, he'd got both the time and venue wrong. He just wanted to get this bloody thing over; whatever the consequences, he didn't really care.

'Come in.' He heard Glasson's familiar voice and entered his sergeant's training office, which was adorned with photographs of passing out parades where Glasson's students met the chief constable before progressing to operational duties.

Glasson sat behind a large desk, together with Chief Superintendent Linda Odell.

'Please sit down, Dominic,' said Odell. There followed a well-documented narrative, delivered by the chief superintendent but obviously written by Glasson, that catalogued Constable Charlton's behaviour since he'd started his career with Parton Constabulary. It didn't sound good.

Dominic had to stifle a yawn at one stage, as the whole process began to bore him. He had decided beforehand he would record the interview on his phone just in case they made any errors that he could use to his advantage.

Some five minutes later, Charlton was out of the room and walking back across to the student area where he could continue his search for Sisters of Mercy tickets. Odell's last sentence had been simple: 'This is your final warning.' Dominic laughed at the thought of her serious face as she summed up their conversation.

Yet Dominic Charlton's police career was about to take a strange path as Geoff Sutton and Joanne Firth approached him on his walk back from the training block. At the same moment, ACC Ron Turner was ringing Odell to inform her that he was dealing with a welfare matter concerning PC Charlton and his parents. It was a sensitive matter and Charlton might have to go on sick leave for a short time. Turner apologised for being so vague, but he would keep her informed. Odell knew better than to question Turner.

Joanne Firth had organised a small office with its own private entrance at the rear of the custody suite at Parton Central Police Station. Charlton had taken some persuading to accompany her and Sutton. They had said that they needed to have a word with him because they were looking at a potential target for drug activity that lived near his aunt's house and they needed him to record some vehicles and sightings. They would supply him with a photograph of the target, as well as his vehicle details.

'This is more like it,' thought Charlton, 'This is living the dream.' He put Odell's recent words and his forthcoming class with Glasson completely out of his mind.

Firth and Sutton sat at one side of the table and Charlton slouched in a seat opposite them. Sutton struggled out of his green barbour. He glanced across at Charlton and fully understood Glasson's anger when he was faced with this lad who thought he was the real deal. Sutton decided to take charge from the outset; Charlton would either listen to what he had to say or walk out of the room.

Sutton placed his phone on the desk to record the meeting and asked Charlton to hand over his mobile. The constable reluctantly complied.

Sutton looked across at him. 'Dominic, we have a proposition for you, a proposition that you're under no pressure to accept. We have an investigation underway into an organised crime group. The Parton Smart Team has already caused the death of one pensioner as well as committing numerous other violent crimes. The problem is escalating, and we need to gather evidence to bring them to court. One of the ways we can do that is by deploying someone close to them. You fit the profile of the group and you're not known in this area. But the operation comes with significant risks both to yourself and the organisation.'

'I'll do it,' Dominic said, butting in. 'Does it mean I won't have to attend Glasson's lessons?'

'Depending on the outcome of the investigation and your participation, it could well end your career with Parton Constabulary – and any other force for that matter.' Sutton's eyes never moved from Charlton's as he wondered what the hell made this lad tick.

'That doesn't concern me,' Charlton answered confidently. 'So far it's been crap and Glasson says I may not last the course. Anything for a change,' he said, almost with some enthusiasm.

Sutton sat back, folded his arms and shot a glance at Firth, who nodded for him to continue. 'We know this gang hang out at a shop called SAMS in Carsten Plaza, a shopping mall on the outskirts of the city. The guy who owns the shop is Nevil Samuels and he sells mobile phones and accessories. We think he's probably involved in some way, taking in stolen mobiles, but he's frightened by the gang and particularly by their leader, Conor Tait. The gang members dress in a similar uniform of hoodies, baggy denims and trainers. They're followers of Goth music.'

A smile appeared on Charlton's face.

Sutton continued, 'They commit their crimes using mopeds. We haven't a clue where they store their vehicles. Most importantly, we believe that Tait is armed with a knife, which he's used to threaten people.' He stopped and looked for Charlton's reaction but there wasn't a flicker of emotion.

'Presumably, you want me to go to SAMS and find out what's happening,' Dominic said nonchalantly.

Sutton leant forward, arms and elbows firmly on the table that separated them. 'You need to listen carefully to what I have to say, Dominic. You are a Police Constable,' he reminded him, it was a statement of his public duty. 'You will be controlled by me and DS Firth. You will not go outside the strict remit we give you. Before any deployment, we'll pick you up and drop you off. You sign a contract on the limits of your involvement in this operation – go outside the terms of this contract and you'll be acting on your own. There are significant dangers and, to put it bluntly, you are a last resort, forced upon us because your profile matches our targets. If you accept, we'll obtain the relevant authority.'

Charlton leant forward, narrowing the space between Sutton and himself. 'I'm in, Mr Sutton. I'm in. Just tell me where and when.'

Firth ended the stares between the two of them by placing two phones on the desk. 'This is your new phone – use it only on a deployment. The other one is for you to contact us. We're working on a story as to why you'd want to go to SAMS and stay there for any length of time. You might have some ideas about that. Now go home to your aunt's, give her a story about exam revision and await our call. It will be sooner than later. We need to act immediately.'

They swapped phone numbers and Charlton shuffled out

of the room.

Firth and Sutton looked at one another; their conversation with Dominic Charlton was an experience neither of them had encountered before, despite having fifty years' policing between them.

***

Ron Turner had just returned from briefing his new chief constable, Christine Mayling, on the progress of the investigation. For the first time since Operation Trust, he felt under intense pressure. He was enjoying his promotion and he knew it would be the pinnacle of his career – but Mayling had slaughtered him at the briefing. Had he considered this? Had he'd done that? He'd given her as much as he could, but it was a roasting, absolutely no doubt about it, something that he had not endured for some considerable time. Despite this, Turner had a grudging respect for the new chief constable. She was strong and had bottle; her arguments were sound.

In one of Turner's proposals he'd suggested that one officer per shift, in addition to officers from the traffic department, should have the authority to make tactical contact with a moped under the direction of the control room supervisor. He was really excited about the idea of *'tactical contact'*, which he considered to be the politically correct term for the police deliberately knocking the offenders off their mopeds. Mayling had refused outright, giving a reasoned argument on the grounds of public safety and the risk to the organisation. The thought of Sutton's proposal with the probationer constable acting as a covert source in the PST wasn't even discussed. There was a never a hope that she would agree to it.

He took a mouthful of strong black coffee as the tune 'Hi Ho Silver Lining' came from deep inside his jacket. Rummaging for his mobile, he answered Sutton's call.

'Sir, he's up for it,' Sutton said. 'I need the authorisation as soon as possible.'

Turner smiled. Had he the nerve to go forward? He considered for a few moments. 'Crack on, Geoff. Keep me informed. Just make sure that he goes through the relevant psychometric tests with Occupational Health.'

He sat back at his desk. There were some things that Chris Mayling didn't need to know about at the moment; she had too much to lose in her career. Turner hadn't anything to lose, even though he knew that he'd receive the bollocking of his life if she ever found out. 'Roll on retirement,' he thought to himself.

15

Conor, Zac, Freddie, Abbie

Conor was bored but he also had a plan, a plan that made him leave his nan's before lunchtime. Not too unusual recently; Zac had noticed that over the past week or so Conor would return to Nan's just as he was getting out of bed. Zac never asked him where he'd been, nor did Conor divulge anything.

Together with Zac, Conor reached SAMS and entered the shop. He didn't give Nev a glance, never mind a grunt of recognition. Abbie and Freddie were already in attendance, mesmerised as they played the gaming machine. It was never a good idea to be late when Conor summoned them.

He called them over to sit at the table. There was no one else in the shop. 'I'm bored and I want some bloody action.' The fact that the PST had just recently agreed to keep quiet for a while had been completely forgotten, and when Conor wanted some action it happened. 'Right, all four of us are in on this. It's pension day and there'll be loads of the old bastards out and about. For the first time we're going four-handed.' Normally they hunted in pairs. 'The first two will act as outriders, create a distraction. The other two will nick the phone. It's our show of force. We're working the new market on the street behind the precinct. Freddie, Abbie, you do the business, nick the phone. Me and Zac will fly the flag. It'll be a piece of piss.'

A smile appeared on his face. 'There'll be a few bizzies around, particularly after the other day in the precinct. We need to stay down the alleys, out of view.'

Conor took his hands out of his pockets to indicate the direction of travel. As he did so, a wad of £10 notes fell to the floor. The other three noticed the large amount of cash but didn't enquire further. It wasn't their place to question him.

Conor stooped to recover the money and continued nonchalantly, 'Hoods up at all times. Don't be seen until we choose a target – Abbie and Freddie will pick the lucky bastard,' he said smirking. There were no questions.

The new market was proving a success for the community of Parton. The timing of its opening was perfect in the run-up to Christmas. White canvasses, billowing like sails in the late October breeze, covered stalls selling everything from the latest electrical gadgets to wool and embroidery. The noise and buzz of the market life was interspersed by traders shouting out to attract customers and providing demonstrations of their latest bargains.

It was just after 1pm. Conor had been correct in his assumption that the market provided targets aplenty; as well as pension day elderly people tended to start their Christmas shopping early.

Zac, out of public view, kept watch over Conor's moped. Tait did an initial cautious walk-through of the busy market area, cleverly avoiding any unwanted attention. Yes, there were more than a few bizzies; Sergeant Steve Barker had diligently supplied two officers each for both the precinct and the market because of the recent robberies. Resources were sparse but you couldn't put a price on protecting the elderly and in doing so gaining public confidence.

Conor smiled at the increased police presence. How on earth were they going to stop the gang on their mopeds? He again scanned the area. The embroidery stall was ideal, offering a ready supply of static targets. It was in an ideal location, opposite one of the delivery alleyways that gave an easy escape route out of the area. More importantly, that particular delivery alley was not currently covered by CCTV cameras.

He reported back to Zac. 'It's on, Zac. Tell them to meet at the bottom of Burns Alley. We can see the embroidery and knitting stall from there. It's bloody perfect.'

Within minutes, all four of the PST were in situ, with Conor barking out final instructions. 'Right, we observe here. Abbie, you pick a target. Me and Zac will go first, create a distraction by heading up Market Street, away from the stall. In the meantime, you and Freddie do the business. We'll meet up at SAMS around four.'

There was no response; hoods were up, and the group were good to go. Conor Tait loved this – he loved the power but, more importantly, the crime gave him the buzz that he craved. The others – well, they did as they were told.

Above the shouting of the market traders declaring their cut-price goods came the unmistakable noise of the mopeds. First two were the outriders, providing a presence to create a distraction. Conor Tait entered the market area after briefly pausing at the entrance, closely followed by Zac. They turned right.

PC 2307 Ollie Hague was on foot patrol when he heard the noise. He was making polite conversation with Jack Willett, a veteran trader with his own particular brand of cheap and nasty footwear. '2307 to control. There is the sound of mopeds, south end of the market. Making my way towards the location now. Definitely two separate sounds, more than one vehicle.'

The Control Dispatcher immediately opened up the Operation Proof protocols on his computer screen and notified his supervisor, Inspector Louise Tranter, the designated critical incident manager.

Ollie Hague started walking purposefully through the market at the same time that Conor and Zac created the distraction. The lads started to bob and weave away from the market, making as much noise as possible. Heads turned and necks strained to watch the two hooded juveniles.

'2307 to control. There are two mopeds heading south in the direction of Trowst Avenue, both riders wearing dark hoodies, no reg plates,' Hague shouted to the control room.

The noise of another two mopeds could be heard clearly as the normal market sounds were drowned by the unmistakable whine of moped engines. Abbie and Freddie sped from the alley directly towards their chosen target; Mollie Grainger was purchasing wool to knit a baby's cardigan for her most recent grandchild. Her open handbag revealed a glistening Samsung J6.

Inspector Tranter immediately alerted the nearest traffic officer in the event of a pursuit occurring. Sergeant Steve Barker also responded as the nearest supervisor, making his way towards Trowst Avenue. Barker had guessed correctly on a potential escape route. He informed Tranter of his location.

Abbie had the gleaming phone in her sights; it seemed to be almost winking at her with a come-and-get-me smile whilst Freddie came to an abrupt halt a couple of yards behind her. She paused for a split second next to Mollie, who was now collecting her change, blissfully unaware of the activity around her. Abbie reached inside the bag and set off again in the same instant.

Freddie saw the successful snatch and waited just long enough for Abbie to begin her getaway. He was looking around quickly, about to follow her, when he was hit from behind by PC Ollie Hague who dived full length and made contact with Freddie's machine, propelling him towards the stall and other shoppers.

The impact made Freddie struggle desperately to stay upright on the machine. He felt himself going – one, two, three hops on his right foot, both hands on the handlebars whilst still keeping the vehicle moving forward ever so slowly.

Hague was back on his feet. He made another move towards Freddie's moped as shoppers stood paralysed, realising what they were witnessing. Yet Freddie was not to be outdone; he was experienced on the machine and helped by a youthful athleticism. Another hop, and both his feet were back on the bike, his momentum restored. Another Hague dive, but this time the young officer hit thin air. The whine of the moped increased and Freddie was gone, heading in the direction of Trowst Avenue. From his prone position, a defeated and almost breathless PC Hague still managed to update the control room.

'Tango 3112 estimated time of arrival to the area five minutes.' The nearest available traffic officer informed Tranter of their location as Barker shouted in, 'Inspector, I've got a visible on a dark moped, one up, wearing a dark hoody. I'm following from a distance, heading south on Trowst Avenue. Traffic is light.'

Barker kept the commentary going. 'It's a right, right, right onto Burton Street. Little or no traffic in the area. Need back up and authorisation. Requesting a trained pursuit officer asap.'

Critical Incident Manager, Inspector Louise Tranter, was in a nightmare scenario. Her nearest traffic officer who had the authority to carry out a pursuit in these circumstances was still some two minutes away, currently she was supervising an untrained officer involved in the chase. She knew full well that a great deal could occur in those two minutes – but could she risk Barker continuing his pursuit? Any accident would translate directly to her decision making. There was no option; call it a lack of bottle, if you like, but the potential consequences weren't worth it. 'Sergeant Barker terminate your pursuit immediately,' came her firm instruction.

Barker continued, but only momentarily. He pulled into a bus stop lay-by and banged his fists against the steering wheel in frustration.

Freddie looked back to see his pursuer parked up. He smiled sarcastically at the driver.

'Inspector, pursuit terminated,' Barker updated Tranter. It was all over as far as he was concerned; an opportunity lost and another victory for the PST.

***

Trish Delaney was in her office updating her policy log. As SIO, she had to ensure all policy decisions were fully documented. The control room had informed her of the incident, which had resulted in both Sutton and Firth leaving the incident room and joining her.

Firth had her airwaves radio, which relayed the pursuit as it happened. Sutton lived it; 'Go on, my son,' he thought as Barker gave chase. He cursed loudly when the pursuit was called off; in his view, it was far too soon.

Delaney interrupted his thoughts. 'Geoff, it's the right call for everyone, including young Barker, and you know it.'

He slumped back in his chair, taking his rebuke like a huffy, scolded schoolboy.

'Geoff, Jo, go to the scene. See what we can gather from this latest crime. I'm off to see Ron Turner before he finds out that we've taken another hit.'

Fortunately for Delaney, she managed to see Turner before he found out from his various informants throughout the force. She smoothed down her black skirt and pushed back her hair; it was vital that she looked confident, however nervous she felt.

'Sir, we've had another crime, this time four mopeds in total. They were followed from the scene by a uniformed officer who initially engaged in a pursuit before the control room inspector aborted the chase. Traffic were still a couple of minutes away.' Delaney looked straight at Turner as she summarised the incident. She thanked her good luck for wearing a skirt that covered her knees, which were knocking as she spoke.

He stared back at her, looking for signs of weakness, anything that would indicate she was not up to the job. Finally, he said, 'The chief wouldn't go with more trained shift officers for tactical contact. I'll talk to her again.'

'Thanks, sir. Sutton and DS Firth have gone to the scene, together with forensic teams and two detectives from the incident room to see what we can gain.' Her knees had stopped knocking. 'We hope to deploy Charlton later today after his visit to Occupational Health.'

'What about the public confidence in us?' Turner questioned his DCI, on the impact that these crimes were having on the force. He knew she couldn't respond, and he just hoped this Charlton deployment never reached the chief's attention.

16

Pete McIntyre

Pete McIntyre had left home earlier that day for a meeting with Alan Strong, Roger's brother. Today was the best time they had to talk as it was one of the few occasions neither he nor his wife, Valerie, were looking after their two-year-old grandson, Ben. Not that they really minded helping their son, Henry, and his wife get through those first few difficult years, particularly when his daughter-in-law, Pat, returned to part-time work after maternity leave. A house move just before Ben arrived had brought the prospect of better schooling but also an increased mortgage, so Pat's contribution to the family's finances was a necessity.

No matter how much they loved their grandson, the child-minding had put additional pressure on the family dynamics. It came to a head the previous week when Val was returning Ben home after a very long day, only to be asked without any prior warning if she was okay for tomorrow.

Val had responded, 'Pete and I also have a life.'

A diplomatic phone call from Pete to Henry later that evening had prevented the disagreement escalating and prompted both sides to adopt a more structured timetable; both parties agreed that should have happened from the outset.

Pete had arranged to meet Alan Strong in Costa Coffee, part of the Next clothing outlet at the North End of the pedestrian precinct. They had met a few times over the years when Alan had been staying at his brother's and popped down to the rugby club for a pint or two.

Pete walked into the café and went upstairs. He immediately saw Alan sitting without a coffee in a relatively quiet area of what was always a busy venue. Pete went over to him and, without any hesitation, gave him a comforting hug rather than a formal handshake. 'What do you want to drink?' he asked.

'Cappuccino please, Pete.'

'No problem.' Pete smiled then joined the queue. As he waited, he looked across at Roger's older brother. He was in his early 60's – and he looked absolutely knackered, with red circles around his baggy eyes. He was scrutinising a wallet of papers, no doubt trying to sort out the estate as well as the funeral, which was sure to attract a huge gathering. Roger Strong had been much-admired, and his tragic death would gather together many mourners.

It was a good five minutes before Pete joined him. Alan looked up, peering over his glasses, and the pair shook hands formally.

'Not sure where I start, Alan,' Pete said, as if he wanted to explain Roger's actions.

Alan interrupted him; he didn't want to go there, not at that moment. 'Pete, can we discuss the funeral arrangements? It's arranged for Wednesday the 10th of November. Apparently, there's a slight backlog for the crematorium at the moment – must have been that recent cold snap,' he said in a thick Cumbrian accent, attempting some black humour to lighten the mood. 'After the crem it will be back at the rugby club. I wonder if you could arrange that side of things. Just let me know the cost after I give you an estimate of numbers.'

Alan continued through a series of questions that he'd already listed and constantly referred to among his pile of paperwork. 'It will be a simple ceremony. Roger had already chosen some songs in a letter of wishes he kept with his will.'

'What are the songs?' asked Pete.

'Well, there's "Chasing Cars" by Snow Patrol, "Proud" by Heather Small, and "She Moves in Her Own Way" by the Kooks when we're on the way out.'

Pete smiled; when they'd had their prolonged drinking sessions at Roger's he always had music playing and not just in the background. 'How's everything else going?' he enquired, looking at the bundle of papers.

'We're getting there,' Alan said confidently. 'The estate is very straightforward. Following his divorce, Roger made another will and it all goes to his son, my nephew – if we ever find him. I haven't seen or heard from him for years, ever since they split up. I know he's not a Strong anymore, not after that bloody divorce.'

'Bloody divorce' was an apt description, thought Pete.

'Anyway, Pete, there's something very personal that Roger has left for you, Stew and Geoff. There are three original Upper Parton Rugby Club ties that were handed down to Roger by his father, a founder member of the club. When the club started there were three teams and each of them had a special tie to commemorate the occasion. Those ties are for you three. He's gifted them in his will.'

Pete tried, but he couldn't speak.

'But why did he do it, Pete? Why did he kill himself?' Alan was desperately searching for the answers to the question that they'd all asked but were no nearer answering. 'The four of you were the closest of friends, closer than any group I've ever known.'

'Alan, I haven't stopped asking that myself. I don't know, I really don't. And sadly, I'm not sure I will ever understand,' Pete said, desperately trying to recover his composure.

Alan removed his glasses and placed them on the coffee table before rubbing his face. 'Can one of you do the eulogy? Roger included that in his letter of wishes.' He showed Pete the paper that detailed the funeral arrangements.

Pete read it slowly; it was written clearly and concisely. The bottom line read: 'Just to make them always remember me, if they outlive me, could either Pete, Stew or Geoff read my eulogy, Lots of Love Rog X.'

'We'll fight over it,' he promised Alan, words he immediately regretted as he wondered how on earth any of them would cope emotionally with the funeral. There was another long, comforting hug between the two of them.

Finally, Alan broke away. 'Must go to the solicitors, Pete. I'll be in touch.' He gathered up his untidy pile of documents and left.

Pete stayed in the café. He had made an instant decision and searched his pockets recovering one of the small glossy flyers supplied by Inspector Foster at the scene of Roger's death. He pulled out his mobile and started scrolling internet sites relating to mental health. Some ten minutes later, he pressed the start-up button of his keyless Honda. He sighed as he placed the car in reverse, lighting up the rear-view camera. He had now enlisted as a volunteer on a mental health counsellors' course. He would never know why Roger took his own life, but he was determined to do something positive, whether it was in memory of Roger Strong or to ease his own conscience.

***

Ron Turner was far from hugging people. He was in Christine Mayling's office, arguing passionately for the need for more officers to be trained in tactical contact.

'Ma'am, if we'd had more trained tactical contact resources on the ground today, we might well have our suspects locked up.'

Turner always gave rank the respect it required and Mayling certainly deserved respect, as opposed to her predecessor, Alan Conting, with whom Turner had clashed repeatedly during Operation Trust.

'Yes, but at what cost, Ron? A risk to the public, to the

officers concerned and finally to the criminals, in that order,' she answered firmly.

Turner looked at her. She had just returned from a civic engagement. As an individual she was impressive; she had a presence that demanded respect.

Mayling rose from her chair. 'Okay, Ron. One sergeant from each city centre shift to undergo an hour's tuition then subsequent test from traffic officers. If successful – and only if – they'll be granted authorisation and their details forwarded to the critical incident commander in the control room under the protocols of Operation Proof. And it needs to happen immediately. Bring them in on their rest days, if need be.'

'Thanks, ma'am,' said Turner. As he left her office, he thought, 'Perhaps now wasn't a good time to inform her of the authorisation he'd given regarding probationer constable Dominic Charlton.'

A few minutes later, he received a phone call from Geoff Sutton. 'Sir, the Occupational Health Unit have just been on the phone. Dominic Charlton passed his tests.'

'Thanks, Geoff. Let's get him deployed ASAP,' replied Turner without hesitation.

17

Joanne Firth

Jo Firth looked across at Geoff Sutton as he replaced his mobile inside his green Barbour. They were both in DCI Delaney's office, having returned from the market with little or no hope of gaining anything forensically. An extended trawl of CCTV would reveal four individuals on mopeds, of similar description, wearing the hoody tops.

Arthur Hails was again the crime scene manager and was at his pessimistic best, although he admitted facial recognition was a reasonable option from the captured CCTV footage of the hooded culprits.

There was no evidence from the PST's numerous offences that provided the investigation team with something to explore. This troubled Sutton more than anything. It was his reasoning behind the extreme and desperate measure of sending in young Charlton.

After Firth updated Delaney about the crime scene, Sutton chipped in. 'Charlton passed his assessment with the OHU. Apparently, he yawned throughout the process. I've just obtained authority from Turner. We're ready to go,' he said confidently.

It was mid-afternoon when he and Jo Firth returned to the incident room and she made the call to Charlton's burner phone. 'Hi, Dominic, it's Sergeant Firth. Can we meet at The Parlour Café on the Springfield Estate? It should be open and it's not too far away from your location. Your normal uniform will be required.' That was a reference to the hoody and baggy denims.

Sutton stared open-mouthed at her; the thought of a deployment briefing in The Parlour, Debbie's café, seemed a little too much to explain.

Firth placed her mobile back on her desk. 'You okay with that, Geoff?' She smiled.

'Just thought Rodney's Pit Stop would be better. It's closer to the Plaza and we want Charlton deployed asap,' he replied unconvincingly.

'No probs, Geoff. I'll ring him back,' said Firth obligingly.

They borrowed a silver Ford Focus from the surveillance unit to carry out their task. It took a fair amount of persuading, but Sutton called in a few favours and promised that there wasn't a chance the unit would be compromised. After changing the number plates, he reversed out of the unit garage. There was no need to monitor any police radio traffic, so it was Radio 2 with Steve Wright and the Big Show that billowed out across the airwaves.

Ten minutes later, he took a left turn into Rodney's Pit Stop. It was the original greasy spoon establishment that stayed open late, with a small car park at the rear and a bus stop immediately outside.

Once parked, Sutton noticed a pedal cycle loosely chained to the only lamppost in the poorly maintained car park. There were no security cameras. He rightly assumed that it was Charlton's mode of transport, organised by Firth via the found-property compound. Before the meeting, two members of the surveillance unit had transported the cycle in one of the unit vans. It had the tall handlebars and small wheels that identified a certain type of rider.

They walked into Rodney's Pit Stop; it was empty apart from a couple of contractors in high-viz yellow jackets, one playing on his phone, the other engrossed in a copy of the Daily Mirror. The silence was disrupted by the sound of a gaming machine.

Sutton looked across and saw the back of someone he assumed was Dominic Charlton playing on the machine. Charlton was dressed as they had requested: black hoody, blue baggy denims and Nike trainers that looked more suitable for a moon walk. His stab vest, which Turner had insisted on being worn, was easily disguised underneath Charlton's hoody.

Sutton went to the counter and ordered a couple of teas. He noticed a can of energy drink carefully balanced on top of the gaming machine. 'So far so good,' he thought. Charlton certainly looked the part and probably felt more natural than he did in his ill-fitting police uniform.

Firth got close enough to ensure that Charlton was aware of her presence then re-joined Sutton, who was looking distastefully at the brown liquid served up as a poor impression of tea.

It seemed like an age before Charlton dragged himself away from the machine and sat with them. He pushed back his hood and scrutinised the document that Firth had placed on the table. It was a necessary contract outlining the rules of his deployment that required Charlton's signature. Sutton glanced across to the two workers; there wasn't a flicker of interest from either of them.

Charlton simply pulled out a plastic biro and scrawled his name, hardly bothering to read the contents despite the fact it was his contract. The signature was endorsed by both Sutton and Firth.

Sutton handed over the key to the cycle's padlock whilst Firth gave Charlton his final briefing. 'Park the bike in the designated area close to the main entrance to the mall. Walk through the shopping area, go into a couple of shops and have a good look around before making your way to SAMS. If there's no one in, speak to Nevil – just make conversation about anything that's pertinent; phones or music. There's a gaming machine on the premises. Use it but don't outstay your welcome. Rodney's Pit Stop closes at 7pm. Ring me on our phone and we can pick you up anywhere within reason. You can drop the bike off, secure it and then pick it up when you need it. We'll take the risk if it's nicked.'

She continued, 'For your own safety we've decided not to use any technical at the moment, so try and remember anything that may be of interest and record it when you're safe. There will be plain clothes officers in the Plaza. If you need them, there's an alarm on the phone linked to both them and us, which will get you an immediate response. It's only to be used in an absolute emergency. We need to control this, so we're giving you two hours maximum from now. Any questions?'

There was no reply from Charlton, not even a grunt; he put up his hood and walked out of the café.

Sutton and Firth didn't move immediately. They drained their cups of stewed tea. The two contractors still hadn't uttered a word to each other; both of them now totally engrossed in their phones. 'A sign of the times,' thought Sutton to himself.

He felt a pang of guilt because he'd failed to return Debbie's call. He'd asked her to contact him after her first counselling session. 'Excuse me, Jo, just have to make a call,' he said, and walked outside.

It was obviously a personal call but, although Firth wondered who he might be ringing, she showed no surprise. She knew Sutton was a long-time widower, but she was one of the few who never involved herself in force gossip and was blissfully unaware of his relationship with Debbie.

***

Dominic Charlton was in his element as he pulled up his hood against the cold and unlocked the chain that secured his newly acquired bike. This beat bloody classroom scenarios and exams on obscure traffic legislation. He was now living the dream.

There was only one light on the bike, at the front. It was all he needed; there was little or no chance of him being stopped by the police. Although the sun was setting, Dominic found the conditions still light enough for him to make good ground using the pavements as well as the road.

Some 30 minutes later, he arrived outside Carsten Plaza. He found the bike park and secured his machine; he thought it looked slightly out of place compared with the expensive bikes that occupied the cycle racks.

He was very relaxed; what was there to be concerned about? He'd have a look around, go for a drink and chat with people who liked his kind of music. To cap it all, he was getting paid for doing so!

He went through the main entrance and straight into WH Smith's. He picked up a packet of chewing gum, thought about walking straight out and smiled to himself before he went through the arduous process of using the self-service till. The complimentary vouchers for further discounts were still spewing out of the machine as he left the shop.

He stood in the doorway and looked at the cavernous space of the shopping centre. The shops were gearing up for Christmas; some were already displaying their festive wares. Charlton knew where he wanted to go; these places were all the same and the areas where his type hung around were usually close to the main information kiosks.

The row of shops led to a central water fountain surrounded by information kiosks, a focal point for the other shopping aisles. There were half a dozen bored youngsters all dressed like him. Whilst it was far too public for the PST, he could always hang around here if he needed time to kill, he certainly wouldn't look out of place. This would normally be Dominic's playground, but for him he was encountering a strange feeling. It was called nerves.

***

Ron Turner had his phone on silent as he sat in the chief officers' conference room at Parton Constabulary HQ. It was the third, and hopefully final, Gold meeting before the major event taking place in Parton city centre.

The term Gold referred to the command structure adopted by the police on the day of the event: Gold was the Commander responsible for the strategy; Silver had the responsibility for designing the tactics, which were then implemented by the Bronze officers who supervised the troops on the ground. It was a tried and trusted method of operating, used not only by the police but by many other agencies when dealing with major events.

The force had heard from the Security Service a few months earlier that the right-wing group British First had decided to hold a rally in Parton city centre on the first Saturday in November. Initially, there'd been some scepticism from the force as to whether or not the event would actually take place, as despite the increase in migrant workers, incidents of racial hate crime in Parton were relatively low. Rumour and innuendo changed to hard evidence as flyers advertising the event started appearing mysteriously around the city and further intelligence filtered through. The British First website was now publicly advertising their march in Parton city centre.

Chief Constable Chris Mayling was determined that Parton Constabulary would not be found wanting. She knew that the problems with the march wouldn't just be with British First; they were more than familiar with the policing tactics that surrounded their events. However, it was also highly likely a last-minute counter-demonstration would be organised – and that's when the real problems would begin.

Turner attended the meeting as Head of Crime and Intelligence to ensure that the force had enough CID resources should there be a major incident, as well as providing accurate intelligence. The major issue would be public order. As with the previous three meetings, this one was both recorded and minuted and had the force media officer in attendance. Chief Constable Mayling was leaving nothing to chance.

The agenda was simple: intelligence update and public order plans. Mayling had the last word, although Chief Superintendent Bruce Urwin, Head of Operations, had been nominated as Gold Commander for the day of the march.

Detective Inspector Howard Broughton gave a comprehensive intelligence update. Broughton was one of the most experienced intelligence officers in the force; always calm, he personified reliability. Each item of his summary had been checked and re-checked to ensure it could be relied upon. Separating the wheat from the chaff was a key part of his role, and effective policing of the event could only be planned with accurate intelligence.

As the meeting moved on, Turner thought Urwin gave a good performance as Mayling hit him with a barrage of questions which he fended off like a boxer sparring for a title bout: What happens if this occurs? What are we going to do if that happens?

Turner's concentration wavered. Under the table, he checked his phone for an update on Dominic Charlton. There was nothing; he was becoming unusually nervous and shot a glance towards his chief constable. If she only knew what he had authorised...

Mayling summarised the meeting; she felt there was no need for another Gold briefing before Saturday's event unless there were significant developments.

As the meeting closed, Broughton spoke up. 'Ma'am, could I have a quick word with you and ACC Turner, please?'

Mayling raised her eyebrows. 'Yes. Ron are you available?'

Turner, agitated, checked his phone again. 'Yes, ma'am.'

Urwin was packing away his papers; it was obvious he wasn't going to be party to their conversation. 'If there's anything I need to know, I will be informed?' It was half a question and half a statement, but the head of operations had made his point. He rightly assumed that they'd be talking about some intelligence reporting that he was not involved in. Mayling and the other two waited for him to leave the room.

Broughton started to speak. 'Ma'am, the original intel for this event came via the Security Service. This was open reporting, available to everyone via the media or social networks. We heard nothing from them after the initial notification and most of the intel has come from other forces who've hosted similar BF marches. However, in the past week or so, the Security Service has supplied a steady stream of more detailed intel on British First. And it's not run-of-the-mill stuff.'

Turner butted in. 'Cut to the chase, Howard. What's your point?' he demanded rudely.

Broughton looked at his chief constable before taking a deep breath. 'I think the Security Service is becoming more confident that the intel they're gathering is spot-on in terms of accuracy. They may have recently recruited someone. The detail suggests they have the right access to the organisation.'

Mayling joined in. 'Does this actually affect our operation, Howard? Surely it's a bonus if we're getting such good intel.'

'That's correct, ma'am. The only reason I'm raising it is that there's a distinct possibility that an informant will be participating in the march. I've checked with my contacts from other forces who've had BF marches and they were never provided with the detail we're now seeing. It's a hunch born out of my past experience,' Broughton explained.

Turner summed up. 'Thanks, Howard. I don't think that Bruce Urwin needs to know. As you said, ma'am, we need to be aware of this scenario, but there's no way we could confirm the individual's identity – nor should we try to do so.' he added confidently.

'We could unknowingly arrest the security service informant. It does happen,' Broughton said, smiling cheekily at both Turner and Mayling.

Mayling nodded. 'Then so be it. Currently, it doesn't affect our operation.'

All three left the room deep in thought; it hadn't been a particularly satisfactory conclusion to their conversation.

***

Meanwhile, Dominic Charlton was making his way slowly but steadily towards the exit point by the multi-storey car park. He had studied the map he'd been given and confirmed his route using the information board. He knew SAMS was on the last row of shops heading to the multi-storey. He saw the flickering lettering of the shop sign some twenty yards away. Most of the other shops were vacant, their flaky painted shutters giving the place a forlorn look.

He stopped in his tracks; he wanted to take his time, take in another shop, to compose himself. For once in his life, Charlton was extremely nervous and that was the last impression he wanted to give. He was sweating, and that had nothing to do with the amount of clothes he was wearing. He could feel dampness on his thighs emanating from hands thrust deep inside his pockets.

He was having more than second thoughts. 'Could he go through with this? He didn't have to,' for a moment, going back to Glasson's boring but safe classroom seemed very appealing. He gritted his teeth as he approached SAMS; it was as if his feet were refusing to move, shuffling as if they were carrying the weight of diver's boots.

Finally, he stationed himself directly in front of SAMS, pretending to scrutinise the items on display. The fact that it was stocked to the hilt with new phones, replacement screens and chargers was lost on him. His heart was thumping against his chest as he arched his neck, not to see more merchandise but to identify the shop's occupants. Gone was the arrogant and confident individual; his whole demeanour had changed dramatically.

Fight or flight; it was now or never. He'd been standing at the display window for what seemed an eternity, but no one had passed him and certainly no one had entered the shop. Despite his efforts to get a better view, he hadn't been able to detect who was in SAMS because of the crammed window display. He looked at his phone, glanced around and checked the time, before finally placing his hand on the door and stepping inside.

He immediately took in the music, which was instantly recognisable – 'Down in the Park' by Tubeway Army was blasting out. The music and the noise of a gaming machine initially confused him but then he saw that there were four customers; two were hanging around the café, sitting opposite each other at one of the four tables, and the other two were engrossed in the gaming machine. All four were drinking from energy cans and were dressed almost identically to himself. That made him breathe slightly more easily.

Dominic tried to control the involuntary shivers underneath his baggy denims. He noted someone whom he thought must be the owner, working behind the counter. The man didn't even look up when Charlton walked in and seemed preoccupied with replacing a phone screen.

Dominic walked purposefully to the counter and took out a phone with a cracked screen; it had been supplied by the force, yet another miscellaneous found-property item. 'How much to replace the screen?' he enquired. There was no 'please' added to his request, and he hoped his words didn't betray the nerves he felt. He felt four pairs of eyes trained on him, burning into his back.

Nev didn't even acknowledge him, which only added to Charlton's anxiety. It seemed ages before his composure returned. He decided to take control. 'Any bloody chance of this screen being replaced, mister?' He deliberately hesitated before adding the *mister*.

Nev looked up, only to be faced with yet another of those hoody types. He didn't like what he saw, but Charlton dropped the phone onto the counter in a way that forced Nev to examine it. 'It will cost twenty-five pounds,' he grunted.

'I'll have it done then. How long?' Charlton demanded, again with no 'please' and certainly no 'thank you', even after Nev said he'd do it now and it would take him thirty minutes maximum.

'I'll wait,' Charlton grunted above the sound of 'Killing Moon', a song by Echo and the Bunnymen. He turned around slowly. The noise of the gaming machine had stopped, as if beaten into submission by the music. He walked to the café area, avoiding eye contact with the other customers, and headed for the hatch. He bought a drink before sitting at a vacant table. The gaming machine noise resumed as Echo and the Bunnymen continued.

Dominic had kept his hood up; of those present, only Nev wasn't wearing the uniform. The young policeman was breathing more easily now and with that came an increased level of confidence. 'It was a strange environment,' he thought, half a phone shop and half a café with what seemed to be a fairly regular clientele.

He took out his other phone and started playing the game *Injustice 2*, whilst trying to listen to the conversation between the other four customers. Conor was brazenly addressing his troops, oblivious to anyone around, such was his arrogance 'The next time we have some fun will probably be Saturday. It's that BF march in the city and there will be lots going on.' Although it wasn't a direct reference to elderly people carrying phones, human nature suggested there would be a few people gathering out of sheer nosiness. 'We'll go four-up again. If anyone gets involved in a chase, just remember the bizzies will always bottle it, if they think there's a risk. The bastards can't touch us,' Tait added. Unknown to the other gang members, Conor Tait had some very good reasons for the PST attending the BF march.

He glanced across and for the first time he and Dominic Charlton caught each other's eye, an indication that the latter wasn't totally focussed on his phone and may have taken an interest in Tait's one-way conversation. The look was only momentary, but it provoked an instant response from Conor.

'Hey, you shit,' Tait said in a more menacing tone.

Charlton ignored the comment and tried unsuccessfully to concentrate on his game.

'Hey, you shit,' Tait repeated.

Again, Charlton ignored the comment, trying to remain cool despite his pounding heartbeat. His mouth was so dry it would have been difficult to respond to the blatant taunting.

Tait's goading had caught the attention of the other three, Freddie, Zac and Abbie. The gaming machine was momentarily ignored and Nev stopped his repair work. Conor Tait had spoken, and everyone listened.

Charlton summoned as much confidence as he could and peered out from his hood, looking directly at Conor. He stared at him but continued to ignore his comments. He had to stand up to Tait to gain his respect but the key to his success would be to gain a level of acceptance without pushing too far.

He waited for what seemed like an eternity; he really didn't know if he should speak or wait for Tait. But Conor had already made a decision. Hands in the pockets of his denims, he walked around the table and grabbed Charlton's phone.

'Piss off!' Charlton went to take his phone back. Tait grabbed his arm with his left hand and produced his flick knife with his right. As he did so, Charlton noted the threatening swastika tattoo on the inside of his wrist.

Tait pressed down with his thumb and the silver blade clicked out menacingly, glinting as it did so. 'It's mine,' Tait said emphatically, pushing forward so that Charlton could feel the knife blade.

Dominic Charlton felt the ice-cold silver steel touch his cheek. He was paralysed by fear. He'd come across bullying in the past, indeed it had affected him significantly at school, but this was a level of violence he had never encountered before. He had no control and he wanted out.

'Nev, how much for this?' Tait waved the phone triumphantly above his head. There was no response from shop owner, who tried to ignore Tait's threats and focused on his phone repairs. He'd already seen and felt that very same knife.

PC Dominic Charlton ran out of SAMS, clearing a path by knocking over a couple of the café chairs as he did so.

Joanne Firth and Geoff Sutton had been enjoying each other's company. They'd anticipated that it would be a couple of hours before they had any news from Charlton. Sutton had tried to ring Debbie but was unable to get a reply. He guessed she was back at work, so he'd left a message hoping that her therapy session had gone well.

A couple of minutes later, Charlton was back at the information desk in the Plaza. He'd run most of the way from SAMS, hoping he wasn't being followed. In his panic he had completely forgot about activating the alarm on the phone he had been given. Eventually he reached into his denims, took out the phone and rang Jo Firth. 'I'm finished,' he said, panting. 'I'm fucking finished,' he repeated emphatically. The few people who knew Dominic Charlton would endorse that he only swore in extreme circumstances.

'Dominic, are you okay?' Jo asked.

'Not fucking really,' replied Charlton, gasping for breath. The once cocky, arrogant, rookie constable had disappeared.

'Where are you, Dominic?' asked Firth calmly, although a worried frown had appeared on her face. Her phone went quiet. 'Dominic are you still there?' she asked.

'I'm still here,' he sniffed. 'I'm at the information desk in the Plaza. I think I'm fucking safe,' he said as he looked around; Charlton still had enough of his faculties left to scour the area. There was no sign of Tait or his gang of followers. 'Are you still close to Rodney's Pit Stop?' he enquired, referring to their earlier meeting place.

'Yep, it's open for another hour,' Firth replied immediately.

'I'll be there in thirty minutes. The cycle ride will do me good. I'm not injured physically.' Charlton stammered his reply, he was shocked, but the feeling was returning to his core and his heartbeat was slowing; there was now no need to swear.

He took some deep breaths as he passed through the exit doors of Carsten Plaza and reached fresh air. He looked around one final time and saw no one. He pushed back his hood and allowed the late October breeze to cool his burning cheeks.

***

As Charlton made his way from the Plaza, Conor Tait and company were reflecting on their day. Before they had been rudely interrupted by an outsider, they were applauding themselves on the success of their latest robbery as well as planning their next venture. The fact that they'd been involved in a pursuit with the bizzies only added to the excitement. It was like a drug; Tait was totally addicted and provided a ready supply to the others, who then scored on the adrenalin rush of robbing old people. They were hooked.

Conor swopped the phone for cash after a few well-chosen words with Nevil. Nev was always reluctant to part with money but his feelings, not just towards Conor but to them all, was now of complete fear. He was totally intimidated; he rightly thought that any disagreement with the PST would end in him being the victim of some violent act.

After Charlton had run from the shop, Nev had somehow plucked up enough courage to turn on Tait. 'What the hell do you think you're doing? Who do you bloody think you are?' he demanded, throwing his arms up in the air as if in a lost cause.

The response was both swift and predictable. Without saying a word, Tait walked to the shop counter. He had the flick knife in his hand, blade still showing. He lifted his hood and made a slicing motion across his throat.

'£20 for my new phone,' Tait teased Nev, waving the phone, 'obtained,' from Charlton in his face. '£20. Now.' He put the stolen phone on the counter.

Nev pondered his response. The panic button that activated a 999 police response was under the counter and within easy reach. His brain said, 'push the bloody alarm,' but his body wouldn't – or couldn't – respond. He was rooted to the spot, totally under Conor Tait's control.

He placed a £20 note on the counter, trying hard to disguise his shaking hand. As with all the other transactions with the gang, he had to make sure it didn't go through the till and his accountancy system, which his wife Joyce controlled.

When Nevil Samuels looked at himself in the mirror every morning, he knew that he was just as responsible as the PST for Enid Benson's death. That thought cut through him as sharp as any knife that Conor Tait had produced.

***

Half an hour later, Joanne Firth, Geoff Sutton and Dominic Charlton were sitting in Rodney's Pitstop. Charlton had recounted his harrowing tale. Sutton was grateful they hadn't fitted the lad with any technical equipment.

They were the only customers. Rodney was dressed in a grey pinafore covering a similarly coloured T-shirt; both items of clothing were probably a pristine white when initially purchased. He was displaying an impressive array of tattoos.

Charlton's hood was down. He sat at the table, both

hands clutching a mug of sweet tea. His complexion, always pale and unhealthy, was now the same colour as Rodney's clothes. Neither Sutton nor Firth could stop him talking but they knew he needed to have this time before they got down to details and, more importantly, any evidence he'd obtained.

Charlton said that the gang were looking at Saturday's British First March as an opportunity for their next robbery. Because he was still scared, and he didn't think it important, he failed to describe the tattoo he'd seen on the inside of Conor Tait's right wrist.

He stopped talking to take a deep breath and a mouthful of tea; his hands had almost stopped shaking. 'I'm not going back. I'm not going back. It's Glasson's lessons for me, or the sack.'

It was early evening when Sutton and Firth dropped off Charlton within walking distance of his aunt's house. 'Let's go for a drink, Jo. There's the Red Fox just around the corner,' Sutton said.

Joanne Firth shuddered slightly but at the same time nodded her head in agreement.

Licensed premises were places she tried to avoid. What Sutton wasn't aware of was that she had a major problem with alcohol. Ten years earlier, a short but essential period of sick leave had been disguised as minor depression and prevented her private problems becoming public. Nevertheless, ten years down the road she still avoided obvious temptations.

They ordered an orange juice and a pint of Timothy Taylors. All Sutton was concerned about now was the evidence against Conor Tait. 'We've got absolutely no evidence to connect him with any crime, other than a public order offence. Our aim was to link him to moped robberies. Using Charlton failed, but we've captured a real nugget of intel about their participation in Saturday's march. We have no proof of him running down Enid Benson, though,' he said, frustrated.

'I agree,' Firth said, trying hard to appear comfortable. 'Charlton's had a major shake-up. Might do him some good,' she added mischievously.

'You're probably right. I'm just pleased he returned relatively unscathed.'

Sutton's phone, on silent, buzzed away in his pocket. He knew he had a busy night ahead. He was due to meet Pete and Stew to discuss Roger's funeral, as well as seeing Debbie after her first counselling session.

Finally, Sutton spoke. 'I need to brief Turner,' he said. 'I hate telling him we've failed to get any evidence, but he can console himself that it looks like the PST will be out and about this Saturday. And there was no damage done to Charlton. It was a high-risk operation and it was his call. Going forward, there's still the possibility of the decoy job.'

Sutton knew that Mayling and her command team had some serious decisions to make. The last thing the force could face was further national embarrassment on the back of Operation Trust.

Firth looked around the pub. The most unpleasant aspect was the smell of alcohol; it was an instant reminder of the occasions when she'd woken up not remembering anything about the night before. When she'd gone to the bathroom cabinet, and not been able to decide between reaching for the toothpaste or the bottle of vodka she kept close by.

Sutton was checking his watch. 'You obviously have to go, Geoff,' she said. She'd had enough, not of Sutton's company but the pub; it was making her feel sick and she needed out.

Sutton picked up his Barbour and they went outside. 'We've got a meeting about Roger's funeral arrangements.' It was the first time he'd mentioned Roger to anyone; he hadn't even had the bottle to ring his daughter Maggie to tell her the news, even though Roger was her godfather.

The two of them said their goodbyes. Moments later Sutton sat in the driver's seat, took a deep breath and tuned into Radio 2 Drivetime show.

18

Geoff Sutton, Pete Mcintyre and Stew Grant

It was approximately 6.30pm on the Thursday evening when Sutton pulled into the car park of the Parton Golf Club. During the journey he turned off his car radio and tried to gather his thoughts. He knew the problem wasn't with the current DJ or the music; it was his total inability to concentrate. His mind wandered from the current investigation and his relationship with Debbie, then there was Roger's tragic death. He was really looking forward to spending an hour or so with Stew and Pete, the company of lifelong mates was so important to them all.

'It's like the Sahara Desert in here, just a half please, Stewy,' Sutton said, as he, 'ordered' Stew to go to the bar.

'Same for me, Stew,' added Pete. There was a certain amount of reluctance as Stew first made sure his lavender cashmere v-neck jumper hadn't developed any unwanted creases before he made his way slowly to the bar. Pete stood and shook hands with Sutton, not out of politeness but a signature of their friendship. Stew did likewise after he had returned from his duties and placed the beer on the table. 'The club looked good,' thought Sutton, as he took a sip of beer and looked around. Although quiet at this time of night with no sign of straggling golfers, battered by the late October weather, the sight of the recently completed refurb had made a significant difference.

'Saw Alan Strong the other day,' Pete began, 'He's struggling and, like us, still looking for answers.'

Pete didn't, at this stage, want to disclose to the others his registered interest in volunteering for a mental health counsellors' course. That would come some months later when Stew Grant appeared at one of his first sessions as someone who needed support.

'The funeral is probably a week on Wednesday, and he would like one of us to do the eulogy. Roger had specifically made this request. I am quite prepared to do it, unless either of you want to?' He looked up, hoping for a positive response but not really expecting one, as both Geoff and Stew made a silent sigh of relief. They all had the greatest respect for each other, but nobody would wish this particular task. 'However, I will need some help in preparation and also a substitute if I break down,' he said with total honesty. They both nodded their assistance, hugely relieved that Pete had volunteered to take on the role.

Pete continued to relay his meeting with Roger's brother, Alan. 'No one has a clue as to the whereabouts of his son or former wife, Alan put an obituary in the Parton Weekly, but nothing so far. For all we know they could be living in another part of the country or even abroad by now,'

'Can't think that she would want anything to do with Roger's funeral, but the son is another matter, he will now be of an age where he can make up his mind about his father, who bloody knows?' said Sutton sadly.

'Do you remember Roger's hole-in-one?' Stew said, completely changing the subject to a lighter tone, 'you've got to mention that Pete, in the eulogy.'

'Yep, it was the 14th and he was playing absolute crap, wanted to walk back to the club house after the first nine holes but we persuaded him to keep playing, even though things didn't improve,' Sutton added. The three started laughing, they knew exactly what was to come next but were not able to contain themselves.

This time it was Pete who continued, he was the first to compose himself. 'The 14th was a 145-yard par three from an elevated tee box, 170 yards off the competition tees. Trees surrounded the back and left-hand side of the green with bunkers covering the front and right. Strongy stood on the tee box, cursing the fact that we had persuaded him to keep playing, and what made it worse the weather had changed, it had started to rain and he'd forgotten his brolly,' tears of laughter began to appear on Pete's cheeks.

Sutton took over. 'He was swearing at us. 'What bloody club should I take? Waste of time anyway, haven't hit a thing above knee height all morning, would have been back at the clubhouse if it wasn't for you buggers, bloody soaked I am.'

Stew continued the tale, dabbing his eyes with his fine pink and blue spotted ironed handkerchief. 'Strongy closed his eyes, took out a club, I think it was a six iron he actually used, teed up his ball. I think he had lost about seven on the round so far.' The laughing between the three was reaching a crescendo, attracting the attention of a few others gathered around the bar.

It was then back to Pete. 'He laced this ball, absolutely creamed it. The first proper strike in nearly two hours of golf. We watched it and it wasn't going anywhere else, it bounced once, twice and three times before rolling into the hole. We saw it all the way in. But Roger had turned his back on the shot as soon as he made contact and refused to look, the daft bugger missed the best shot he'd ever played and his one and only hole-in-one,' he spluttered, now hardly able to speak. 'It cost him an absolute bloody fortune, marvellous, Strongy was never the first in getting out his wallet.'

The three of them couldn't speak never mind drink, but they did have the full attention of all those present. It was a timely reminder of their friendship and the good times that they had shared. On reflection, they also realised that this short get together at the golf club was a necessary and integral part of the grieving process. All three were really struggling in coming to terms with Roger's death, particularly given the circumstances. Stew knew he would be waking up at 3am the following morning pacing around the house, whilst Pete had opted for a discussion at the local pharmacist resulting in a purchase of some herbal sleeping remedy.

All three exited the club together, walking across the car park to their respective vehicles. Sutton sat in the Karoq and finally rang Debbie. 'How are you?' a direct reference to her counselling session. Despite all that had gone on today, Sutton was very aware that it was Debbie's first therapy meeting, it had been a long time coming and she had taken a great deal of persuading.

'I'm good, Geoff, can I come and see you?' she asked.

'Certainly, why don't I pick up something on the way home and we'll eat in about an hour?' Sutton suggested.

'That's just what I want,' Debbie said with feeling.

19

Zac Ewart

Unknown to Zac Ewart and the others, Conor had been diversifying his activities in recent months. He had thought for some time that their arrangement with Nev wouldn't go on forever. He also took the logical view that Samuels was so deeply implicated in their crimes and crucially, lacked the bottle to grass on their activities.

With that in mind, Conor Tait took stock – other than his nan and the other members of the PST, Conor Tait had no friends. He basically hated people. A little internet research made the British First an appealing organisation for him to join. As a group they seemed like-minded people, who generally disliked society. Further research and a few posts on social media saw Conor make a short trip to Asha's tattoo parlour, one of the new shops in Carsten Plaza. After a fair amount of pain, Tait walked out a short time later with a swastika tattoo discreetly adorning the inside of his right wrist.

Conor Tait, however, was bright in an evil way, he knew that British First would be desperate for funds and wouldn't really care how those funds were sourced. It didn't take long for young Conor to become a fully-fledged BF member, due to a few stolen phones that he had passed their way. The promise of a regular supply was an appealing fundraising proposition, which was gaining impetus among his new-found fascist acquaintances.

He'd been promising his closest confidant Zac Ewart a night out for some time had Conor Tait. There was never a chance that Zac would suggest something to Conor, but there was no doubt recently Conor's habits had altered, something that had become increasingly noticeable. There had been a few occasions that Conor had returned back to Nan's, just as Zac was having his breakfast; that, and a couple of Saturdays when he had just disappeared – not a word of explanation.

It had felt strange to Zac when he was alone in the bungalow, with Nan at The Haven. Conor would return perfectly happy but without any explanation as to where he'd been or what he'd been doing, and Zac never asked. It wasn't his position to do so. Today was slightly different in that, upon his return, Conor informed him they would be going out.

They had arrived back at Nan's early that evening. She was watching the six o'clock news when she was invaded. Some five minutes later, Nan Tait left her cosy seat in the warm lounge to take up her usual post in the kitchen where she listened to Radio 4 and took orders for tea, whilst Conor and Zac watched a rerun of some Extreme Sports on iPlayer. After twenty minutes or so, the pair of them were tucking into egg and chips surrounded by tomato sauce and accompanied by a couple of well-buttered slices of bread. Zac was just wiping up the remnants of his plate with his last slice of bread when Conor announced, 'We are off in a couple of minutes.' Zac took one final mouthful of his bread and followed his leader out of the door, without so much as a question. They left their plates in the lounge and hadn't bothered to say goodbye to Nan, never mind thank her for tea. This was the night out that Conor had promised Zac.

Hoods up, they made their way back to Nev's small lock-up, which acted as the PST's garage. The temperature had dropped a couple of degrees as evening met up with night.

Zac took comfort that he was the chosen one, going out with Conor alone and outranking the other two members. It was only a couple of hours earlier that they had deposited the mopeds, after Conor and had made the briefest of acquaintances with the traumatised Dominic Charlton.

Tait scanned the area; what made this location so good was that there was no housing close by, no snooping people. There were six containers in total, surrounded by a metal fence with a gate that appeared to be secured with a large chain, inside the entrance was a metal post approximately fifteen feet in height, on which was perched a rusted and totally useless security camera. The containers resembled an old-style western film where cowboys made a circle of their stagecoaches when facing an Indian attack. Closer scrutiny of the compound showed that Nev's container, where the PST housed their vehicles, was the only one in reasonable order; the others were rusted over, most with their doors flapping open in the evening breeze. The chain wrapped around the entrance gate was equally rusted and was only placed there because the PST used it, giving a false impression of security. The reality was that the heavy wraparound chain just about prevented the gates from blowing open in a moderate breeze. Happy there were no unwanted observers, Conor and Zac unlocked Nev's container, removed their mopeds and set out.

'Follow me Zac,' he instructed. Conor, as always, took the lead.

The two members of the PST were off to the final local BF meeting before their march this coming Saturday. For Conor Tait he was, 'going to work', developing a business relationship which he hoped would provide a reliable outlet for the PST stolen phones if, or when, Nev went AWOL.

Their journey was relatively uneventful, Conor knew the way, and Zac had past experience of follow my leader. Keeping to the minor alleyways and deserted pavements, the noise of the mopeds permeated through the otherwise silent night. Another right then a sharp left, Conor entered a narrow and rundown street on the outskirts of Parton city centre. It was an old 1930s terrace that no doubt once was a sought-after area to live but had now deteriorated significantly. Half the houses in the street were boarded up and the others displayed watery light through some grainy net curtains. Conor pulled up outside 41, Parton Rise, an end terrace with shafts of light trying desperately to make a surprise appearance to the outside world. They parked the mopeds outside and wheeled them into a small cellar underneath the stone steps that provided access to the front door. He pushed the rotted wooden cellar door that scraped, groaned and gave way to nothing but darkness. 'Zac, put it in here,' Conor ordered. As ever, Zac followed Conor's directions despite not having a clue where he was or, more importantly, what on earth he was doing.

Mopeds parked in the cellar and without giving out any further dialogue, Conor led the way up the steep stone steps to the large front door. He ignored the bell and door knocker as he leant across to the front window and knocked loudly on the glass, struggling to make an impact as he heard one of Skrewrdriver's distinctive rock anthems beating out. Tait recognised 'The Voice of Britain', one of their most famous tracks, from a previous British First meeting.

Conor entered the house, having carefully avoided a snarling Pit Bull Terrier chained to the drainpipe by the front door. He walked into the hallway before turning immediately right into the front room. Zac followed slowly but obediently, like a well-trained pet. He was frightened and didn't want to be here. He entered the front room and the sight that met Zac Ewart's eyes only increased his fear. His feet stuck to the carpet, which was a dark red and black floral design. The walls were a flaky cream colour decorated in red paint with various swastikas drawn in different angles, together with a Death's head and the number 88. Above the redundant fireplace was the title **BRITISH FIRST**, again in the same colour. The curtains he had only seen from the outside looked even worse inside. Conor noted there was a total of fourteen people crammed into the room listening to the loud music and drinking Diamond White cider whilst smoking cheap cigarettes. Discarded cans and cigarette butts littered the carpet. Tait made a mental note that most, but not all of those present, were in their early twenties. There were a couple of dark green settees punctured with cigarette burns parked around the room. There was no heating, but despite the cold many wore cap sleeved T-shirts, displaying tattoos that replicated the emblems that appeared on the walls. Male or female, it didn't matter; everyone seemed to have their hair so closely cropped it was impossible to determine its colour. Zac Ewart thought immediately of Nan Tait's bungalow and the warmth of her living room. He didn't want to be here. The atmosphere and the people in attendance made him nervous and uncomfortable.

'Tel, you old bastard, meet this little shit,' Conor tapped the tallest of the group on his shoulder and pointed to Zac.

'You a friend of Conor?' the male introduced as Tel, turned around and spat on the sticky carpet. He looked threatening, with a large tattoo displaying the letters BF along the centre of his forehead.

'Yep,' Zac replied quietly; far too quietly for Tel, and much to his obvious annoyance he repeated his question.

'You a fucking friend of Conor?' he shouted above the music.

'Yep I'm Zac,' he shouted, desperately trying to be confident.

'A friend of fucking Conor's is a friend of us all. Here, take a can,' Tel thrust a can of Diamond White in Zac's direction. Zac's trembling right hand took hold of the cold object whilst his left attempted to release the ring pull. He took a long swig then as the icy liquid collided with the back of his throat it took a U-turn as Zac spluttered most of the cider out over the filthy carpet. It only added to his nerves, but Tel laughed, whilst Conor looked away embarrassed at his guest. Zac just didn't want to be here. To him it seemed that everyone in the room looked angry, as if they wanted a fight. The way they dressed, most wearing braces and boots, it was intimidating. That didn't seem to bother Conor, he obviously knew at least some of the crowd, but it certainly frightened Zac. He literally hung onto his leader's coat tails.

'Any fucking phones, Conor?' Tel continued shouting.

'Soon Tel, soon,' came Conor's quick response, whilst Zac look confused, before the music was turned down a decibel or two. Conor's business plan with regard to the supply of mobile phones was initially known only to Tel, who in turn had been given the green light to proceed by the BF hierarchy. Unbeknown to Conor, Tel was about to go public on their business arrangement.

Tel addressed the group. 'Saturday is our day; we gather at the Bird and Feather just off the city centre precinct at 12 noon. Have a couple there, then march down the fucking precinct somewhere around 2pm, we will then have some more booze around 3pm, I've booked a room at Walter's, it's close to the precinct itself and Ronnie here is the fucking landlord,' Tel pushed a large and older individual to the front of his audience.

'Good on you Ronnie,' shouted a girl, raising her arms as she did so, revealing a swastika on the inside of her right wrist, whilst Ronnie seemed almost embarrassed with his newfound fame as he looked down at the gleaming, big black Doc Martens boots he had purchased that morning.

Tel continued, 'We are expecting over 200 to 250 fuckers to travel from most parts of the country. Weather looks good. We need to let the fucking bizzies know the route of the march, but not our expected numbers, or our two fucking venues: Bird and Feather and Walter's. We are not expecting bother, so we may have to make it; we need to attract some fucking publicity. I'll have a megaphone and if I shout "88", Mick, I want a fucking window to go in.' Tel pushed the smallest of the crew to the front and Mick faced the audience with a huge grin across his face, revealing two missing front teeth. There was no hiding his delight to be awarded the opportunity of causing bother. 'There is still time for a counter demo from some fucking lefties, or worse some do-gooders but that will only assist our cause and publicity,' Tel added in response to a few rumours that had been flying around on Facebook.

'Shaz, could you do a couple of fucking banners and provide some whistles for the day.' Shaz was now un-recognisable from her true identity of Susan Ibbotson; Gary Thornton's best undercover operative in the Direct Action section of the Security Service, who had infiltrated the group some months previously. Shaz raised her left hand holding her can of Diamond White high above her head. 'Conor and a couple of his friends will join us on their machines, they may even nick a couple of fucking phones for us,' Tel continued, as Conor smiled politely whilst Zac looked away hoping he wasn't going to be pushed to the front of the gathering. It was now patently obvious that Conor's stolen phone business plan was no longer a closely guarded secret.

Shaz shouted, 'Go Conor, fucking go,' lifting the same hand and can of cider above her head.

'Most importantly,' Tel said, lowering his voice, there was a pause as he sought to build up the excitement. 'And this isn't to leave the room, our fucking leader, Barry Harrison will attend the march and speak to us at Walter's.'

Shaz was up again, arm raised, but this time jumping up and down spilling her cider. 'There's only one Barry Harrison, one Barry Harrison …' Conor and the others joined her in the monotonous chant, whilst Zac looked away, embarrassed, before Tel finally brought things to order. He was hoping to avoid another outburst from Shaz, who had appeared to have consumed more Diamond White than the rest of them put together. No one knew that before Shaz had consumed any of the cheap and strong cider, a quick trip to the toilet was necessary to drain it away replacing it with nothing stronger than tap water.

'Right, that's all I have to say, see you on Saturday at the fucking Bird and Feather.' Tel finished his less than eloquent briefing and Shaz walked forward and gave him a big hug, making sure everyone saw this outward display of affection.

As she exited the meeting, Shaz clung to Tel thinking of what excuse she needed to make so she could complete her prior arrangement and contact her boss Peter Havelock at Thames House at the agreed time. It was important he knew about Barry Harrison's presence for the forthcoming rally, the possibility of disorder and the two venues involved. Although she noted Conor and his team's planned appearance at the event, she was distracted by the news of the BF's recent fundraising venture, which she would develop further with Tel before reporting back to Havelock.

She smiled inwardly to herself, another couple of Diamond White cans supplied to Tel should do the trick; it normally did.

As they were clear of the premises Zac summoned up enough courage to ask Conor a question. 'Conor, why are you knocking around with this group? It's not even our music and they don't ride mopeds?' he asked in a manner that justified the question.

Conor looked directly at Zac, it wasn't often he was asked a question by a member of his team. 'It's simple Zac, Nevil Samuels won't go on forever. He's a prick, a pathetic little shit. Given the chance I am sure these goons will pay us well for any phones,' he answered confidently. Zac was there and then satisfied and immediately diverted his eyes away from his leader.

20

The Haven

Hilda Tait was really glad that the boys had disappeared some time earlier that Thursday evening; she didn't have to make any excuses when her neighbour Charlie Drummond came to the door. She and Charlie had a meeting to attend. Although he had secretly helped the police earlier in the week, Charlie had received no contact, no update, absolutely nothing and Drummond was a man of action.

The usual murmurings over coffee about how Parton was not the place it used to be, was a normal conversation among the elderly. However, feelings had escalated over the past few months when older members of the community had become targets for the moped thieves. It had reached a crisis point with the death of Enid, an attack on her good friend Muriel and then another robbery at the new market. To add insult to injury, now Parton city centre was to host a British First march which will no doubt attract a great deal of unwanted publicity to the area. 'There will be police on every corner,' seethed Drummond inwardly. Charlie sent off a few emails, text messages and contacted those with Facebook accounts, an extraordinary short notice meeting was arranged at The Haven.

Charlie knocked on Conor's nan's door. He hoped that Conor was out, but he also knew there wasn't much chance he would get off his arse and answer the door. He was correct on both counts. 'Evening Hilda, you all set?' Charlie asked, as she opened the door, tied her navy blue and white headscarf tightly underneath her chin and pushed her fingers deep into her brown-leather gloves, another lovely Conor present.

'All set, Charlie,' and the two of them made their way to The Haven. They chatted aimlessly on the way, about the changing weather as well as their various health ailments. Charlie paid particular attention when Hilda mentioned that Conor had popped out earlier this evening with his mate Zac, but she didn't disclose anything further. Time passed quickly and they reached The Haven both realising just how well they enjoyed each other's company.

The turnout was amazing with over forty members present, representing the many societies that existed in this popular community venue. They were all brought together with a common goal. Teas and coffees were being served and there was a general buzz of anticipation around the hall. Charlie Drummond wasted no time; he fully appreciated the efforts of his fellow members attending at such short notice.

'Thanks so much for coming. I will try and keep this brief.' He felt a small surge of adrenalin, which reminded him of the military briefings he had attended in a former life. 'British First, a far-right group, are marching through the city centre precinct on Saturday afternoon. This is one of a series of marches taking place in city centres throughout the country.'

'Could you speak up Charlie, please?' asked Iris Smith, as she manipulated her hearing aid.

'Sorry Iris.' Charlie continued, his voice louder now, 'These marches have resulted in violence, damage and general disorder in other parts of the country. Pardon my language but it's bloody disgraceful and with that in mind we are making a stand for the good people of Parton. Why is this group coming to Parton? We have enough disorder and damage already and we as a group are being singled out as targets. Sadly, Enid Benson's death was the last straw. And we can use the BF march to highlight our cause because of the amount of publicity they always attract.' A ripple of applause was led by Hilda Tait. It echoed around The Haven. 'Our first priority is that no one gets hurt, so we will walk through the new market when British First walk through the precinct, we will meet here at 1pm on Saturday. I know that we are obliged to inform the police and make them aware of our event.' Charlie added, growing in confidence. 'Hilda, can we organise some coffee and mince pies?' he smiled down at her. 'Those of you who are struggling to walk can use the centre wheelchairs, family and friends can assist. Please bring anything that supports our cause, such as placards and banners.'

'Large photos of Enid,' Iris shouted up, hearing obviously restored.

Hilda looked admiringly at Charlie Drummond; she really liked him, standing upright in his corduroy trousers, brogue shoes and thick woollen jumper hiding his Ryedale checked shirt. That was all that needed to be said with Charlie adding that he would circulate everyone confirming the march details in the hope for further support. There was also a sensible suggestion from the audience to spread the word around with a few phone calls as not everyone had email addresses or mobile phones.

The whole meeting took barely ten minutes and it wasn't long after clearing away the empty cups that Charlie, who was also a key holder, locked the doors of The Haven as Hilda waited for him patiently. They walked and talked their way back to Meadowland Crescent. It was as if they hadn't a care in the world. She couldn't remember how or where it happened, but at some stage on their walk back home Hilda linked arms with Charlie, it just seemed so very natural that she hardly realised her actions. However, Charlie became immediately aware and without Hilda knowing, he smiled broadly.

When they got home, Charlie found the business card supplied by Parton Constabulary and emailed them with the details of The Haven march. As for Nan she closed her front door and smiled inwardly, linking arms with Charlie had been her first male contact since she became a widow so many years ago.

21

Debbie Smith

Geoff Sutton was running late, he knew it, but he had an important call to make, one that he had been prevaricating over for far too long, with good reason. He still had not informed his daughter of Roger Strong's death. Sutton knew how very fond Maggie was of her godfather who, on his part, took his duties very conscientiously. He never missed a birthday and always took time out to visit her whenever she made a visit to Parton. Maggie, for her part, always called him Uncle Roger. He pulled into the local Marks and Spencer's Foodhall car park, before scrolling down his contacts. Sutton was half hoping there would be no response as he called Maggie's number.

'Hi dad, how you doing?' was the bright and cheery response he always got when he managed to get an answer.

'I'm fine Maggie, where are you?' he enquired, not wishing to begin a difficult conversation if she was somewhere public.

'Just going through the front door now,' she replied putting the key into the lock of her recently purchased flat. Sutton gave her a little time to get sorted before restarting the conversation.

'Maggie, I've got some really sad news for you.' There was silence at the other end. Sutton knew from his past experience there was no easy way of getting this done and he came straight to the point. 'Your Uncle Roger has died, Maggie. I'm so sorry.'

Maggie continued her silence, which was broken by the occasional sniff which Sutton immediately recognised. 'How? Why? He wasn't ill, as far I was aware, Dad. He must have had an accident,' Maggie said in a statement rather than a question.

'Maggie love, Roger, committed suicide,' Sutton said, as quickly as he could. The sniffs had increased to sobs as Maggie slowly came to terms with the news.

'Geoff, I am with her now and will stay with Maggie,' Sutton instantly recognised the voice of her boyfriend. He was so glad to hear his voice. 'I will send you a text later, just to update you on how she is getting on,' Christopher said compassionately.

'Thanks Christopher, that's really appreciated,' Sutton said in a relieved tone and ended the call. He sat back in the car feeling guilty that he hadn't been with Maggie when she received the news but quickly realised that would have been impossible given her current job in London.

He made a quick visit to the new Marks and Spencer's; a stir fry meal deal was in the offing, he avoided the black bean sauce option, not one of Debbie's favourites, and found a couple of bottles of an Australian red. He was really looking forward to meeting up with Debbie. After her aborted birthday meal and Roger's death it had been a nightmare couple of days.

The three-bedroom semi was really more than he needed. Sutton really lived in two rooms, the living room and bedroom, only nature made him enter the bathroom and kitchen. He dived into the house abandoning his green Barbour as he ran through to the living room. Using the timer for the heating was beyond Sutton, and he needed to get some heat into the house before Debbie arrived.

He unpacked his shopping, but not before he had consumed a bottle of Peroni which hardly touched the sides. Some ten minutes later, Sutton was almost there – a bottle of red opened to breathe, he had already tried a mouthful or two, and his stir fry was well on the way. Phil Collins was doing his bit, with more than a little help from Alexa, a recent birthday present from Maggie, and the house was warming up nicely.

The front doorbell rang, Sutton responded immediately, 'Come in,' there was no response; Debbie couldn't hear over the combined noise of 'Against all Odds,' and Sutton's cooking. He turned the music down and marched to the door.

'That smells so good.' Debbie entered the small hallway, her gorgeous brown eyes smiled at Sutton, before she threw her arms around him and hugged him close. He could smell the Coco Chanel perfume as Sutton briefly experienced the intimacy that he'd always missed in their relationship.

'And a good evening to you; that's a lovely welcome,' he said, as they disengaged. He became momentarily distracted, as the smell of burning food entered his nostrils and he walked back to the kitchen hoping to avoid a disaster. He was relieved that the food appeared unscathed and looked back from the cooker to see Debbie helping herself to a large glass of red wine. Sutton took in the sight before him; he had been attracted to her for such a long time, but just didn't have the courage to ask her out. But seeing her here and now, confirmed to Sutton the strength of his attraction. She was dressed casually, skinny denim jeans, a sky-blue blouse unbuttoned to reveal a small gold chain. A black jumper was draped around her shoulders. There was nothing dramatic about the way Debbie dressed, it was casual, but it was also highly attractive to Sutton.

'That's just the ticket,' she said, taking another large gulp of wine, and as her eyes danced, Sutton struggled to concentrate on the cooking.

'Just about ready,' he said, reaching up for two large plates and served the food. Sutton would never get marks for presentation. He crashed the plates down on either side of his kitchen island where the two chairs were located, narrowly avoiding any spillage. Sutton quickly glanced around the room and immediately recognised the tell-tale signs of a single male existence; no napkins, a pinboard with a single picture of him and daughter Maggie on holiday. The icing on the cake was the roller blind that remained broken from sometime last year.

He had ordered Alexa to stop and sat down opposite Debbie. He took a large gulp of his wine before they both reached for the salt in unison, touching hands as they did so. Despite the length of their relationship they smiled at each other nervously.

'Well, how did the session go?' Sutton said, trying to wrap the noodles onto his fork without making himself look a complete idiot.

'Really, really helpful,' was Debbie's positive reply. 'I'm going again next week, the session was positive, and I really liked the counsellor,' she added enthusiastically. Sutton nodded approval between mouthfuls. 'What sort of day have you had?' Debbie asked with concern.

Sutton kept it brief. 'Pretty hectic Debbie, we still haven't secured enough evidence to make progress on Enid Benson's death. Pete, Stew and me just met up to have a chat about Rog's funeral. His brother wanted one of us to do the eulogy and Pete's got the job, he's been speaking with Alan, Rog's brother.'

Debbie listened intently and took a mouthful of wine. 'Are they any further forward in finding out why Roger hung himself?' she asked.

'No, not at all. I doubt we ever will,' Sutton replied quickly. 'And we are still no further forward in finding out the whereabouts of his ex-wife, but more importantly his son, who's a beneficiary named in his will. They could be anywhere.' He looked away and Debbie knew immediately the conversation was causing him to reflect.

She changed the subject. 'This is lovely, Geoff, it really is,' she said, as she nonchalantly picked up a fork full of noodles.

'And you're lovely, Debbie,' Sutton said, smiling, but slightly embarrassed at such a cheesy remark. 'Alexa, George Michael.' 'Time for some background music,' he thought, as he looked across at his Debbie.

It was a short time later when Sutton cleared away the empty plates. He took what was remaining of the red wine and their two glasses. 'Comfy seat?' Sutton suggested.

'Geoff, I've got a better idea,' Debbie's eyes were now both serious and sensual. 'Let's go upstairs, lead the way.' Sutton hesitated and faced her directly. He was stunned and felt paralysed. It was only when Debbie walked to him and kissed him passionately that his paralysis left him immediately. He struggled to hold onto the wine and glasses as he led the way upstairs.

The intimacy in their relationship that Geoff Sutton had craved for so long was satisfied that night. For Debbie, it was a release from the shackles and nightmares of her abusive past. They both lay there, side by side, before Sutton broke the silence. 'More counselling for you,' they both laughed loudly.

The alarm went at 7am the following morning. They turned to each other and repeated last night's love making. Sutton now thought they were truly a couple.

22

Chris Mayling

It was Friday morning, the day before the British First march, and Chris Mayling unusually had her door closed. Unless she was chairing a meeting Mayling had a strict 'open door' policy. No matter how busy, she always made time for people; something that Ron Turner thought was strange to say the least. On this particular occasion Mayling needed quiet, she had just received a secret intelligence document giving her the latest update on tomorrow's high-profile event. She sighed inwardly after reading the document for the third time. Mayling knew that with Barry Harrison – the BF's leader – attending the rally it would guarantee a national media interest and turn up the pressure on both her and Parton Constabulary. To add to the chief constable's consternation, she had also received notification of The Haven march. Her main concern was that her force was losing community confidence, which would attract Home Office attention.

She sighed again and poured herself a cup of percolated high-quality coffee, instantly the thought of a quiet weekend at home and regular updates from the commander on the day had disappeared. The intelligence and possible high-profile consequences required her to take control. There was no doubt in Mayling's mind that the risk of major disorder, together with force reputation, had escalated significantly. She had already called a press conference for this afternoon, as knowledge of a counter-march by The Haven had just been publicly announced. It was her force and she would now be the officer in charge, Gold Commander on the day. Without taking her eyes from the briefing paper she reached for the phone on her desk and keyed in Ron Turner's extension.

'ACC Turner speaking,' came the brusque but polite answer.

'Ron, it's Chris here, I've just read the latest intel brief for tomorrow's march, please organise a Gold Meeting in the conference room; 2pm will do, I have a press conference due at 4pm.'

'Yes ma'am,' came Turner's obedient reply.

'Ron, I would also like you to have look at this latest intel and advise me before the meeting,' Mayling requested with authority.

'Yes, ma'am,' Turner repeated himself. He put the phone down and made his way to Mayling's office. Ron Turner knew, both by the tone and her urgency, that there were problems, but he appreciated the way she had asked for advice, albeit he knew the chief constable would make up her own mind.

Some twenty minutes later, Turner was back in his office studying the document. 'Shit, they must have someone close,' he thought to himself, awfully close; a direct reference to the Security Service intelligence. Turner stared over the paper and immediately recognised the concerns shown by his chief constable; the warning signs were all too obvious. There was mention in the briefing of the venues for the start and finish of the British First march; Turner was well aware of the Bird and Feather as well as Walter's, both premises carried with them some notoriety. What more concerned Turner was the nugget of intelligence obtained by Dominic Charlton during his traumatic deployment. How does he possibly explain to Chief Constable Mayling that he authorised this course of action with a problem probationer constable and that we now know the PST will also be present on Saturday?

Turner went through a tick list of attendees for the Gold meeting that afternoon: Head of Operations, Chief Supt. Bruce Urwin and DI Howard Broughton, Intelligence. He then nominated DCI Delaney and Geoff Sutton, due to their involvement in Operation Proof.

DO NOT DISTURB was printed boldly on a card and placed on the door of the force conference room. It was 2pm. Chief Constable Chris Mayling sat at the head of the table, Ron Turner on her right. Apart from DI Howard Broughton, who had written the document, all the other attendees were digesting a newly sanitised intelligence brief. Mayling gave them a five minute period to read the contents. She activated the recording device, which was an additional accuracy measure to the minutes taken by her secretary.

'Ladies and gents, the goal posts have changed in line with our recent intelligence. I will take charge and be Gold Commander tomorrow.' She looked at Urwin directly, 'This is no reflection on you Bruce, but the risk to the force has been raised to a level which I consider is commensurate to my rank, you will perform the role of Silver,' a reference to the fact that Bruce Urwin would now be responsible for setting out the tactics from Mayling's strategy.

Urwin did not deflect her gaze and responded immediately, 'Yes, ma'am.'

The chief constable continued, 'We have ten uniform serials available for policing the march, plus CID staff whom I want to be proactive, on the streets, as overt as possible. We need to identify the male named as 'Mick', either on the march or hopefully before, according to the intel he's the one nominated to cause damage.' Mayling was in full command, giving out her orders. 'If one window goes in there will be alot more.' She then turned to Howard Broughton as the intel manager. 'Howard, can we expect any more intel coming through before the march?'

'Unless something major breaks, ma'am, I will be very

surprised if we get anything further,' Broughton respectfully replied. Turner looked on and thinking inwardly, shot a glance towards Geoff Sutton who was looking directly at him.

'Bruce, I want a serial of officers at the Bird and Feather as soon as it opens, the same applies with Walter's. British First is going to know we are on their case from the outset. We need firm policing and we are not going to be found wanting. Trish, anything at all from The Haven side of things and the Parton Smart Team?' she turned to Delaney.

'They feel aggrieved that they have been singled out as vulnerable targets by the PST and see this as an opportunity to highlight their concerns, particularly with all the media attention British First will be getting. Understandably they see them as unwelcome guests in the town,' Delaney reported.

'I share their sympathy,' said Mayling. 'Any developments on the Op Proof investigation; that may go some way to satisfying their concerns?' she asked a very pertinent question.

'Nothing significant planned before tomorrow,' Delaney said in a disappointed tone.

Within thirty minutes or so Mayling thought she had covered all necessary issues, or so she believed. She looked to her right at her sounding board. 'Ron, anything else?'

Turner looked down and shook his head. 'No, ma'am.' He'd been really impressed with Mayling; she was firm, positive and in charge. But what was really occupying Turner's mind was how could he get Charlton's' intelligence into the arena without giving any background as to where or how it had been obtained. The last thing Turner needed was another Mayling probing question, particularly in this forum.

'Thank you for your attendance ladies and gents. It's a test but we will be successful tomorrow. I'm off to face the press.' She switched the recording to off and the ever-efficient Steve, her secretary, promised the minutes would be circulated within the hour.

'Ma'am, what is our response if the PST actually attends, considering the fact that The Haven have announced an event of their own? There will be plenty of potential targets,' Sutton said, quietly but firmly. Geoff obviously was well aware of Charlton's information which had not been addressed. Mayling nodded towards Sutton immediately recognising it was a matter that had been overlooked.

'This is an important point, any views?' she scanned the room, reactivated the recorder and then summarised Sutton's question.

Turner recovered his composure, 'This is an opportunity; we need to get ahead with Operation Proof, we have a crime in action strategy to deal with them, 'tactical contact', I think is the correct term,' he was gagging to say, 'knock the buggers off their bikes', but was well aware of any recording in progress. He was also extremely grateful to Sutton for cleverly bringing this issue to the table.

Delaney entered the discussion. 'We do have an option of an officer dressed up as a pensioner who will openly be using a mobile phone to attract an attack from the PST; a decoy operation. In addition, as I said before we haven't got anything currently planned, but we could potentially stretch a point and arrest a suspect by the name of Conor Tait, as a disruption tactic. Take him out and it would almost certainly guarantee there would be no PST attending the city centre tomorrow,' Delaney looked around the room nervously. Turner looked directly at her and naturally got involved.

'If an arrest is made now, others would be tipped off, we would lose any chance of recovering the mopeds and forensic evidence linking them to the serious crimes already committed.'

'But we would keep safe the good citizens of Parton, something we have failed to do recently,' Mayling interrupted and looked directly at Turner.

There was silence around the room, everyone knew it was

the chief's constable's call and whilst others looked down at their briefing documents Ron Turner closely watched Mayling. She placed her elbows on the table, her reading glasses on the tip of her nose, her hands placed together pointing upwards in a praying position with her thumbs cupped underneath her chin. You could hear a pin drop as she took in the options available. 'Can we guarantee that Conor Tait will be housed tomorrow?' she enquired.

'An obvious but practical question,' thought Turner.

Delaney responded. 'Ma'am, as far as we are aware, he always stays at his grandma's in Meadowland Crescent,' she said confidently.

'Bruce, views please.' Mayling was keen to seek the views of her head of operations; he was more objective and not directly involved in any ongoing criminal investigation.

'Arrest Tait tomorrow morning and detain him throughout the march for interview and any searches to take place. I have no knowledge of the investigation, but you might get lucky and recover evidence. He might even admit to his offending,' Urwin said with a sarcastic smile.

'I agree with you Bruce,' said Mayling. 'For the minutes of the meeting: my rationale is that public safety is paramount, however, if he isn't arrested, we then go to the decoy job and keep the tactical contact operation available. Thank you for your views. We have some good people around and we will be successful.' She scanned the room one final time making eye contact with each and every one in attendance, before ending the meeting.

'She was a good boss,' thought Sutton to himself; he had been really impressed with his first impression of Chief Constable Mayling.

'Geoff, can I have a word please?' Turner whispered to Sutton as the meeting broke up. The two of them remained alone in the conference room. 'Is it possible to ask the Security Service for a favour, we need to get the identity of Mick, the chief is spot on, he's the catalyst to any bother planned by the BF – what will he be wearing? Where he is in the march? It will be real-time intel, but we need to arrest him before he starts smashing windows. If not, it is a complete guess that someone spots him or hears a name. Have you any contacts we can ring in London? I know Howard Broughton has tried and failed. And by the way, that was a good call in mentioning the PST involvement on Saturday.' Almost praise from Ron Turner!

The hope was that Sutton's previous long experience in the field of intelligence would have provided him with a few national contacts.

Sutton shot him a glance; he knew it was a good call if they could gain that level of access. He started to rack his brains. 'Leave it with me, sir, will give you a call.' They both finally left the conference room, Sutton holding the door open for his senior officer; 'Old habits die hard,' Turner thought to himself, as he led the way.

Sutton was head down, deep in thought as he made his way to the canteen, he just needed the time to collate his thoughts and recall any contacts. He tried to make an Americano from the newly installed coffee machine located immediately adjacent to the food checkout. Due to his ignorance of all things mechanical he received appropriate instructions from one of the canteen staff. 'Come on Geoff me boy, you place the coins here, place your cup there, press that silver button for your drink and it's sorted,' Eileen said in a maternal manner. In Sutton's case the simple instructions were a necessity.

He took a seat on his own, a quiet alcove, out of earshot of any unwanted listeners, and far away from the training staff of the force driving school who were regulars on a Friday afternoon. He placed his Barbour over the chair, and placed his phone on the table, almost burning his mouth after taking a large gulp of coffee. Sutton began to scroll through his list of contacts.

23

Gary Thornton

In Thames House, Gary Thornton was back behind his desk after updating the director general with the progress made on British First coverage. He was able to report on the excellent infiltration work by his undercover operative providing intelligence which had been forwarded to Parton Constabulary for their event taking place tomorrow. Thornton was feeling pretty pleased with himself. It was a situation that didn't look possible a few months previously. The DG had nodded his approval at the excellent progress being made, which usually was as much praise as anyone received.

He looked out of the window and checked out the forecast for tomorrow's park run via his smartphone. He had made a New Year resolution to recapture some fitness, which, as a young man in his twenties, made him an excellent 1500 metre runner with Belgrave Harriers. His fitness campaign was planned to follow his annual NHS health check prior to his forthcoming retirement. Scrutiny of the forecast came to an abrupt halt with the familiar noise of his ringtone, Lindisfarne's 'Run for Home'. He immediately recognised the contact, Geoff Sutton, but instinctively wondered why on earth he would be ringing him 'out of the blue'.

His mind quickly wandered back to the last national conference they had attended together. The conference subject had been intelligence sharing between the Security

Service and the police. It took place at the Crowne Plaza Hotel, on the outskirts of Birmingham. They had met previously at other national events. Thornton and Sutton had one of those strange relationships where they immediately enjoyed each other's company and contact was only ever through a work environment which they both understood and wanted. He smiled inwardly as he reminisced over a late-night drunken game of snooker on the final night of that particular conference, just the two of them, drunk as skunks, desperately trying to pot the elusive black in order that they could finally go to bed. He picked up his mobile.

'Geoffrey, long time, no hear; you're in town aren't you, a long way from the bleak north and you want to meet up for a beer?' Thornton knew full well that this wouldn't be the case and the call would be work related.

'How are you doing Gary?'

'Yep good Geoff, now I guess this is not a social call, but what do I owe this absolute pleasure? And honestly, it is really good to hear from you, young Sutton.'

Geoff started, 'Gary I'm after a favour; we have this march tomorrow in the city centre with British First (unbeknown to Sutton, Thornton was nodding to himself but also wondering where this conversation was going). There is some intel that suggests when a command is given during the BF march a bloke called Mick will smash a window. I'll cut to the chase Gary, is there any chance of a heads up on Mick's identity? So, we can then get close to him and step in before it happens? Our problem would be if one window is smashed it will just escalate into major disorder. I suppose we are talking about real-time intel.'

There was silence from the other end as Thornton worked out the scenario. He totally saw Sutton's point of view, a real issue for the officers on the ground, but his priority would be to protect his asset and the safety of his agent, Susan Ibbotson (aka Shaz). Any risk of compromise had to be avoided.

Thornton's years of experience took over. 'Completely off the record Geoff, if we had a source with that sort of access and I'm not saying we have, how could we then supply you with that info without any compromise?'

'I honestly don't know,' Sutton replied.

'In addition, at this late stage Geoff, even if we had a source, we could have difficulties in making contact.' Sutton could fully understand the difficulties in this whole situation. There was silence between the two; a recognition of each other's problems.

'Leave it with me Geoff and I will come back to you, probably by close of play, if not later this evening on this number, if we are able to assist.'

'Thanks Gary,' Sutton said knowingly, glancing around the sparsely populated canteen from his location.

'Thanks for nothing at the moment Geoff, I am not admitting, saying or doing anything,' Thornton replied firmly and ended his call.

'I will miss all this aggravation,' Thornton thought to himself as he sat at his desk quickly thinking over his recent contact with Sutton. The easiest thing would be to do nothing. But Sutton was no fool - he was aware they had a very well-placed source that Thornton had to protect. Nevertheless, he picked up the phone to request his deputy, Peter Havelock, attend his office.

In a matter of minutes, he ran through Sutton's request giving Havelock the opportunity to contribute. 'I had no plans to contact Sue before tomorrow's march, but that in itself may cause problems.' He looked around, thinking out loud, 'I could send something as bland as a dentist appointment text, nothing out of the ordinary, but I would give my mobile instead of the dentist's as a point of contact. It shouldn't attract undue attention to anyone else and she would obviously recognise my number and hopefully reply.

If anyone else picked up her phone and saw the message they would think nothing of it.' Thornton listened intently to Havelock, he was a good operator and his idea was typical of his inventive practical approach.

'I'm quite happy to authorise that contact, but how does Sue then identify Mick on the day?'

Havelock smiled to his boss. 'That's not a problem, from the previous reporting Mick isn't the sharpest knife in the drawer, that's probably why he's always nominated to start the bother, he's one of the few who couldn't care less if he gets locked up. He always carries the same banner at the marches, always with the same words – PISS OFF HOME –in red lettering. It's unique to him and I suppose any BF member can identify him when they want to instigate trouble. We would just need Sue to confirm he would have it with him on the day. She could easily send me a text when they assemble at the pub; pop out for a fag or something and I could notify yourself.'

'Seems straightforward Peter, it would be Sod's law he forgets the banner on the day,' said Thornton, pessimistic as ever. 'Whilst this is my call, do you think that there would be any chance that Sue would be compromised, that's my priority?' Thornton asked Havelock seriously, labouring the point.

'Personally, I can't see any risk to Sue. The BF aren't surveillance conscious and use social media to publicise their actions,' Havelock continued with confidence, adding helpfully, 'I also know Sue would highlight in some way if she thought there was any danger.'

'Thanks Pete, take it as authorised and I will wait to hear from you around lunchtime tomorrow.'

Thornton picked up his mobile and rang Geoff Sutton, who looked down at the screen, he had remained in the alcove of the canteen hoping for a quick response. 'Go ahead,' Sutton said in a business like tone.

'If we have any information available, I will ring you tomorrow lunchtime Geoff,' Thornton said abruptly.

'Thanks Gary, I owe you a game of snooker,' said Sutton, a huge grin appeared across his face – unknown to him that grin was replicated by his friend at the other end of the country.

'You might not hear from me Geoff,' Thornton reminded him as he ended the call.

Sutton contacted Turner immediately. The update that followed saw an unusual sight, a Turner smile. It only ever took place behind closed doors and with no one present. They had decided that no one else needed to know this information. If and when they got the call, Turner would be informed by Sutton. It would then fall upon Turner to pass that information to Bruce Urwin who, as Head of Operations during the march, would then direct resources.

The conversation was ended, and Sutton's thoughts were brought back down to earth with a sharp slap on the back from Jim Glasson.

'Sutton, I was wrong, totally wrong,' said Glasson. Trust Jim to hunt him out in this private part of the canteen. The slap on the back had brought Sutton back from his focus and telephone call with Gary Thornton. However, he was totally confused by Glasson's remarks and hadn't a clue what he was talking about. 'What a student!' Glasson exclaimed. He was obviously on a roll as he continued enthusiastically, now taking a seat next to Sutton, who had other more pressing matters on his mind.

'Jim, calm down and please explain,' Sutton said, not really wanting to engage.

'Bloody Dominic Charlton haven't a clue what's happened, but I don't care. He's polite, eager to learn, a completely different bloke, never seen such a change in someone. First I heard was that he had gone sick, next he's straight back in class, without attitude, must be the drugs he was on,' Glasson gave Sutton a knowing wink.

'Well that's good news Jim, really good news,' Sutton had eventually caught up with the theme of Glasson's conversation.

'Just had an exam, Charlton came out top of the syndicate, unbelievable,' Glasson enthused, not recognising it was the wrong time and place to have this conversation as far as Sutton was concerned. 'I'm now really looking forward to taking him out on foot patrol this Saturday afternoon. Just for a couple of hours, the first time they meet the public in uniform. We always pick somewhere quiet first time out. Better make sure we are well clear of the city centre, with the marches going down,' Glasson said, the voice of experience.

Sutton's concentration picked up when he heard about Charlton's proposed foot patrol, immediately thinking back to his failed deployment. Such was his very brief encounter with the PST there was never any chance that Charlton's encounter had scuppered his police career if he ever wished to pursue it. 'It must be his excellent teacher,' said Sutton, returning the slap on Glasson's back. 'Sorry Jim, I'm late for Ron Turner and couldn't face another of his bollockings,' Sutton lied, as he removed his Barbour from the chair.'

'No problem Geoff, we'll have a pint before I head out to grass,' said Glasson, referring to his forthcoming retirement, before biting into his fruit scone covered in strawberry jam which oozed out and headed down his chin. 'Not the most attractive of sights,' thought Sutton as he headed out of the canteen.

His phone rang, Trish Delaney. 'Geoff, I need to plan this decoy job in case we don't get hold of Conor Tait first thing tomorrow morning, are you available?'

'Yep I will be there in five minutes, Trish,' Sutton replied immediately, still trying to banish the sight of Glasson attacking his fruit scone.

24

Decoy

Having hopefully put that one to bed, Sutton was in Delaney's office, together with Joanne Firth, to plan the decoy operation. He always felt that there was a welcoming atmosphere helped by freshly cut flowers and a constant smell of the coffee machine. Unlike Delaney, Sutton had previous experience of this type of decoy operation and Ron Turner had only authorised the job on the basis that it was planned and prepared by Sutton.

The concept was fairly simple, working on the premise that a cop would act and dress as a potential target for a crime to take place. In this particular case it would be a constable made up as a pensioner to act as bait, for the PST to commit one of their robberies. The target would have with them a good quality smart phone which would become available for all to see. Minders in the form of plain clothes officers would react, both to safeguard their colleague and arrest offenders. Whilst the outline was simple, as ever the devil was in the detail, and Sutton was in full flow, his mind totally focussed on the job.

It didn't take Sutton long before he finished outlining the plan. He thought the chances of the decoy job going ahead would be extremely slim as it was far more likely that Conor Tait would be arrested first thing in the morning. Everyone knew he always slept at his nan's.

Delaney looked down at her notes and took another sip

of coffee and changed the subject. 'What about his arrest?' she queried.

Sutton nodded in anticipation of this question. 'I've lined up Ben Linton's team of officers.' Linton was the sergeant on one of the two specialist teams of officer's within Parton Constabulary who were trained in dealing with major disorder, crime searches and other operations. Sutton had worked with Linton on Operation Trust and had been impressed with his leadership and professionalism.

He continued, 'His team are detailed with the march tomorrow afternoon, but they are coming in early to carry out the arrest of Conor Tait and search of the address. I have told him it is really low key, the last thing we need is Hilda Tait to have a heart attack. He also confirmed to me that they have past experience in decoy operations so if for some unknown reason Conor isn't present at the address, Linton's mob will then resource the decoy job. I am meeting with him later to supply a full briefing.'

Delaney nodded her approval.

'What time do you want the arrest to take place?' Firth enquired.

'8 am, it won't take long to search her premises, hopefully we will find some evidence and we can tee up interviews just after lunch, which should ensure Conor is out of the equation at the time of the marches. From what we know of the PST if Conor is absent, they are rudderless. Unless we recover anything incriminating from the searches, we've nothing on anyone else,' Delaney said confidently.

Neither Sutton nor Firth responded further, there was more than enough to consider as they exited Delaney's office: Firth to prepare an operational order and Sutton to brief Ben Linton's team.

25

Ben Linton

It was late afternoon when Sutton made his way to the crew room of Ben Linton's team of officers. It was located within the headquarters' building. The crew room had one long table in the centre surrounded by lockers for the team members which stored the specialist equipment required to carry out their duties. The team were out and about performing a normal routine disorder patrol without their sergeant who was currently being briefed by Sutton. There was a mutual respect between the two, Linton experienced, knowledgeable and very straightforward to deal with as Sutton provided him with the intelligence and background.

The arrest of Conor Tait the following morning was covered very quickly. Linton asked few questions but made notes. 'Any warnings for him,' he enquired.

'He's been known to use knives,' Sutton answered, 'but it's not anticipated he would direct that towards the police.' Sutton highlighted the low-key approach although he didn't need to provide any great detail, Linton knew the area well. They moved on to the search phase, Sutton highlighted any phones, sim cards, tablets or computers, but was nonspecific regarding potential clothing other than hoodies and trainers.

Linton was his normal helpful self. 'If we find something and are not sure of its relevance, presumably we can get in contact with either you or Jo Firth,' he stated. 'Will there be anyone else in the property apart from Conor and Hilda

Tait?'

'Possibly Zac Ewart, he's a known associate of Conor who stays at the address fairly frequently, but the whole purpose of arresting Conor is purely disruption, Ben. We've got absolutely nothing on Ewart, unless we recover anything from the search.' They then moved on to the unlikely scenario of Conor not being present at the premises and the decoy operation.

'We've got the ideal target,' Ben smiled, he was referring to Ronnie Watts, and gave Sutton a pen picture of his abilities. 'He can do an old grandma or grandpa, young businessperson, you name it he can be it. He should have been on the stage. He's slim build so can easily wear his body armour under whatever clothing he chooses, he really looks the part Geoff, and he will have pepper spray with him.'

They both consulted a map to ensure that everyone understood where they would be operating. Linton assured Sutton that all members of his team were more than familiar with Parton city centre. 'Hopefully, we won't require Ronnie to dress up in anything other than his uniform when we have arrested Tait. See you here 7.30am and we will go and get him.' Sutton and Linton stood up and shook hands, Linton towered above him. 'It was a firm handshake from someone who has a significant presence,' thought Sutton.

He was eager to finish duty and get home; primarily there was the excitement of seeing Debbie, last night's passionate memories were still to the forefront of his mind and the prospect of further intimacy tonight made him feel like a young adolescent. But more than that Sutton knew that last night was a significant moment in their relationship.

He even forgot to remove his Barbour as he jumped into the driver's seat. It was 6pm as Sutton completed a right turn into Springfield Green housing estate where the Sutton residence was located. He passed the Falcon pub and turned left into his cul-de-sac. His heart skipped a beat as he saw a vehicle he instantly recognised on the driveway. Debbie had beaten him home. She had obviously used the key he had given her before she left this morning – another positive sign.

He opened the door. 'Debbie I'm sorry, tea will be a few minutes.'

'Tea can wait,' came the reply from upstairs.

26

Ron Turner

Turner locked and left his office at the same time as Sutton entered his house. 'No chance of a weekend walking in the Lakes,' he thought to himself, as he prepared for another major policing event tomorrow. He turned left, passing the small waiting area for those who had appointments with the chief officer team. He was surprised at this time on a Friday to notice a Police Federation representative, together with someone he took to be a probationer constable. It was a system that Mayling had introduced on her arrival to the force. Any new recruit, upon the first weeks of joining, could have an audience with a member of the chief officer team if they so wished. Turner thought it a complete waste of time; he'd dealt with a couple of them who had complained about the food, or their uniform not fitting properly. 'Total trivia,' was Turner's thought. But this particular officer caught his attention – he looked once, then twice. He had a young, choirboy appearance. Turner felt as though he should know this youngster, but how could he? Ron Turner had never actually met Dominic Charlton.

Chris Mayling groaned as she viewed the early evening diary appointment that had just appeared on her phone, which she scrutinised after her press conference that had lasted a good deal longer than anticipated. It had been awkward, but she had expected nothing less. Difficult questions came from all four corners of the room regarding public confidence in the police, as the British First march gathered momentum and the crimes against elderly victims remained unresolved.

The appointment, for some unknown reason, was marked 'urgent' and the probationer constable had specifically requested an audience with the chief. 'It's my own fault,' she thought to herself, these interviews were my idea. She headed wearily back to her office.

Some ten minutes later Mayling sat behind her desk, hands underneath her chin supporting the bottom jaw which otherwise would have hit the floor, as Charlton told his story. It began with his initial meeting with Geoff Sutton and DS Joanne Firth, followed by an interview with the Occupational Health Unit before being deployed in plain clothes to a mobile phone shop, where he was threatened with a knife. Mayling could not believe her ears, 'No one in their right mind could, let alone would, authorise this deployment,' she thought to herself. She desperately fought to contain her anger as Charlton ended his account without a care in the world and leaving her with the words, 'I thought you would like to know.'

Mayling pretended to make notes, but she knew Charlton's account word for word – committed to memory – as Dominic's federation rep remained silenced, studying the carpet and occasionally checking his watch, wondering why he was still at work after 6pm on a Friday evening.

Mayling obtained assurance from them both that they were not to repeat any of this conversation outside these four walls, and long after they had vacated her office Chris Mayling remained, gathering her thoughts. For the good of Parton Constabulary nothing could alter tomorrow's plans for Operation Proof, but bloody Ron Turner had some questions to answer. Whilst their relationship was relatively new, she knew there was only one person in the force who had the necessary rank to authorise this type of operation.

27

Conor, Zac, Abbie and Freddie

The PST met as normal at SAMS, treating the owner with total disdain (nothing new there) and played the gaming machine, listening to an old gothic rock album from Bauhaus. Unusually the group rarely consumed alcohol, ironically because they were riding their mopeds; it was one of the few matters where they adhered to the law. The rationale was that it could affect their ability to carry out their robberies, perverse but logical. However, Conor's attendance at British First meetings had introduced him to Diamond White cider and he had decreed that tonight the group would have a can or two, with the mopeds safely locked away for the night.

They had brought their own drink to SAMS, much to Nevil's disgust, and although he tried initially to remonstrate, he was greeted with a tirade of abuse from Conor and then the team. Not for the first time Nevil's courage let him down. As the evening wore on and Nev looked forward to his 8pm finish and closing the shop, he wondered how on earth he would get them to leave. They were getting increasingly louder and more abusive and it wasn't only Conor, they had all taken his lead, 'Thank goodness for a lack of customers,' he thought to himself. Nev's humiliation was total; there was only one owner of this shop and it wasn't Nevil Samuels.

Nevil glanced down at his watch in trepidation at having to ask them to leave. It was 7.55pm, he looked at his watch yet again and noticed his hand was shaking, he groaned inwardly, pathetic, absolutely pathetic. 'Right time to go, leave this shit hole,' shouted Conor above the music. He looked across at Nevil after finishing on the gaming machine and grabbing his half-drunk cheap cider. The others, all armed with similar drinks, immediately rose from their seats and responded to Conor's orders.

'Back to mine?' Abbie said. 'Paula is out for the night,' a direct reference to her hardworking mother who had another shift working behind the bar at the local pub. Abbie had bravely made this alcohol fuelled suggestion but looked towards Conor as she did so, an obvious sign to seek his approval. 'We can hang out there,' she suggested.

'Good call Abbie, we can also plan for tomorrow,' Conor sanctioned. Meanwhile, the most relieved person in Parton breathed a huge sigh of relief, as Nev felt a drink for him tonight was not out of the question.

An hour or so later, after having stopped off at the local Nisa store for them each to purchase another litre of Diamond White, Freddie Ingles, Abbie Liston, Conor Tait and Zac Ewart were all holed up at Paula's house. Freddie and Abbie had adopted their normal pose, entwined around each other on the large settee, watching an EastEnders omnibus on iPlayer. Conor and Zac, although in the same room, were engrossed with another machine, this time the PlayStation. They all continued drinking and Conor knew that any hopes of planning for tomorrow had evaporated. It was a good night and they finally all passed out in Paula's living room, oblivious to her returning from work.

It was around midnight when Paula arrived home, viewed the carnage in her living room, sighed deeply, switched off the relevant electrical equipment, and made her way upstairs to bed. 'Some life they have,' thought Paula to herself, little did she know that was soon to change for her daughter and guests.

28

Joyce Samuels

It was shortly after 8pm when a beleaguered Nevil Samuels finished pulling the shutters down on his shop. A reconcile of today's takings had taken minutes. Tait and his cronies had dictated the closing time and made their way to wherever. The Plaza was empty of customers at his location, the night-time economy consisting of a bowling alley, cinema and a few fast food eateries were all located adjacent to the main entrance and nowhere near SAMS.

The final shutter in place felt like the last nail in the coffin for Nev. With his back to the metal grills, he slid to the hard-tiled floor, legs stretched out in front of him, back upright against the shop with his chin on his chest; he was in the depths of despair. His life at home was totally dominated by Joyce, his life at work by Conor Tait and his mates. Whilst Nev had relayed to Joyce of being abused by Tait, he immediately regretted informing her, knowing full well she would blame this on his inadequacies. He now pushed his chin forward looking upward. What had been domestic bliss had turned into a living nightmare for Nev, as his work had become a replica of his life at home. Joyce often recognised and highlighted his weaknesses. During the early years of their marriage when they both got home, they shared a good-natured minute by minute account of what had occurred during their day, now they barely spoke at all.

From his forlorn position he looked around at the desolate shopping mall. He felt so alone, bereft of friends, love and comfort. Nevil finally dragged himself to his feet and began the walk to the nearest exit. He had an allocated parking space which, in happier times, he had negotiated with the local NCP, probably the best piece of business he'd completed over the last year or so. On his walk back to the car he repeated the phrase, *'Get a grip of yourself Nev, show some courage.'*

Samuels located his old style, dark blue Vauxhall Astra, the radio didn't work, and he couldn't afford to have it mended. Some twenty-five minutes later, he was parked up in the driveway of his home. He had nowhere else to go. His heart sank with the prospect of seeing Joyce. She would only insult him, making him feel even more devalued. He locked the car door and forced himself to walk to the house, *'Get a grip of yourself Nev, show some courage.'*

As soon as he entered his property, without warning or premonition, she started, 'He's home children, he's home, no doubt with more stories of bullying from the young ones.' A direct reference to the PST threats Nev had discussed with her. Joyce made sure that everyone in the house could hear her words. Ironically, she hated herself for doing so, her reactions were born out of the sheer frustration she felt towards her husband. Although she didn't show it, she loved him and knew in her heart Nev Samuels was a good man and a good father.

Joyce approached Nev, *'Get a grip of yourself Nev, show some courage.'* Her eyes were wide and staring, now in a quieter tone, almost whispering, 'Nev Samuels you are useless both to me and our children,' she spat the words out, and then, almost with a reflex reaction, she grabbed the lapels of his jacket and pulled herself forward to rest her forehead on his chest. The tears began and Nev could feel Joyce's sobs as they began to dampen his cheap shirt. *'Get a grip of yourself*

Nev, show some courage,' he repeated inwardly but this time firmly.

Nev took hold of Joyce's wrists and removed them from his jacket lapels. He looked directly into her tear-stained face. Without saying anything – he didn't need to – Nevil turned on his heel and walked out of the house, retracing his steps to the Astra, which took what seemed an age to start before it eventually spluttered into life. He reversed backwards, not looking or checking his rear-view mirror, just staring at the front door of his house. *'Get a grip of yourself Nev, show some courage.'* This time the words were louder and said with a greater confidence. He made the return journey back to his allocated parking bay at the NCP Car Park in the Plaza. He needed time to think and once parked up he checked his phone. Already there were three missed calls from Joyce. He took a blanket from the boot of his Astra before retracing his steps to SAMS. A few minutes later Nev was tucked up in the cramped stockroom. He switched off his phone, not before sending Joyce a loving text. He would ring her tomorrow.

He knew he would endure a sleepless night, but for once Nevil felt in control and ready to act. *'Get a grip of yourself Nev, show some courage!'* he shouted, content in the knowledge he couldn't be heard.

His new life had begun.

29

Graham Buttle

As he had predicted to himself, Nev had hardly slept a wink but he was surprisingly alert and absolutely clear about his next course of action. Firstly, he sent a text to Joyce. It simply read: *I love you Joyce, will ring you later today xxx.* He knew that ringing her at this exact moment would be a mistake and open up a prolonged discussion.

He walked back to the Astra, which eventually started, before making his way to Parton city centre. Parked up, in the few bays available for the public, Nev entered the foyer of the police station. He observed the walls covered with various posters, giving numbers and helplines of various agencies. It wasn't a welcoming environment and the stench of a strong disinfectant permeated through his nostrils. He paused momentarily, thought about turning back, *'Get a grip of yourself Nev, show some courage,'* the words from last night remained in his head. He was momentarily distracted by a missing person poster of a child who looked identical to his youngest son. But Nevil Samuels was focussed, heart pounding against his chest, he took a deep breath and pressed the desk bell designated for enquiries.

The half glass screens opened to reveal a young civilian operator wearing a black polo shirt and epaulettes. Twenty-year-old Graham Buttle was a young dedicated member of Parton Constabulary support staff, who harboured ambitions that one day he would become a fully-fledged police constable. He'd already applied once but failed the assessment centre; the feedback was along the lines of him requiring more life experience. His disappointment only heightened his determination that one day he would achieve his lifelong ambition.

'Yes, sir, how can I help you?' Buttle smiled towards Nev.

'Could I speak in private?' Nev said earnestly.

'Certainly, sir, please take a seat I will be out in a minute,' he replied in a genuinely concerned manner.

Buttle politely obtained his supervisor's permission, as he would need to cover the front desk while Buttle was dealing with Samuels. It had been quiet so far this Saturday morning although with the British First march later they were expecting a busy shift. He grabbed a pen and paper before ushering Nev away from public view and into one of the adjacent interview rooms. He flicked the occupied sign on the door and sat down opposite Nev, placed his notepad on the desk, picked up his cheap force Bic pen and started with the formalities recording Nev's name, address and date of birth.

Buttle completed the formalities before Nev took control. 'For a while now I have been handling stolen mobile phones for the Parton Smart Team,' the words came out slowly and softly. Buttle listened intently but really wished he had the reassurance of his sergeant present, but checking with his sergeant now would interrupt the interview; he recognised Samuels was in full flow.

Nev named all the team members. 'The leader is Conor Tait, the others are Zac Ewart, Abbie Liston and Freddie Ingles; they make up the rest of the PST.' He informed Buttle of the robberies, gave specific mention of Enid Benson's death and the fact that Tait had threatened him with a knife when he wanted to put an end to his own involvement. Nev gave mention that he had some potential evidence on his own CCTV system.

Buttle followed the limited training he had received and let Nevil speak. He made copious notes. After Samuels had finished, he allowed him to read through, sign and date their accuracy.

This time it was young Graham Buttle who took a deep breath as Nev handed back the signed paperwork. He had tried so hard to remain professional and maintain a calm persona, but his mind was bursting to relate the contents of his interview to Sergeant Jack Wilshaw, the whole of Parton Constabulary knew the impact that the PST had caused. Even Buttle knew he had obtained an account of a major significance.

He closed the door of the interview room and only then realised his knees were knocking together. The foyer remained empty as Buttle walked quickly, realising help, in the form of Wilshaw, was only yards away. 'Sarge, I need some help, please,' Buttle said, always polite but with increased urgency, to his balding and vastly experienced supervisor.

'Well, Graham if you haven't committed a murder, it's solvable,' it was his stock phrase, but it was always said in a reassuring fashion. He listened intently to what Buttle relayed. Wilshaw had been around the block, and his unflappable manner was the envy of many higher-ranking officer.

'We will take him through to custody as a voluntary attender. Judging by what you tell me he won't have a problem with that. The immediate problem is the intelligence he has supplied about the PST and I will deal with that,' he nodded towards Buttle. 'Graham, it's a job well done as far as you're concerned, and no you haven't committed a murder,' he smiled at his young protégé and rang an old and very trusted colleague in Geoff Sutton. However, the call went to voicemail, Sutton was currently pre-occupied with briefing Ben Linton's team, who were about to make a visit to Hilda Tait's bungalow.

'Geoff leave it with me,' Linton said confidently, 'I'll do the knock myself and speak to the occupant. I will contact you if we have any problems,' he added referring to the planned arrest. 'We will then secure Conor and bring him to the City Central Station,' a direct reference to the main cell complex.

Sergeant Ben Linton, together with another member of his team, approached the home of Hilda Tait, the remaining officers stayed in their van some thirty metres away, out of sight and parked up behind some disused garages. Linton was unaware of the twitching of a net curtain at the neighbouring address; Charlie Drummond didn't miss much. Hilda was in the kitchen, clearing up after breakfast and listening to the *Today* programme on Radio 4. Her kitchen was the nearest room to the front door. She heard the knock, and without even pausing to think who it might be at this time in the morning, opened the door.

'Good morning, Mrs Tait, can we come in?' asked Linton calmly and politely.

There was a pause as Hilda tried to gather her thoughts at the sight of two uniformed officers at her front door. 'Yes,' she finally managed to respond, unsure of what was coming next as she ushered both officers into the kitchen. 'Just hold on,' Hilda rushed to turn down the volume on the radio. 'Please come through,' politely directing both officers, through the kitchen, into the comfort of the sitting room. Linton knew immediately Conor wasn't present. Despite the relatively early 'knock', Conor would have been at his confrontational best with the sound of two police officers at the door.

Ben Linton asked the obvious question, to which he already knew the answer, 'Mrs Tait, is Conor here?'

'No, he's not officer, he usually is, normally stays here with his friend Zac,' she added helpfully. 'It is really unusual for him not to stay, I was becoming a little worried. I actually don't know where he is,' she paused again for another moment, realising what she had said, then her right hand went to cover her mouth, it stayed there for a second or two before the same hand dropped to her waist, the colour quickly drained from her face. The penny had dropped for Hilda, it was if she had just solved a puzzle. 'He's had an accident, hasn't he?' she said very slowly, wide eyes staring towards Linton.'

'No, Mrs Tait, not that we are aware of, but we would like to speak to him. If we hear anything we will be back in touch but if he returns could you, please give the control room a ring.' Linton supplied a business card with all the relevant contact details of Parton Constabulary. 'Thanks, Mrs Tait,' said Linton with a sincere smile, he recognised her as a warm woman, 'A typical grandma,' he thought as the officers said their goodbyes.

Linton's visit to Meadowland Crescent had not gone unnoticed by Charlie Drummond who had decided he was the original nosy neighbour.

Hilda Tait leant against the kitchen sink and wondered. She was nobody's fool and though she hated to admit it, she knew that Conor was more than likely in trouble. It was what the officers *didn't say* that actually concerned her. She sighed; she had been in denial for longer than she could remember, she knew it but would never admit it. *Not my Conor,* she tried to convince herself and looked at the new washing machine he had purchased as a recent present. 'How did he afford that?' her thoughts were ended with a sharp knock on the door. Charlie Drummond wasn't the only one who didn't use the doorbell. She opened the door for the second time this morning and saw her lovely Charlie.

'Everything alright with you Hilda, couldn't help noticing the two officers walk past my door just before.'

'Come in Charlie, would you like a cup of tea?' she could do with the company and someone to speak with; Charlie Drummond offered both. She told him the police were looking for Conor but wouldn't say why. 'He's not a bad lad,' Hilda said, desperately wanting Charlie to reassure her.

Whilst Linton was trying to locate Conor Tait, Sgt Jack Wilshaw had been unsuccessful in his attempts to contact Sutton, who had just realised his phone was still on silent. He was expecting an update from Linton on Conor's arrest which was taking longer than he expected when he noticed a couple of missed calls from Jack Wilshaw. He rang him back immediately and a smile appeared across his face. 'Retirement do?' Sutton enquired.

'Not a social call, Geoff, but I know you're involved in Operation Proof. There's a guy by the name of Nevil Samuels just been in at the front counter and he's fully admitted being an outlet for the phones stolen by the PST, apparently he has a shop in the Plaza. He names them all and states they are responsible for the death of Enid Benson. I've asked for him to be taken into custody, initially as a voluntary attender,' Wilshaw, spoke confidently to his longstanding colleague. Sutton's eyes widened, they already had some good intelligence on Nevil Samuels, but this was now prima facie evidence on the team, finally some *proof.*

Sutton acted without due course to supervision. 'Arrest him for handling, Jack, we can then interview, decide on his disposal, possibly caution him and use him as a witness,' Sutton was thinking out loud.

'Not a problem Geoff,' came Wilshaw's reply.

'And thanks Jack, that's really good news, we will have an interview team to you within the hour,' the conversation was ended. Sutton's phone immediately rang again, it was Ben Linton, who informed him of the news that Conor Tait wasn't at his nan's address.

Sutton updated Trish Delaney in her role as Senior Investigating Officer, it was the bad news then the good news type of report, first Tait's non-arrest, and then the fact that Nev Samuels was in custody. Delaney took in the information; the decoy operation would now be actioned. She would inform Ron Turner whilst Sutton would give the go ahead to Ben Linton and his team.

Having returned to the enquiry desk of the police station, Graham Buttle's heart rate had slowed a little as Nev Samuels had been placed in custody. Buttle's actions that Saturday morning had guaranteed that any assessment centre in the future would be a formality in the next round of new recruits to the force.

30

Paula Liston

Chief Constable Chris Mayling had risen at 7.30 that morning, she recognised it was an important day for Parton Constabulary; publicly humiliated after Operation Trust, they were back in the national spotlight with the British First event. She knew that if the policing operation was a success there would be little or no reporting in the national press but get it wrong and Parton Constabulary would be headline news. Mayling more than anyone knew that her force policed the community with the public's consent and confidence, should things go wrong today the force would take an irretrievable step backwards.

She looked out of the window of her smart city centre quayside apartment to see the sun shining. She cursed her luck; experience had taught her that bad weather tended to curtail the enthusiasm of demonstrators. She would be at work by 10am but in the meantime would review the force's recent inspection report on Safeguarding; 'bloody inspections,' she thought, as she took a professionally bonded booklet from her bulging briefcase and sat down next to her freshly brewed cafetière and sliced melon. Mayling began to read but her concentration wandered to yesterday evening and her short and worrying interview with Dominic Charlton. Her insistence for Ron Turner to postpone his retirement and be promoted to Assistant Chief Constable had been an inspired move; he was dedicated to the force and instrumental in repairing the damage caused by Operation Trust. That said, his use of Charlton as an undercover deployment was downright dangerous and reckless. It wasn't just Turner implicated, now that she was armed with the names of Geoff Sutton and Joanne Firth, there was collateral damage in this scenario, and they could hardly use the excuse of carrying out a lawful order.

There wasn't much chance of her being able to concentrate on this bloody inspection report, let alone Operation Proof, she would be working with Ron Turner in the next couple of hours. Mayling wondered what the possibilities were of Turner having something else, equally as reckless under his sleeve … 'Surely not,' she thought.

Mayling walked into the Gold room at 11am, having previously been updated on the Nev Samuel's arrest.

'Good morning, ma'am,' she received numerous polite and respectful greetings as her rank deserved. There was warmth in her reception. In the relatively short time in her post, Mayling had gained respect from everyone.

The incident room resembled a PC World display with a bank of monitors streaming live pictures of Parton city centre. There were eight control room operatives, supervised by a sergeant, with one Inspector, Louise Tranter, who was the acting Critical Incident Manager, deliberately chosen because she had been involved in the previous chase with the PST. Tranter reported directly to Bruce Urwin, the head of operations who was already in the senior officer's suite along with Ron Turner, who was advising on all crime and intelligence matters required on the day. Mayling strode purposefully into the suite.

'Bloody good news about the PST,' she said, confidently looking Ron Turner directly in the eye. 'Now anything new about the march?' her eyes scanned between the two senior officers. 'Any news on the whereabouts of Conor Tait?' she looked again at Turner, fully aware that they had missed their target earlier.

'No, ma'am,' Turner replied immediately, 'but his description and those of the others involved have been circulated to all city centre officers, we have the necessary proof now of everyone involved.' Mayling nodded. 'They will be interviewing Nev Samuels in the next hour or so and I should be able to give you an update well before the march is due to start,' Turner added with some confidence.

'Well, time to relax gentlemen; we still have some time before the event assembles. I have an inspection report to review and will be in my office if needed, and if not, will be back here at 12 noon,' the chief constable made her exit.

At approximately the same time, Conor Tait, Zac Ewart, Abbie Liston and Freddie Ingles had just about surfaced after last night's excesses. Paula Liston, despite being the last to bed was the earliest to rise, and rather than read the riot act to Abbie she thought it more prudent to put the frying pan to good use. She knew a full breakfast for the gang would 'hit the spot' and gain her the much deserved praise that she craved. Paula knew she had spoilt Abbie, but it had been extremely difficult. As a single parent she worked unsocial hours abandoning Abbie to her own devices for long periods; something she had now grown to regret.

'Come on you lot it's ready, help yourself,' she called out making sure everyone could hear. It took minutes for them to gather around the kitchen table, grabbing anything that was on offer.

'Lovely stuff Paula,' Zac said, munching through a bacon and egg roll, the yoke running down his chin like a small yellow stream.

'Thanks Mum,' Abbie walked around the table to give her mother a large hug. All was well; Paula instantly forgot the state of the house last night and leant back against the cooker. For a short time only, Paula enjoyed the company of Abbie's young friends.

Eating breakfast took only a few minutes. 'Time to get on our way,' Conor had spoken and when he did, they all reacted. He had plans today and those plans included all of them. He wanted to get the mopeds from the lock-up in plenty of time before the BF march. He was also well aware of The Haven members marching in the adjacent street, and despite the large police presence the temptation to 'do a job' and have some fun was too good an opportunity to miss, with the chances of getting caught, minimal. Once they had used and abused Paula's hospitality, the PST, all hooded up, were on their way, a thirty minute walk. Conor used this time to provide them with an outline plan. They were attending the British First march on the mopeds and he wanted Freddie Ingles to move between them and The Haven parade in the neighbouring street. His role was to inform Tait if there was an obvious and easy target. Conor would then decide if the job was on.

Meanwhile in the custody area of Parton Central Police Station, Nev Samuels had been interviewed under caution regarding his involvement in the PST's crimes, and although his account would need corroboration, Samuels had been more than helpful. Joanne Firth, recognising an opportunity, enquired further. 'Nev, can you take me to the lock-up where you say they kept their mopeds?'

'That's no problem whatsoever,' he replied confidently. With Samuels still technically in custody, he was discreetly handcuffed, placed in an unmarked car with Firth and two other detectives. It was an excellent opportunity of securing more evidence of the team's criminality and recovering their vehicles. After a fifteen minute drive, Nev broke the silence. 'We will have to walk from here or you'll damage the car,' as the single track road ended. They parked their vehicle some 300 metres away from the containers and continued on foot.

There was a quiet excitement among the four members of the PST as they had just finished using the small petrol can to top up their small machines. 'Ready to go and time to hole up for a while,' thought Conor to himself, as they set off; the gang were on their way to a standoff point close to the city centre. Neither Conor Tait nor Jo Firth knew just how close they were to each other.

'Did you here that?' said Firth to one of her colleagues, cupping her ear. Firth and the other officers all stopped, but the strong northerly wind was able to suffocate the unique noise of the mopeds heading off in the opposite direction. Nothing further was heard and certainly nothing seen as they followed the directions of the handcuffed Nevil Samuels, but the police had missed the PST by a matter of minutes.

The Parton Smart Team were out and about, at the same time as a frustrated police team, together with Nev Samuels, returned to the custody area at Parton Central Police Station.

'You will be released on bail, but still under investigation,' Firth said formally to Nev Samuels after they had returned to the police station. 'We will be in touch, but you're free to go.' As a safety measure a personal attack alarm was in the process of being installed at SAMS should the PST wish to take retribution. Fortunately, the team members were unaware of Samuels' home address.

Nevil walked through the sliding doors of the police station and into the fresh air. He was no longer a prisoner, domestically or criminally. He was seemingly walking on air as he made his way to his car. For once the Astra started first time and he phoned Joyce. He spoke confidently not letting her interrupt and controlled the conversation which he ended with words, 'I love you Joyce Samuels.' He knew the forthcoming police investigation would have major implications but for once Nevil Samuels had regained his composure and some of his confidence, a fact recognised by his wife.

The journey home for Nev took longer than normal; it was approaching lunchtime with many traffic diversions now operating around Parton city centre as the policing operation for the BF march and The Haven protest gained momentum.

31

'Mick'

It had been an average performance from Gary Thornton in the Wimbledon Common Saturday Morning Park Run. He slumped, exhausted in his kitchen, gagging for a drink when his phone rang, it was Pete Havelock, his deputy, who was always bright and breezy. 'Gary, I have just had a text from Sue, our man Mick has his banner with him, nice red letters: PISS OFF,' Havelock said mischievously.

'Thanks Pete,' Thornton managed, still breathing hard. 'See you Monday and have a good weekend,' he ended the call.

Sutton was in Trish Delaney's office when Thornton rang him. 'Sorry Trish, I will have to get this,' he said in a formal and polite manner, before heading off to her unoccupied secretary's office. 'Gary, any news?' Sutton enquired urgently.

'Yep, your man will have a banner with red lettering saying PISS OFF, the only banner with those words; dilute it, Geoff,' ensuring that Sutton would make the intelligence sanitised in order to protect their source.

Moments previously, after responding to Pete Havelock's text, Susan Ibbotson, aka Shaz, smiled to herself, replaced her phone and stubbed her fag out onto the pavement. She would discuss her exit strategy on Monday. She was becoming increasingly bored with her current deployment and needed a fresh challenge to avert the dangers of complacency. She quickly reverted back to Shaz and returned inside the Bird and Feather, as the first members of the BF began to gather.

'Pint of fucking cider please Mick,' she shouted her order to a shaven headed youth. He was minus two front teeth and carrying a red lettered placard. He made his way happily to the bar, a small brick secreted within his large inside jacket pocket.

'No fucking probs Shaz,' Mick grunted, always willing to please a pretty lady.

Chris Mayling had been back in the Gold room for over an hour. She had been moving between the senior officer's suite and communications room containing the huge bank of monitors. She'd completed a full briefing with both Urwin and Turner.

'Boss, can I have another quick word please?' Turner enquired of Mayling. It was clear that Urwin was not going to be part of that conversation. Once alone Turner wasted no time. 'Ma'am, we have some actionable real-time intelligence. We can identify Mick, the lad who's nominated to cause some damage; he'll be the only one with a placard, displaying PISS OFF in red lettering. In order to protect the source can we take out a small group, with him included, and conduct a stop and search, more than likely they will find something if he's the guy who's going to smash a window. It would give the appearance of a random police tactic.'

Mayling didn't speak, she couldn't. The only thing that passed through her mind was, was this another one of Turner's kamikaze escapades? She looked directly at him, smiled and nodded. 'Thanks Ron,' and they both returned back to the communications room.

Chief Constable Mayling surveyed the cameras, people were gathering, she opened her policy log and handed it over to her nominated scribe, a young constable on an accelerated promotion career path. One day that constable would hope it would bring her the same responsibilities that were now incumbent on Mayling, but for now she had more than enough on her plate. She had to get this right – pen shaking in her right hand she was poised to make the first entry.

The current state of play was as follows: British First were just beginning to gather in the pub, The Haven protestors would soon be at their community centre and the PST were hidden away in the disused bowling club, close to the city centre. All police had been briefed, and an advanced serial of officers were already at the Bird and Feather with other resources deployed at strategic positions; Ben Linton's decoy team, who would only go live immediately prior to the beginning of both marches. 'Senior officers present: myself, ACC Turner and Chief Superintendent Urwin. Time 12.45pm,' Mayling dictated to her scribe. 'Yes, ma'am,' came the instant reply.

Operation Proof was up and running.

32

The Haven, British First
and the Decoy

The Haven

Charlie Drummond had his clipboard at the ready, ticking off names as members of The Haven gathered at the community centre. He had walked there with Hilda Tait, she again linked arms with him, and Charlie felt very proud to have Hilda by his side. With the weather being good, the turnout was excellent, albeit, Henry Buckingham had called Charlie earlier; trouble down below was the last thing Drummond needed to hear. There were an assortment of walking aids clattering around the centre as Charlie, as sprightly as anyone half his age, began barking instructions which were largely ignored by the gathering throng who seemed more concerned with helping themselves to the free refreshments on offer.

Charlie was grateful the city centre was their planned marching route; he was of the opinion that for many of his fellow protestors whilst the mind was willing, the flesh was weak. He hoped that Hilda Tait would again be on his arm as they marched through the city centre. If that proved to be the case, he couldn't be prouder. Charlie Drummond led from the front; he was well aware that their march was only a short distance but had requested the photographer with the

Parton Weekly to attend the finish where he secretly hoped he would be asked to make a speech thanking everyone for their support. Charlie had just about assembled 'his troops'. He had borrowed a megaphone which, given the number of attendees fitted out with hearing aids, proved an excellent acquisition. The Haven marchers slowly made their way from the centre and began the short walk to their starting position; Charlie had given themselves plenty of time and Hilda was on his arm.

He could hear in the distance the noise of whistles and a beating drum from the neighbouring street, their parade was, as would be expected, far more sedate. He looked across to his right and Hilda Tait smiled brightly at him, for a moment Charlie Drummond felt he was walking on air but his mood changed in an instant, he shivered, not because of the cold but because he believed he could clearly hear the sound of a moped. He couldn't be a hundred per cent sure and it was quickly drowned by a beating drum, but a deep frown of concern spread across Drummond's face.

British First

There was a roar that could be heard throughout the city centre as Barry Harrison, British First Leader, entered the Bird and Feather. 'There's only one Barry Harrison,' Shaz led the inane chant, quickly to be joined by the rest of the gathering.

Harrison was an unlikely leader of British First. He looked so different from his followers, impeccably dressed and groomed; he always wore a light-coloured suit, wearing a red rose in his lapel. Today it was a pale blue number with trendy, highly polished, black pointy shoes. Born in Peckham from a working class background, Harrison had graduated with a 2:1 honours degree from Churchill College, Cambridge. Politics and economics were his chosen subjects before securing employment in the City. He used both influence and intellect in his activities. In response to the crowd chanting his name he nonchalantly waved a hand in arrogant recognition of his followers.

Tel, the local BF commander made a beeline straight over to Barry and threw himself at his leader, Tel's sweaty frame embraced Harrison's pristine suit. Shaz thought Harrison looked more like a pimp than anyone who may harbour political ambitions, but she was fully aware that he was nobody's fool. Without making it obvious, she viewed the whole scene with utter dismay and checked the time on her phone.

'Mick want another?' she shouted out an offer to return his previous favour. It also gave her the opportunity to purchase something non-alcoholic; she needed to be fully focussed at march time.

'Cheers Shaz!' came the toothless but yelled response.

A few minutes passed before Tel instructed Mick to round them up. This literally meant him standing on a bar table and shouting at the top of his voice.

'Shut up, fucking shut up!' he screamed 'Time to get ready you bastards, outside in five minutes, down your fucking drinks!' he yelled manically and within a few seconds had finished his full pint.

It was the normal mix at any demonstration, a few with megaphones and placards, some with tabards to act as their own stewards, a group with whistles, and one youth carrying a huge drum. Shaz looked around and noted Harrison playing the room, a conversation here, a nod of acknowledgment there, 'Paying lip service to his minions,' she thought to herself. The group reluctantly began to leave the pub and take up their own starting positions.

Conor Tait and the other members of the PST were at their usual city centre standoff point behind the disused bowling clubhouse. He checked his phone for the time, 'Another five minutes or so,' he thought to himself, it didn't take long to get where they would need to be. He began discussing their holding position before they would finally deploy themselves on the British First march, as agreed with Tel. He and Zac would go to the BF march and ensure Tel saw them, with Abbie and Freddie roaming The Haven protest looking for targets. 'If one is identified, we will regather at the holding position and plan the strike. Me and Zac will do the business today,' Conor grinned, excited at the thought.

Chris Mayling, in the command suite, looked up at the screens and noted the marches beginning to assemble. 'An entry in the policy log to the effect that all officers policing the British First march are tasked to identify a male carrying a placard with distinctive red lettering, PISS OFF displayed. No action at this time – just identify at this stage,' she said firmly, looking across at Ron Turner.

The drunken few were finishing off their drinks at the Bird and Feather before joining the rear of the march. Shaz always liked to start at the back and therefore was always one of the last to leave, it was often a good opportunity to obtain some intelligence and potential evidence from discarded items. On this occasion what she found caused her a major headache. She placed her pint glass back on the bar counter and stumbled over something as she did so. She looked down and for a moment froze completely, a placard bearing the words PISS OFF in big red letters was staring back at her. Shaz was numb, 'That stupid shit, Mick, he's left his fucking banner!' she shouted, but no one took any notice. Shaz had two options: leave it in situ and try and get a message through to Havelock or run out into the gathering march and find Mick.

Although she ran the risk of arrest or some other police intervention, Shaz knew Mick would be at the front of the protest, he always was. 'Bollocks,' she thought again of Mick probably half-pissed and shouting his mouth off, armed with a brick in his pocket ready to smash the first window. Shaz picked up the placard and ran out of the pub barging her way through to the front row of the march. She heard him long before she saw him, despite the noise of the other activists. This wasn't surprising as Mick never spoke, only shouted, and was even distinctive above the drums and whistles.

'Mick, you stupid bastard, you forgot something,' she said, passing the placard he'd abandoned at the bar along the line at the front of the march, towards its intended destination. It had reached the bloke standing next to Mick who immediately took the opportunity to proudly hold it aloft, with an obvious, 'Finders keepers,' mentality.

'No Shaz, you have it!' he screamed back towards Shaz, an act of what Mick considered genuine kindness.

Shaz's heart sank. 'I can't Mick!' she yelled back at him. 'I've been given a sign that Barry wants me to carry and it's back at the pub,' Shaz lied, thinking on her feet like every good undercover operative. She knew that whatever Barry Harrison said would be gospel with Mick.

'If Barry says so, Shaz,' he said, as with a degree of difficulty, he grabbed the banner from the now disgruntled fellow BF member, standing next to him. Mick hoisted the sign high into the air, displaying the words PISS OFF in bright red letters. Shaz looked up, relieved to get rid of the placard but only to see the eyes of a uniformed officer who had observed her actions with some interest, having noted the banner's description as previously circulated by the control room. Unfortunately, the officer was unable to hear their conversation above the noise of the gathering demonstration.

Performing his duties diligently, he immediately contacted the control room relaying what had taken place. Following the update, Ron Turner had been called into the senior officer's suite by his chief constable.

'Which individual is it, Ron? Someone who initially brought the banner to the front of the march, although that person looked female, or one of the two males who then lifted it aloft?' Mayling was asking Turner a straightforward question.

'I don't know, ma'am, I really don't know,' he replied.

'Well bloody find out Ron, find out, and quickly,' she said sharply. Turner noted the change of tone, she was under pressure; they all were. He made his way out of the command room and contacted Sutton relaying the identity issue. He was the only person Turner could think of who might be able to assist.

When Sutton first received the call from Turner he panicked and called Thornton as his Security Service contact. It went straight to voicemail. 'Shit,' he thought to himself, waste of a call, there was no way on earth that Thornton could contact the source at this late stage. Sutton needed to act, quickly but logically. He slumped back in the chair of an empty office he had located and thought for a moment or two. He then rang Turner. 'It's the last male to hold the banner at the front of the march,' Sutton said before any questions. He tried to sound as confident as he could but there was a momentary pause at the other end.

'Geoff is that a guess. I have to inform the chief?'

'Sir, it's the last male to hold the banner at the front of the march,' he repeated firmly, but politely. Turner walked through to where Mayling was waiting and repeated verbatim what Sutton had told him. He said the words as confidently as he could.

Mayling called for her loggist. 'For the benefit of the policy document ACC Turner has informed me that intel suggests a person identified as a potential target is now reported as being in the front row of the march. He has been identified carrying a banner scrawled with the words PISS OFF in red letters. Please fully record that entry,'

Mayling's eyes never deviated from Turner, who looked directly back at his chief constable. In that moment of recognition, Turner now knew that Mayling was fully aware of Dominic Charlton's deployment. It was far more than a gut feeling of lost trust between them, as he thought back to the constable accompanied by his federation rep who was waiting to see her last night. In that moment his worst fears of Mayling finding out about his authorisation had been realised. He was in the shit but even more so if this march goes belly up, particularly as he had fed through this latest piece of intelligence.

At the same time Sutton was still in his newly acquired office, he reviewed his thought process. He had guessed that the subject must have forgotten the placard which had been returned to him. He couldn't think that their subject would actually willingly give up the banner with the event witnessed by a cop, who was only carrying out his duties. Yes, it was a guess, and Turner knew it, but there was a certain logic behind his thoughts. Sutton just hoped his logical thoughts were correct.

Sutton stopped musing over his conversation with Turner; he was detailed to be on the ground with Firth now that she had finished with Nev Samuels.

Decoy Operation

Ronnie Watts, the cop who was dressed to become the target in the forthcoming decoy operation, smiled back to himself in the mirror, it had taken him the good part of an hour – he was literally made up and he liked what he saw. 'Now for the final item,' he said to himself, rummaging in the bag of tricks he kept deep inside the locker within the crew room. He deliberately removed a very distinctive black and white headscarf. This would be instantly identifiable for all officers who would be given his full description. In the event of someone wearing a similar item in the march he pushed another, equally identifiable, headscarf of a different colour in his coat pocket.

It was ten minutes later, covert earpiece in place, when the very same PC 1995 Watts returned to the crew room ready for action, only to be greeted with wolf whistles from his team members. Linton quickly called them to order. He had received an update from Sutton that the mopeds weren't at the lockup and therefore there was every chance they would be attending the march searching for a target to attack. There was a thought that Watts could attend The Haven and latch onto their group but there was a slim chance that despite Ronnie's excellent disguise, he could be compromised; far better if he wandered about in the designated areas in the city centre. Linton detailed four plain clothes officers to act as minders for Watts, ensuring not only that he wasn't in danger, but also to notify supervision should they spot the PST on the plot. Most importantly, Linton mapped out to all his team where Ronnie Watts would be allowed to walk, leaving no one in any doubt that officer safety was paramount.

Linton's team was just one of many police resources assigned to Saturday's events; Sergeant Steve Barker was supervising a serial of officers working the demonstrations in the City Centre. His team were split into four cars, two officers per car. Their role was simple: in the event of a pursuit involving the mopeds, they would be first responders. Each driver had successfully passed the mobile tactical contact course held recently by the traffic department. Barker paraded the group of constables and gave them the latest intelligence and a description of PC Watts' clothing. They went immediately mobile in preparation.

Ben Linton's phone rang, a buzz of excitement rang around the crew room, unlike many other deployments, there was a really good chance this job would come off and the atmosphere reflected that expectation.

'Right guys, we're good to go.' Ronnie Watts picked up his walking stick and carried out a radio check, via his covert earpiece. He had a nominated driver in an unmarked car that would take him into the pre-agreed zone and join up initially at the rear of The Haven march.

At the same time Conor Tait started up his moped, the others followed suit. Hoods up, they set off for their own rendezvous out of sight of CCTV and the two parades.

'At 2 pm, both marches commence,' said Chief Constable Mayling to her loggist. 'Over to you Bruce,' she nodded to Bruce Urwin, her silver commander. He gave the order and the two nominated uniformed inspectors, one with British First and the other with The Haven, confirmed their instructions and allowed the stewards of both marches to move forward.

33

The March

With both marches underway, Urwin soon gave the instruction for an intervention in the British First event. He wanted four people on the front right flank of the march to be stopped and searched, starting with the male carrying the banner displaying PISS OFF in large red letters. Critical Incident Manager, Inspector Louise Tranter, gave the order clearly and calmly asking for an update when complete. You could touch and breathe the tension within the room. Ron Turner stared at the screen and took a deep breath. He watched, waited and *bloody hoped*; he was in more than enough trouble. Chief Constable Mayling looked across at Ron Turner while Bruce Urwin viewed the screens.

Sutton was on the ground with Firth when he heard the instructions being given, he knew what that meant. He stopped in his tracks and took a deep breath. Minutes later a call came into the control room. 'Can we have some transport, please? One arrest; goes by the name of Mick, conspiracy to commit criminal damage, a small rock or brick recovered from the suspect.'

'Transport on its way,' came Tranter's immediate reply.

Mayling smiled across at Turner who was trying his best to look calm and composed. 'Log update on the arrest, please,' Mayling said firmly, her confidence restored.

On the ground Firth glanced across at Sutton, they had both been listening into the radio transmissions. 'Geoff are you ok?' she enquired, noticing his worried frown.

'Fine now, thanks Jo.' His mobile rang; it was Gary Thornton, from the Security Service returning his urgent call. Sutton chose to ignore it.

The decoy constable, Ronnie Watts had quietly joined the rear stragglers as they set off on The Haven march. No one seemed to notice 'this outsider' with the distinctive head wear. He made sure that he had his mobile within clear view inside the open shopping bag. Ronnie Watts peered through his clear lens, round-rimmed spectacles, perched on the end of his nose and glanced across at his covert team members, who, between window shopping kept a close eye on their colleague.

The Parton Smart Team were now very close to both marches, hidden away in one of their favourite alleyways, not covered by CCTV, but within immediate striking distance of the precinct.

Conor began to instruct his team. 'Ok, me and Zac will skirt the British First march, I need to know that Tel and his gang have seen me, whilst Abbie and Freddie go scouting for targets at The Haven march, meet back here in five minutes.' With that there was a whine of the machines as the PST went mobile. Within moments they were on the plot, Conor skirted the front of the parade to loud whistles from Tel and his mates.

'Go Conor go!' Tel screamed at the top of his voice like a child on a roller coaster, with his arms held high. Zac took the opportunity to circle the back markers. Shaz noted their activity; she also observed the escorting uniform officers speaking directly into their airwave radios, 'Unwelcome guests,' she thought. Meanwhile the remainder of the team, Abbie and Freddie, performed similar tasks with The Haven march; Abbie circled the front and Freddie the rear, surveying The Haven group for likely targets.

The screens in the command suite streamed the ongoing

activity. Silver Commander Bruce Urwin calmly gave the instructions via the critical incident manager for all staff to monitor this activity but not to intervene at this time, public safety being his main priority. PC Ronnie Watts took the opportunity to cast the bait, coming to a stop he leant on his walking stick and removed the mobile from his shopping bag, just momentarily lifting it to his ear before replacing the item back in the bag. 'Just enough show,' he thought to himself, whilst the mopeds were in the vicinity, before rejoining the rear of the march. The fact that his protest contained so many infirm people was a distinct help in making up any lost ground.

Steve Barker and his team of mobile officers listened into the most recent transmissions with gathering tension; a pursuit was becoming more than a possibility.

As agreed, the PST regathered at their own meeting point.

'We have a dead cert,' said Freddie excitedly, 'There's a granny at the very back of The Haven march wearing a black and white checked headscarf and walking with a stick. Too good to be true, - she's got an open shopping bag. You can even see the bloody phone!'

'This is mine,' thought Conor to himself. He was absolutely buzzing. 'As planned, I'll hit this bastard,' Conor instructed, 'with Zac as back up. Abbie and Freddie, create diversions on the plot,' he looked around at them, they all grinned back, they loved their sport.

Geoff Sutton and Joanne Firth had a free role on the ground walking between the two marches and acting as eyes and ears. They had heard the noise of the mopeds. 'Let's have a look at The Haven march, Jo,' Sutton said to Firth, as they moved from the BF march to latch onto the front of the slowly moving Haven group.

Ronnie Watts scanned everywhere and checked his minders were in place. A shiver ran up his spine, he had a sixth sense that an attack was going to happen. He thought he heard the mopeds above the din of the whistles and drums. He reached inside his shopping bag and took out his phone, but this time he also fished out his pepper spray which he discreetly tucked underneath the fingers holding onto to his walking stick.

The PST were on plot, and Ronnie's minders, as if in tandem, broke their own cardinal rule: never let your eyes divert from your subject – easier said than done. They had to ensure that the two outriders were not an immediate threat to their colleague. But Freddie and Abbie had an objective, create a momentary distraction, buzzing around like bees in and out of a hive. It was all that was required. Conor was now on the plot as Zac emerged unannounced from a nearby alley. He immediately identified the target nominated by Freddie; the description was spot on. She was on her phone, perfect timing.

Conor Tait struck, and attacked Watts from his blind side. Whilst the officer knew an attack was imminent, the speed caught him unawares, his minders started running, they were only a few yards away, but that distance was crucial. With immaculate timing, Tait had already grabbed for the phone. Ronnie Watts stumbled slightly, realised the phone was lost, but immediately discarded his walking stick, freeing up the pepper spray which he discharged at the same time, aimed directly towards Tait's hidden face.

It wasn't a direct hit but there was enough contact of the noxious substance to halt Tait momentarily in his tracks. He wiped his eyes blindly, the wrong tactic given the nature of the spray.

'Go Conor go!' Zac screamed at his leader, as Tait weaved around just avoiding Watts' minders. Make ground, any ground, Tait was desperately trying to regain his senses.

Watts bellowed into his covert radio, 'An attack, spray discharged on offender, officers giving chase towards the front of The Haven march.' Given his circumstances it was a remarkably composed broadcast.

Charlie Drummond had never felt happier for years; here he was the leader of a community display of solidarity. The loud noise of the British First march seemed miles away as his group made their slow progress along the short designated route. Charlie smiled as Saturday shoppers turned and looked on, showing their support with spontaneous applause. He then felt a nudge on his arm, it was Hilda.

'Charlie, will just have to tie my shoelace before I fall over,' she shouted above the noise and moved to one side as she did so, in order that the people following were not obstructed. As is the case with any movement at her stage of life, Hilda bent down slowly to her polished brown shoes. She stretched down, making inward groaning noises, completely oblivious to the increasing sound of nearing mopeds.

Conor continued to blink and rub his eyes with one hand, whilst steering with the other. He was almost totally reliant on Zac's shouts of directions, as he hadn't a clue where he was, despite riding in the streets he knew like the back of his hand. Meanwhile, his eyes felt as though they were burning holes deep inside his throbbing head. He was desperate.

Sutton and Firth heard the now familiar and haunting sound of an approaching moped, they looked around from their position towards the front of The Haven march.

'Conor left, left!' Zac screamed at the top of his voice, still trying to direct his leader to safety as the pursuing cops chased them down. It was too late; as Hilda Tait began tying her errant shoelace, her grandson collided with her. She collapsed backwards, blood oozing from a head wound, mangled reading glasses lying next to her. On impact Conor Tait spun around, causing him to become even more disorientated before man and machine parted company. He staggered around like a crazed drunk, still vigorously rubbing his burning eyes. Zac Ewart also came to an immediate halt, dumped his machine on the ground and stood still, wide eyes staring at the scene, unable to move; his mind drowning in a lake of confusion between escape and the need to remain with his beloved leader. This momentary confusion proved his downfall as he was brought to the ground by two members of Ben Linton's team assigned to act as Ronnie Watts' minders.

Seconds later, Conor Tait joined Zac on the hard concrete, as the remainder of Watts' minders had pounced. Whilst the noise of the right-wing protest could be clearly heard, absurdly there was now a deafening silence in the immediate space around The Haven protest, broken only by the sound of two abandoned mopeds, engines still running, wheels still spinning. Sutton shouted through to the control room after giving the location.

'Ambulance urgently required we have an elderly female with a head injury. Transport required for two arrests and we also require two mopeds to be forensically recovered,' Sutton barked out his requests clearly. Charlie Drummond was kneeling alongside Hilda, cradling her, as the blood oozed through her greying hair.

'Stay with us Hilda, stay with us,' he repeated, the former war hero choked back his emotion.

In the command suite, Mayling prompted Urwin as the events unfolded, 'Bruce any sign of the other mopeds,' just as she said those words Sergeant Steve Barker, on mobile patrol duties, shouted in.

'Control we have two mopeds exiting from the march area, we are following and request authorisation for tactical contact?'

Critical Incident Manager, Inspector Louise Tranter, looked across to the command team and Urwin walked through to her location. Urwin had planned carefully for this potential scenario and had also appointed an experienced traffic officer to advise. 'Any thoughts?' Urwin asked the officer urgently, beads of sweat just beginning to appear on his brow. Urwin knew this was a crucial accountable decision.

'Roads are relatively quiet, they are currently heading to an unbuilt-up area, seems ok,' was the reply from the traffic officer.

'Tactical contact authorised,' he said to Inspector Tranter, who immediately relayed the message to Barker. The loggist recorded Urwin's authority with both Mayling and Turner tuned into Barker's commentary.

'It's a left, left, left onto Rose Street, then a right, right, right, onto John Street, speed 30mph still making up ground and too far away to make contact, traffic still light,' Barker said, trying so hard to control nerves against his fears, whilst his partner for the shift sat almost glued to the front passenger seat. Google maps were scrutinised, Urwin knew the area and was concerned about a play park half a mile away, a locality popular with parents and toddlers, particularly on a weekend.

'Louise, tell them to abort,' Urwin said immediately to the critical incident manager.

'No keep going, Gold's commander's call,' said Chris Mayling, overriding Urwin's last instruction. They all turned and looked at their chief constable. 'He may have the opportunity to take them out at these traffic lights, there's no other vehicles or pedestrians in the immediate vicinity,' Mayling said with both confidence and authority, turning to her loggist, 'Please make a written record of both my decision and the rationale.'

Totally unaware of the events on the march, and operating on a different radio channel, Sgt Jim Glasson was in company with his current star probationer constable, Dominic Charlton. They had enjoyed a pleasant couple of hours on foot patrol, some three miles west of the city centre. It had been uneventful, Charlton had admonished a few youngsters for cycling on the pavements, whilst listening to some locals surprised at seeing a police officer on foot patrol but at the same time complaining about litter and dog excrement. Charlton heard the police sirens becoming louder, as they approached a set of traffic lights.

'It's no change, no change, approaching traffic lights ahead, currently on green. We may have an opportunity,' Barker continued his commentary, sweaty hands gripping the wheel ever tighter, while his colleague and front seat passenger pressed the release button on his own seat belt, anticipating a chase. Abbie Liston and Freddie Ingles made their way towards the traffic lights as they changed colour, amber then red. A red signal was never a guarantee that they would stop but it could cause confusion in their mind. The pair were in panic mode, fight or flight, their leader gone, the two of them rudderless. They had decided to return to their holding position at the disused bowling club. The sirens behind them just added to the mayhem, Freddie noticed the traffic lights change, they normally would go straight through on red or up on the pavement to avoid pursuers, but he just wanted to check with Abbie; for an instant, they closed up together, side by side, slowing towards the lights. Barker anticipated, remembered his training if there are two together, aim for the middle. He checked left and right – no other traffic – GO FOR IT.

He slowed ever so slightly, his back clinging to his seat through fear and sweat, and then accelerated smoothly towards the target. The front centre of his vehicle made firm contact with the rear of the two mopeds, similar to a well-aimed strike at a bowling alley. The two riders spilled either side like a parting of the waves; Freddie prone, Abbie scrambled to her feet, extricating herself from beneath the machine and began running. Dominic Charlton, without prompting from his sergeant, gave chase whilst Barker's partner detained Freddie.

'Go Dom, bloody go,' shouted an out of breath Glasson

unable to manage anything other than a trot. Abbie ran through the park but Charlton, as ungainly as ever but running high on adrenalin, was not giving up and began to close the distance between them, before the inevitable happened and he eventually brought her to the ground with a textbook rugby tackle. He was subsequently joined by an exhausted Glasson a couple of minutes later.

'Great stuff, Dom, great stuff,' Glasson repeated himself as he sought his own recovery from the chase. 'Don't forget the caution,' he reminded his protégé. Dominic Charlton had a grin from ear to ear as he realised he had made his first ever arrest. An arrest that was so important, not only to him personally, but significantly to the good people of Parton. The PST had been captured.

Returning to the British First march, Tel was trying frantically to drum up some aggro but many of his key players were struggling to muster much enthusiasm, primarily due to the amount of strong cheap cider consumed at the Bird and Feather earlier that afternoon. The whistles were becoming more infrequent and the drummer had moved to the rear of the gathering with the sole intention of abandoning the march when he saw the next pub. Barry Harrison knew this was rapidly becoming a complete waste of time: a waste of his time more to the point. He checked his watch and wondered if he could get the earlier train back to London, first class of course, rather than spend any more time with this drunken bunch. There wasn't a hope of him delivering his prepared speech, as planned.

No one among the British First crowd were aware of what had gone on nearby, and nor did they care about the serious injury to Hilda Tait.

34

Doctor Patterson

Sutton and Firth followed the ambulance carrying Hilda Tait to Parton General. They needed an update on her condition as soon as possible. Charlie Drummond accompanied her in the rear of the emergency vehicle; he refused to be parted from his Hilda. The attending paramedics gave nothing away regarding her injuries at the scene.

'Hold on in there, Hilda,' Charlie said quietly, holding her hand, with tears streaming down his face. He looked around at the array of equipment.

'Keep talking to her Charlie, keep on talking,' said the paramedic encouragingly, whilst holding the IV drip inserted into her arm.

Parked up, Sutton reckoned they were probably a good ten minutes behind the ambulance when they got to Accident and Emergency. He saw Charlie Drummond as they entered the waiting area and for once Sutton didn't take in the sad faces of either injured people or concerned friends and relatives. Charlie looked totally dischevelled, gone was the proud ex-military man with the upright stature and smart appearance, he now looked considerably older, stooped, and with his shirt tail hanging out.

'How are you doing Charlie?' Jo Firth said sympathetically, immediately thinking what a stupid question to ask. She then reacted naturally and far more appropriately, giving Charlie a huge comforting embrace. Sutton now scanned the waiting area, the sight of wheelchairs, anxious faces and a general atmosphere of trauma, hit him like a brick. Today's events had kept him apart from the pain of Roger's tragic death, but now, here, in the public area of A & E, without any warning it had caught up with Sutton. Head down and to avoid any public embarrassment he headed for the gent's toilets, locked himself away in a cubicle and was violently sick. He didn't care if anyone came to use the facilities. He just needed a short time to recover his composure.

Sutton emerged minutes later; Firth was looking anxiously around, neither she nor Charlie had seen his disappearing act. 'Seen a doctor, Geoff?' Firth asked, presuming he had been making enquiries regarding Hilda Tait's condition.

'No, not yet Jo,' he replied quietly. Firth knew through his drained pale complexion that something was wrong but didn't enquire further.

A door to the right of reception displaying a large NO ENTRY was pushed open from the inside. 'Next of kin for Mrs Tait,' called a confident voice. Charlie, Sutton and Firth made their way towards the young male with a stethoscope hanging limply around his neck, dressed in an unbuttoned white coat and pale blue clogs.

'Doctor, we are not sure who is her next of kin, I am both a good friend and a neighbour. I came with her in the ambulance,' Charlie said helpfully.

'And we are both police officers, investigating the incident regarding the injuries to Mrs Tait,' Sutton said politely, interrupting Charlie.

'I am Doctor Patterson, please come this way.'

Sutton followed the clogs as they all made their way through to Patterson's office, where the doctor then made a half-hearted attempt to clear a dirty coffee cup and tidy away a half-eaten sandwich, before asking them to sit down. Charlie Drummond took a huge breath as he sat down, Firth reached over and held his hand which Charlie gladly accepted and gripped tightly. Patterson leant forward, elbows on knees, closing the space between himself and his three guests. Firth felt the grip on her hand become even tighter, almost causing her pain.

'Mrs Tait is going to be fine I'm pleased to tell you. Slightly concussed, with a small wound to her head which will require stitches and we will keep her in overnight for observations, but I'm confident there is no lasting damage, although obviously, she's very shaken.'

'Can I see her?' Charlie asked immediately.

'Give us ten minutes or so and we will call you through,' Patterson said assuredly. 'But please keep your contact short, Hilda needs rest more than anything,' he added with authority.

They all returned to the waiting area; Sutton and Firth said their goodbyes to Drummond, they needed to get back to the station, armed with the news that Hilda Tait was going to be fine.

It seemed the longest ten minutes of his life for Charlie Drummond before he got the call and walked through to the bay where Hilda had been taken. He had taken the opportunity to purchase some chocolates from the League of Friends kiosk. He peeled back the curtain and was greeted with a loving smile from Hilda, her face was bruised, and a large bandage was wrapped around her greying locks but that didn't deter Charlie from affectionately planting a kiss on her forehead, placing the chocolates on top of the small cabinet next to her bed.

'They are as lovely as you, Charlie,' Nan Tait said the words with meaning and looked straight up at Drummond. 'Charlie please tell me one thing; do you know who was riding the moped? They say I have had some concussion, but I can remember the moped coming towards me.' Charlie looked at her, eyes never wavering, now standing upright looking down at her on the bed.

'It was Conor, Hilda, your Conor,' he emphasised your.

Hilda cried out and put both hands up to her lips, shaking her head in denial, 'No, no.'

'Hilda, it was Conor,' Drummond repeated.

'You're lying, Charlie Drummond, you're lying,' she repeated, in total denial.

Drummond looked deep into the eyes of Nan. 'Hilda, I don't lie,' this time Charlie spoke firmly. Hilda closed her eyes and nodded. With both arms she reached upwards in order that Charlie could join her in a loving embrace.

'I need you, Charlie Drummond,' Nan said, kissing the side of his neck as she held him close.

Hilda Tait had been finally forced to admit that Conor Tait was not the angelic grandson she previously believed. At last Charlie released himself from the warmth of Nan's embrace and drew the plastic curtain across, closing his view of her lying in the hospital bed. As ordered, he knew she had to rest. He also knew at that moment he had a partner to share his life and final years. He smiled because Charlie Drummond was a happy man who would no longer be lonely.

Whilst Charlie was visiting Nan, Sutton and Firth made their way back to Parton Central Police Station.

35

Freddie Ingles

Zac Ewart had already been booked into custody when Conor Tait, handcuffed and bungled into a marked police car, entered the holding area at the Parton Central prisoner area. He was placed in a metal gated area, not too dissimilar to a caged animal on display at a local zoo. He said nothing apart from a few choice words directed at his arresting officers. At this time, he neither knew nor cared whom he'd hit with his moped. His immediate concern was the irritation of his eyes caused by the pepper spray rather than the fact he'd been captured.

His eyes were clearing slowly, this was his first ever time he'd been in custody. With blinking eyes, he looked around the brightly lit arena; the centre stage was taken by a central console where the custody sergeant was housed behind safety glass. Despite the rank, a custody sergeant was the officer in charge of this domain.

Tara Shipley was behind the consul when Tait had been brought in, her 2pm till 10pm shift had been remarkably quiet, although she was banned for saying that word within the custody empire. They had been half expecting to be run ragged if the British First march had 'kicked off.'

'Next,' said Sergeant Shipley, without even looking up as Tait was escorted by a civilian detention officer and the circumstances of his arrest were outlined to Shipley. 'Name?' no answer came from underneath the hoodie. 'Name?'

Shipley repeated the question, again no answer from Tait. She always politely asked the same question twice; if nothing sensible was forthcoming, it was her unwritten rule that the conversation had ended and so did Conor Tait's brief appearance before her.

'Take him down, Cell 3 please, got better things to do with my time,' she added for good measure to no one in particular. Shipley was known for being firm and fair, but she didn't stand for any nonsense. She also knew there was every chance she would obtain Conor Tait's relevant details from Sutton and Firth who had recently entered the custody suite. A few minutes passed before Tait was housed in Cell 3 and Firth had supplied Shipley with the new prisoner's particulars.

Once Tait had been detained, Sutton and Firth took the opportunity to meet with Trish Delaney in her role of SIO (Senior Investigating Officer) and review where they were with the investigation. It was all positive and a much relieved Trish Delaney knew it. The Parton Smart Team had been caught in the act of committing a robbery, but not only for this offence – where there was clear CCTV footage – as now they had Nevil Samuels on board; crucially they had evidence of other crimes, most importantly the death of Enid Benson. The chances were that they would be able to recover some of the stolen phones from SAMS. The interview teams had already been allocated. They were expecting Freddie Ingles and Abbie Liston to be in custody very soon after having attended a local health centre following their *'accident'*.

Sutton took a large sip of Delaney's frothy coffee and took in the aroma of the flowers that seemed to change almost daily. 'Let's try and teach Conor Tait a lesson,' said Sutton out loud, as a wide grin appeared across his face for the first time in a few days.

With Delaney's agreement, they returned to the cell complex armed with a download on Firth's phone incorporating the scene of Conor's accident with his nan. They agreed with Custody Sergeant Shipley on a welfare check for their prisoner, which may assist in the identification process. Tait had, after all, initially refused to give any details. Armed with the cell keys, Sutton and Firth made their way to Cell 3, opened the door, to find Tait lying prone on his blue plastic mattress.

'Conor,' said Sutton firmly, as before there was no reply. 'Conor have a look and listen to this.' No movement at all from the lifeless body on the mat.

The recording contained audio. Sutton and Firth squatted down, in order that any words spoken could be clearly heard by the prisoner. The clip showed Conor stealing the phone from Ronnie Watts who, in discharging his pepper spray, screamed loudly for assistance. It then showed Conor manoeuvre his moped in an attempt to evade capture, together with Zac Ewart. Zac could be heard shouting his instructions before Conor collided with one of the pensioners, tying her shoelace at the front of The Haven march. At this point there was a loud shout of distress perfectly captured on the clip.

Firth leaped backwards and pressed the alarm button at the cell entrance, as the shape on the mattress catapulted itself upright and lunged towards Sutton.

Conor Tait screamed out loud, 'That's not Nan, that's not my Nan!' Sutton was expecting a reaction, but he had got more than he anticipated and although he stepped aside, he caught a glancing blow to the right side of his head. Custody resources arrived before Tait could capitalise on his advantage and the sight of another can of pepper spray by the custody staff put an end to Conor's physical resistance, but not his screaming.

'That's not Nan, it's not my nan, you bastards!' he repeated – another total denial of the obvious. 'I want to see her, I want to see my nan!' Tait continued to rant uncontrollably.

Sutton's pride was hurt far more than any physical injury.

He chuckled to himself as he and Firth walked back down to the custody sergeant's consul. By this time Freddie Ingles and Abbie Liston had arrived in the custody area having replaced Conor in the holding cage. Unsurprisingly, Tait was the only member of the gang who had been anything other than compliant.

The fact that it was their first time in custody had been enough for Zac, Freddie and Abbie to be totally submissive. 'Next,' Sergeant Tara Shipley began the same routine, always necessary when booking in her next inmate. Freddie Ingles, still handcuffed, shuffled towards Shipley's platform accompanied by the diligent detention officer. Freddie was in tears, not from any physical injury sustained during his chase and collision, this whole custody environment had hit home; 'What would his dad ever think of him,' he thought to himself. He wondered if his dad even cared.

'Just make sure he hasn't got anything remaining in his pockets, Derek,' Shipley instructed one of her custody staff. Without removing the cuffs, the detention officer did a final check removing a small black wallet from his denim jeans pocket. He then placed the item on the custody sergeant's desk and in doing so a small passport sized photograph fell to the ground. Sutton reached down, turned it over and there looking back at him was a picture of his lifelong friend, a very young Roger Strong.

Sutton shivered and choked. 'Freddie, who is this?' Jo Firth asked him.

'It's my dad, but haven't seen him in years,' Ingles replied between sniffs. Freddie Ingles was Roger's estranged son.

Sutton stared at young Freddie; it had been more than a few years since he'd last seen him and there was no way he would ever have recognised him. 'Geoff, are you alright?' Firth asked, not for the first time today.

Sutton recovered slightly and spoke to the custody sergeant. 'Tara, I need to speak to Freddie. This has nothing to with the enquiry or any other criminal investigation,' he said quickly, composing himself. Sutton had known Tara Shipley for a number of years.

'Not a problem Geoff,' it was an immediate reply from the custody sergeant, born out of the mutual respect between them.

Within a couple of minutes, Sutton and Firth were sitting opposite young Freddie in an interview room within the custody area. He was relieved of the handcuffs but was still visibly upset at his current predicament. Sutton thought that the news he was about to impart wasn't about to assist his current circumstances. 'Freddie there is no easy way to say this, but your father has passed away,' Sutton said quickly.

'What did you say?' Ingles leant forward not believing what he thought he had heard.

'Freddie, your dad is dead,' Sutton said, louder this time, and with some finality, considering the gravity of his statement. Freddie's head dropped, could his young life be any worse. He had really hoped that someday soon he would ignore his mother's protests and recontact his dad after all these years. Firth comforted Freddie Ingles, he and the others from the Parton Smart Team had caused so much grief, yet in reality he was an exceptionally vulnerable young man. He just sobbed and sobbed. Sutton looked down, he hadn't the bottle to tell him the circumstances of his dad's death; it would be just too much at this time.

Sutton returned to the main custody area to advise Tara Shipley. 'Tara, might be a good idea to get a doctor for Ingles,' as he explained the news he'd just delivered.

It was 5pm, Chris Mayling and her command team were about to stand down. There were only some ten British First marchers who made it to Walter's without Barry Harrison, who was currently in his first-class carriage on a train heading back to London. Mayling personally thanked everyone for their help. 'Job done,' she thought to herself, and a satisfied, if relieved smile appeared across her face. 'We will debrief on Monday, gents,' she said directly to Turner and Urwin, 'but it has gone well, thanks again. Any news on the Smart Team investigation, Ron?'

'Looks very positive, ma'am, the live footage we have of today's crime will ensure an initial charge and with Nevil Samuel's evidence it is looking very promising.'

'Excellent, enjoy your weekend,' Mayling added, in a sarcastic tone in the knowledge that it was fast approaching Saturday evening. 'Ron, I would like to see you first thing Monday morning, 8am.' It was Mayling's final words as she left for a press conference that would be a great deal easier than yesterday. As for Ron Turner, he didn't have to guess the purpose of her request to see him on Monday.

Turner phoned Sutton just as he was leaving the custody area. 'All ok Geoff? Presume you're now off to the rugby club?' Turner knew full well the importance that Sutton attached to his Saturday ritual of golf, rugby, then a few beers, all with his mates.

'I am boss. Just to let you know, there's every indication we will get full confessions from the Smart team, well at least three of them. Conor wants to see his nan, which is possible, but only on the basis that he supplies us with the full story. Once he's spoken, the others will follow suit, the interview teams have been briefed. I get the impression that even his nan, Hilda Tait, has decided to give us a witness statement. The rumour is that she now wants nothing to do with him. There is more than enough CCTV and we can also obtain the necessary DNA samples to match the profile found on Enid Benson's mobile phone.

'I think they're knackered, boss,' Sutton summarised his thoughts on the evidence against the PST.

'Thanks Geoff,' an unusual comment from Turner, who failed to mention his concern over Mayling discovering Charlton's deployment. He hoped that above anything else he alone would take all the flack going.

Sutton and Firth walked together through the car park; Trish Delaney had told them to go home, she would get a further update from the interview teams later tonight, bed them all down and she would return tomorrow and personally supervise the charging process, after consultation with the CPS.

Some thirty minutes later, Sutton parked up at Upper Parton RFC. He decided to put the car to bed, after a few beers he would be walking back up the hill later. He hadn't arranged to see Debbie that night as she had arranged to cook a meal for her brother Billy, to celebrate his birthday.

He walked into the warmth of the clubhouse; Sutton was home. Pete McIntyre and Stew Grant were sat at their table. A vacant chair, carrying the name plate of Roger Strong with the Upper Parton scarf, was sited close by. They had been joined by a few other club members who had plucked up enough courage to go over and reminisce about Roger. Sutton approached his mates; he was knackered both physically and emotionally.

'Stew, your shout,' he targeted Stew, smart as a carrot, in his club waistcoat and matching bow tie.

'Bollocks Sutton, what time do you call this? Get your own,' Sutton smiled to himself, as if he was going to get any sympathy from these lot and walked to the bar.

A few minutes later Geoff Sutton, armed with a pint of their favourite hand-pulled brew, took a huge gulp, coughed and spluttered. He smiled as the contents of the drink hit the back of his throat and then headed downwards. He proposed a toast, raising his glass: 'Raise your glasses to Roger Strong, one of us, rest peacefully Rog.'

'Roger Strong,' came the immediate response from the others.

A couple of pints later, Sutton failed to notice Debbie sneak up on his blindside. 'Any chance I can stay again tonight? Billy cancelled last minute, he has man flu!' she whispered in his ear before stepping back and winking.

Regardless of any embarrassment, given they were in the middle of Upper Parton RFC Clubhouse, Sutton gave Debbie a prolonged and loving embrace.

36

Chris and Ron

Ron Turner rose early the following day. He didn't get much sleep, something noted by his wife, who also passed comment on the fact that he had hardly spoken to her since he returned home following the conclusion of the march. He was a troubled man and the question he continually asked himself, did he have any alternatives other than to resign?

A quick breakfast before Ron and Sheila made a getaway for the hills. Weather permitting, they had promised themselves a long hike in the beautiful Parton countryside on his one day off. Walking was their favourite joint hobby and the couple had plans to move to the Lake District when Ron eventually finished work.

Much to Sheila's frustration nothing was said for the forty-five-minute car journey. After forty years of marriage she knew her husband's reaction to a serious problem. He would discuss the matter with her, only when he was ready. Ron eventually told the tale of Charlton's deployment and of the officer's subsequent meeting with Mayling on Friday night. 'She knows I authorised the job, Sheila. I am sure,' Ron said disappointingly. 'And what is worse she probably knows about Sutton and Firth's involvement,' he added sadly.

'Well what are you going to do?' Sheila posed the obvious question.

'Resign. I think,' Ron said unconvincingly. 'If she lets me off with a severe bollocking, how can we possibly work together in the future?' he continued.

'But you like her Ron, and she rates you. More importantly you still enjoy the job. Ride it out and see what Mayling has to say on the matter.' Sheila was as succinct as ever.

Chris Mayling worked on her day off reading the Safeguard inspection report, as well as considering the future of her assistant chief constable.

Turner was in his office at 7am on the Monday morning but he hadn't arrived before Mayling, door open as ever, she was reading the latest crime statistics. Turner walked straight into her office.

'Boss I was out of order,' Turner said, closing the door. It was the last words he spoke, as for the next five minutes Mayling gave him the biggest bollocking of his long career. He was hardly allowed to breathe never mind speak. He thought, 'Perhaps it wasn't the right time or place to inform her that as a result of Charlton's deployment crucial intelligence had been obtained.' Turner just sat and took it, looking for comfort, he felt for his letter of resignation in his jacket pocket.

Mayling was about to request his resignation when, without thinking, she continued talking. 'That said Ron, you are my most valuable asset in this force. I cannot afford to lose you, but more importantly I don't want to lose you. What has been said behind these closed doors will remain between us and we move on,' the words were said with some feeling and compassion. There was a pause as Mayling realised the impact of her words. She couldn't do without him, despite his gross error of judgement. Mayling finally looked at Turner smiling. 'You've got some balls Ron, to pull a stroke like that.' It was almost said in admiration.

Turner removed his hand from the resignation letter in his jacket pocket. 'What about Sutton and Firth? It was my decision, mine alone,' Turner said, almost pleading for punishment.

'Ron, they prompted Charlton's deployment. That will be my decision, mine alone,' Mayling repeated his words. 'And now Ron, we both have work to do.'

Turner returned to his office suitably chastised but job still intact. He would see Sutton and Firth at Enid Benson's funeral due to be held later that day.

Enid's funeral was almost a rerun of The Haven march, in terms of attendees. Hilda Tait attended despite medical advice to the contrary and Charlie Drummond never left her side.

Over a milky coffee at The Haven, Turner took Firth and Sutton to one side and informed them of his conversation with Mayling earlier that day. He reinforced the fact that as authorising officer, he alone should take responsibility for Charlton's deployment, but she had maintained that this would be her decision.

Epilogue

It was Roger Strong's cremation and Geoff Sutton, Pete McIntyre and Stew Grant stood sombre, side by side in the Parton Crematorium, their respective partners and Sutton's daughter Maggie, occupying the pews immediately behind them. All dressed in dark suits they wore their commemorative Upper Parton RFC ties that had been gifted to them as part of Roger's will. Pete had delivered a terrific eulogy, humorous, personal and emotional. Stew had leapt to his aid and finished the final sentence as it all proved just too much for him.

It was the final prayers and the curtains closed around the coffin. Sutton looked forward and to his right, Alan Strong, Roger's brother, stood with his immediate family occupying the front row. They were joined by young Freddie Ingles who, thanks to a few strings pulled by Ron Turner, attended his dad's funeral whilst still on remand. He also received special disposition in that his handcuffs were removed during the service. Even from his vantage point Sutton could see that it was one occasion too many for young Freddie. The minister touched on the circumstances of Roger's death reminding people not to pursue personal recriminations. He informed the gathering that there was a collection for the Samaritans. Despite the minister's words, for Sutton, McIntyre and Grant, the closest of comrades, they would always have recriminations; Roger's death was such a waste.

Sutton, McIntyre and Grant joined together, arms around shoulders, as they left the crematorium, only pausing for a moment or two whilst exchanging pleasantries with Alan and his family. Freddie Ingles had already been whisked away by the prison authorities and back to his remand establishment.

Outside in the final throws of sunshine that signalled the end of an autumn afternoon that soon would make way for the chill of winter, the three of them made their way back to Stew's spotless Lexus SUV. Sutton glanced quickly back at the depressing sight of people streaming out of the crematorium whilst another funeral party was about to make an entrance for the next service.

There were no words between them during the twenty minute drive back to the wake, naturally at Upper Parton RFC. Stew parked up and they walked to the clubhouse, again as a three and never again as a four. It was now dark, and the clubhouse lights shone brightly. They once again saw Roger's chair adorned with a club scarf. They cried openly as they walked towards their table and chairs.

After recovering their composure Stew Grant went to the bar, with Pete and Sutton taking their usual seats, at their usual table. Sutton switched his phone back on, before replacing it in his suit pocket.

Meanwhile back at Parton Constabulary HQ, Chief Constable Mayling had a nightmare scenario that had just arrived on her desk. After due consideration, her secretary was tasked to send out a diary appointment to discuss the matter with an officer whom she had specifically chosen for the task.

Sutton's phone vibrated in his pocket. He studied the recent email; an appointment with Mayling. 'Shit,' he thought that if he was to be sacked or bollocked, it would have taken place by now.

Unbeknown to Geoff Sutton, was there one final job for him?

Previous title by the author

Trust

Retired DCI Geoff Sutton now works as a civilian at Parton Constabulary. Life is quiet as he follows his usual routine of golf and watching his beloved Upper Parton RFC - but all that's about to change...

Walking home one evening, Geoff sees a familiar van. When it's still there the next morning he decides to act - and what he and his colleagues find inside is beyond their worst nightmares.

Geoff's experience is needed and he soon finds himself playing an integral part in an investigation that rocks the local force.

A dead prostitute, a missing foster child, a senior police officer whose love affair makes her careless... Geoff and his colleagues reveal blackmail, murder and kidnap as they untangle a web of deceit and corruption.

And Geoff is forced to ask himself: who can you really TRUST ?

Lightning Source UK Ltd.
Milton Keynes UK
UKHW011434250820
368800UK00001B/52